SNAKE RIVER SECRET

a Mary MacIntosh novel

Maureen Anne Meehan

www.maureenannemeehan.com
info@maureenannemeehan.com

Table of Contents

Chapter 1

I awoke slowly Saturday morning, sluggish and exhausted from the O'Connor trial. It was my first shot at being a big-time lawyer in a small town, and the experience kicked my butt. My name is Mary MacIntosh and I'm a trial attorney, as you've probably gathered, working for Harry Harrrison–a well-known big shot lawyer in the small town of Jackson, Wyoming, near Yellowstone National Park and the Grand Tetons. It wouldn't be such a bad job if Harry would give me more responsibility. I've been working for him for seven years and all I do, it seems, is the boring stuff that Harry doesn't want to do. I'm told that I'm an attractive woman–tall, lean and physically fit–but I rarely see the light of day, or go on a date for that matter, because I'm always at Harry's beck and call. I don't mean to complain. I love my job overall, but I need more in life.

I crawled out of bed, opened the door to my apartment and stared at the headline at my feet. "Killer is Still on the Loose."

I read the rest of the article in bed, scanning to see if my name was mentioned as one of the lawyers on the case. Tucked into the third column of the second page I found, "Neither Harry Harrison nor Mary MacIntosh could be reached for comment." I called Harry to see if he'd read the paper yet.

"I'm reading the article now," Harry said. "I still can't believe it." There was a pause on the other end of the line and Mac could hear newspapers rustling. "Nevermind."

"Nevermind what?" I asked.

"I don't want to think about the O'Connor case anymore. I have an excruciating headache. You should have joined our 'Thank God the

O'Connor Trial is Over' celebration last night. I cracked the Château Léoville Las Cases St. Julien. It scored a perfect 100 from Wine Spectator. Deliciously bold. You would have appreciated it. Anyhow, changing the subject again, did you hear from Lela last night?"

"No. Why?"

"She didn't show up. I'm a little worried, Mac. I tried calling her, but there's no answer. She was supposed to come over to our house for a celebration drink after the verdict."

"When I saw her at the office after the trial, she said that she was heading over to your house after she stopped by her place to change clothes. Maybe something came up. It was a Friday night, after all, and knowing Lela, she had a hot date lined up. Partying with her boss might not have been high on her list, Harry. No offense."

Lela, our legal secretary, almost always had a Friday night date. Young, single and a Shoshone Indian beauty, she had no problem filling her social calendar.

"But she would have called me if she couldn't make it," Harry said. "She might have had other plans, Mac, but she would have at least stopped by for a drink and if she couldn't, she would've called. She always calls if there's a problem. I couldn't sleep past four this morning worrying about her. Call me if you hear from her."

"She already has one father."

"Lately, I think she needs two."

I heard Harry let out a deep sigh. I pictured the silk laden pillows propped up behind him as he reclined in his poster bed wearing his black terrycloth robe while reading the Saturday morning paper. Normally, he would have devoured the sports page first, but after the most publicized trial of his legal career, he undoubtedly focused on the front-page headlines.

"I'm heading out for my morning run. I'll drop by her place and check on her. I'll take my cell and call you when I find her hung-over body curled up in bed. She'll probably yell at me for waking her up."

"Good. Thanks. Call me if you hear from her. I'll call the Chief. Maybe he knows where she is."

* * *

Lela's father, Ed Washakie Duran, was one of several Shoshone Chiefs in the greater Wind River Range. His Washakie name meant "The Rattler," which was not a comparison to a snake, but an allusion to the rawhide buffalo rattle that his great grandfather, Chief Washakie, used to scare Sioux Indian ponies during his many daring raids in the early 1900's. Chief Washakie was remembered in Wyoming as one of the fiercest warriors, yet one of the most effective peacemakers in history. While other tribes such as the Sioux, Crow and Cheyenne fought the white man with vigor, Chief Washakie realized that a union with whites was wiser for his people than trying to fight the invasion. Other warriors who fought against General Custer and Crook were famous for their massacres, but Chief Washakie was happy to keep his tribe alive and well. Despite his peacefulness, however, he was infamous for the battle at Crowheart Butte where legend has it that he charged a neighboring Bannock tribe over hunting ground rights and was declared the winner when he paraded around with the Bannock chief's heart dangling from his spear. Chief Washakie was buried at 102 years of age as the only Indian chief to attain full U.S. military honors, but such honors had a high price. Ed Washakie Duran was worthy of his namesake: a peaceful leader of his tribe, a proud rancher, and a devoted father to Lela.

Ed's ancestors had trained him well in the fleeting and enduring pangs of fright, terror and horror. As chief, he passed many tribal warrior tests of bravery, endurance, compassion and vision, but ancestral explanations and anecdotes failed to adequately prepare him for the phone call he was about to receive from Harry.

* * *

Millions of years of rocky cliffs have been cut like jewels by the sinuous flow of the Snake River flowing through and beyond Jackson Hole. The wider banks of the river flow peacefully, and in the light of a setting sun, look like golden garland on a Christmas tree. In contrast, the narrow chutes of the Snake River Canyon boast torrid rapids that look like a kettle of bubbling water boiling over. The Snake River got its name from the

Shoshone Indians, who used a serpentine hand movement for their tribal name–a motion that early settlers and trappers misinterpreted as a snake and applied it to the river, which flowed through Shoshone territory. The peaceful calm and the raging torrents of the Snake River are like the Yin and the Yang of Lela Duran.

Harry hired Lela after she dropped out of high school. As I understand it, Lela got pregnant during her sophomore year at a post-football season party hosted by Harry's son, John, the quarterback for the team. After Lela got pregnant, John tried everything to get her to return and get a diploma.

Rumor around town was that John was the father of the baby, but Lela never substantiated paternity. John, wanting to take responsibility, even had Harry talk to her. The minute Harry laid eyes on Lela, he realized why his son admired her. She had long, straight black hair that fell to her waist, like the tail of a prized Palomino. Her skin was more olive than dark, but her eyes were the color of obsidian, wide and knowing. She had straight teeth and thin, perfectly heart-shaped lips, always lined in red lipstick. She was average height and weight–not too thin or too thick.

After dwelling on my conversation with Harry, I started to worry about Lela too. I tied my running shoes, grabbed my jacket, and took off on foot toward her apartment. It was a brisk morning in May. The winter snow was melting from the tips of the Teton Mountains. I could smell the smoke from fires burning in neighbor's fireplaces–and indication that winter had lingered into spring–something not uncommon in Wyoming. The air was crisp and fresh and I thought about many things on my way to Lela's–most particularly, about Greg, my new boyfriend.

As I got closer to Lela's, I started wondering whether I was being overly paranoid. Maybe she needed a break from us. We'd been working around the clock for months during the O'Connor trial. Once it was over, maybe she didn't want to see or hear from us until after the weekend.

After seventeen years of working for Harry, Lela was his right arm. She kept his files in perfect order, filed the pleadings in the right court at the right time without being asked, arranged depositions by the mere eavesdropping in on a conversation, and packed his briefcase with the next day's files before he left for the day. Lela knew the clients as well, if not better, than Harry or me and most of them dropped in unannounced to see her, not us. The holiday greeting treats were addressed to her first, us second. *Holiday greetings . . .*

I thought of that horrifying morning last Christmas when I was assaulted at gunpoint at the office. I had arrived around my usual time and turned around to hang my jacket on the hook behind my door. There he stood, tucked into the corner of my office, his dark, beady eyes burning through me like lasers. He was a heavy-set man with a navy blue ski cap pulled down over his face. Panic overwhelmed me, to the point where I couldn't scream for help, as I backed slowly toward my desk, hoping to get close enough to grab the phone. When I saw the gun in his hand, I realized that the phone wouldn't save me. He grabbed me by my ponytail with his black-gloved hand and jolted me to the ground, and with the gun pressed against my right temple, he duct taped my mouth and in a low, gruff tone he said, "Take all of your clothes off." I remember that his breath smelled like a stale cigarette. It was Lela who comforted me after the assault. She understood my shame and humiliation of being forced to strip. Lela was reliable and comforting.

The more I thought of my conversation with Harry about Lela, I decided that maybe he was right. It wasn't like Lela to not show up. She was reliable. I called Harry from my cell phone and told him to meet me at her apartment.

When Harry arrived, I followed him up the cobblestone sidewalk. Walking with a slight limp from a Stanford University football career-ending knee injury, Harry turned and flashed me a nervous, toothy grin. The deep crags around his eyes from years of squinting at fine print were deeper this morning, likely the result of little sleep. He's known around town for his elegant Savile Row custom-tailored British clothes and today he donned a Burberry striped button-down shirt, blue jeans and Sergio Rossi side-buckle leather shoes. Although his dark hair was thinning, he'd never let the color fade. He was handsome for a man in his late fifties.

By the way, like I said earlier, my name is Mary MacIntosh, but Harry calls me "Mac." I'm a thirty-two-year-old tall Irish gal with long, curly auburn hair, freckled cheeks and a wide smile. Harry hired me upon law school graduation because he didn't want to hire a young lawyer with bad habits acquired from working for another attorney. Harry told me that if I was going to have bad habits, he wanted me to have his bad habits. Harry's the closest paradigm to the father that I didn't have. My father died when I was young, and the man my mother remarried was more interested in gaining a mother for his children than serving as a father to me. Harry pulled me under his sophisticated wings, introducing me to food, wine and the finer things in life—like how to be a lawyer without losing your mind.

Harry punched in the access code to Lela's apartment building and then pulled the heavy wooden door open. As we climbed the flight of steps leading to her apartment, I could feel my adrenaline mounting.

"That's strange. Her door is wide open," I said.

Harry jerked his large hand toward me, silently cautioning me to stay back. He took a few steps into Lela's apartment.

"Lela? Lela? Anyone home?" Harry shouted, but there was no response.

"Lela?"

I inched behind Harry, close enough to smell his Polo cologne. At that moment, I sensed a wrongness about the place, like a snowstorm in August.

"Harry, her purse and keys are still here," I whispered. "Lela would *never* leave her apartment without her purse."

"Sshhhh." Harry held his hand up to me again, signaling for me to stay put.

"Maybe she was on her way out and forgot something."

Harry looked back and held his finger to his lip. I stopped talking. He silently walked down the short hallway toward Lela's only bedroom. I followed him. Her bedroom was in shambles. Her bed was unmade and clothes were strewn all over the floor. Her closet door was open and its contents had been emptied. Her dresser drawers had been ransacked and her nightstand lamp was shattered. Harry pushed by me and headed toward the bathroom door, which was slightly ajar. He knocked as he pushed the door open further. He ripped back the shower curtain, anticipating the worst. The tub was empty.

I bolted back into her living room. "Hey Harry, look at this." Lela's coffee table was covered with a brightly colored Navajo blanket on top of which sat a half-empty bottle of wine with a tall tumbler next to it with a quarter of the way full of a yellow liquid.

Harry leaned down on one knee to smell the contents in the glass tumbler. "Smells like wine."

"Lela's a Southern Comfort and Coke drinker."

"I've offered her wine many times, but she's always turned me down. She won't even try a sip of my finer vintage." Harry braced his hand against the arm of the couch and grimaced as he stood, looking down at his knee. There was a large stain on his jeans.

"Is your knee bleeding? Do you think that one of the pins in there popped out? Should I call -"

"No. My knee is fine. The carpet is wet."

"Wet?" I took a closer look at the burnt orange carpet. "That looks like . . . blood?"

"Don't touch anything, Mac." I shoved my hands in the front pockets of my blue jeans. "Look here. This chair has been moved. You can see the imprints on the carpet where it used to be."

I walked around the couch. "Harry, there's a broken vase here. And Lela's other matching Navajo blanket is missing. It's usually hung over the back of this chair."

"I'm calling the police," Harry said. Harry pulled out his Hermes handkerchief and reached for Lela's telephone.

"Wait. Use my cell." I dialed 9-1-1 and handed my phone to Harry.

"They're sending over a squad car," he said, trying to figure out how to turn my phone off. I grabbed the phone and clicked the right button. "Do you have the Chief's number on your cell?" Harry shook his head no.

I pulled my Blackberry out of my purse and scrolled down to Duran, then plugged my cell into my Blackberry, direct-dialing the Chief.

"Ed, this is Harry. Have you heard from Lela?" He hadn't. "You need to come to Lela's apartment. I'm afraid that something has happened."

I'd never seen Harry this shook up. Lela was a diamond that he had perfectly cut and polished. He couldn't place a value on her because he had never been forced to. When I first came to work for Harry, Lela had already been there for nearly eleven years. She knew more about practicing law than I did, and was helpful in bridging the gap from law school to reality. She'd become my friend, inviting me to join her friends for happy hour and other social events, and over the years, I felt like I'd gotten to know her pretty well. But as I looked around her apartment, I wondered if I knew her at all.

Lela didn't drink wine, as far as I knew, and she swore that she only used Noxema on her face, but her medicine cabinet was full of skin products. While waiting for the police to show up, I walked into her bedroom and looked around, careful not to disturb anything. Dozens of pictures of Lela with her family adorned the walls of her bedroom, which were painted scarlet red. Red candles were perched on the windowsill above her unmade bed.

Afraid of leaving a fingerprint behind, I slipped my right hand into my coat pocket and reached for the handle of her top bureau drawer. I pulled the drawer open far enough to see leopard print undergarments. I poked through her lingerie and beneath the pile of red and black lace panties lay a wad of green bills.

"Harry, in here," I shouted. I pointed to the money bound tight in a rubber band.

"That looks like a lot of money. The top bill is a five hundred. Must be a couple of thousand dollars here, at least." He looked at me in astonishment, like a father discovering marijuana in his teenager's sock drawer.

"She has a slew of expensive cosmetic products in the bathroom, too. She swore to me that she didn't believe in that stuff. It's like she had a private life that we didn't know about."

"Harry?" a voice called out.

"Back here," Harry said as he shoved the wad of bills back in the lingerie drawer.

Deputy Sheriff Tim Marshall walked in Lela's bedroom. Tim Marshall's salt and pepper hair was combed directly back off his high forehead, forming a bit of a peak, exposing a large, z-shaped scar on the left side near his temple. His gray eyes were deeply set, framed by a thick, dark unibrow. He had perfectly white-capped teeth, like the tips of the Tetons, and nearly as pointed. A waft of cigarette odor filled the room as soon as he spoke.

"What's goin' on?" he asked. Harry filled him in as we edged back toward the kitchen.

"When you arrived, what did you see?" Tim asked, while pulling out a notebook from his shirt pocket.

"The door was wide open and her purse and keys were on the table. I called out for her, but she didn't answer, so we checked the rooms. She's not here. There's a stain on the carpet I think you should look at."

Harry showed Tim the stain on his pants from where he knelt on the wet carpet. Tim touched the stain and then examined his finger. "I need to call in forensics." He made the call. "While we're waitin' for them to show up, let me ask you a few questions. When did you see Lela last?"

"I saw her at the office last night around five o'clock," I said. "She was organizing all of the O'Connor trial documents into boxes for storage. She said that she was coming here to freshen up and then to Harry's for a drink."

"So, you were the last person to see Lela," Tim said, in an almost accusatory tone.

"I don't know whether I was the last person to see Lela, Tim. I'm the last person I know to have seen her. She obviously came home and perhaps had wine with a friend. I don't know whom she saw after she left the office."

Tim's a decent cop and was recognized on the force as a specialist in forensics, but his biggest problem, in my opinion, was that he opened his mouth too often when he should be listening.

"What's the name of her friend that she's always hangin' around?"

"Sheila Fall is her best friend."

"Oh, sure. I think I know her. Doesn't she work at Albertsons?" Tim asked. I nodded. "Maybe we should give her a call and see if she knows where Lela is."

"I'll call her, but I hope it's not too early. Sheila works the night shift."

Lela introduced me to Sheila several years back at a happy hour. I'll never forget watching Sheila walk in to the bar, her tight Levi's and a very low-cut magenta top getting whistles from all the male patrons. Her bleached- blond, over-permed frizzy hair clung to her shoulders and every finger was adorned with a ring. Her false fingernails were so long that they curled in the shape of a U. When she told me that she worked as a checker at Albertson's, I wondered how on earth she could punch anything on the checkout keypad with claws like that. I dialed her number. It rang four times before anyone answered.

"H-h-hello," a voice whispered, hardly audible.

"Sheila? It's Mary MacIntosh. Have you -"

"What the fuck time is it?"

"Sorry to wake you. It's almost ten in the morning. Listen, have you seen or heard from Lela lately?"

"Shit no. Haven't I told you never to call before noon? It's Saturday morning."

"She didn't show up at Harry's house last night and we're worried about her. When was the last time you talked with her?"

"Hhhhcccm. Shit. I've got a fucking hair in my mouth. Just a minute. Hhhcccm. She called after the trial was over and said that she was gonna have a drink with Harry and then she said she might meet me later at the Cowboy. She didn't show."

"That's not like her, is it?"

I heard Sheila whispering to someone in the background. "Down the hall, first right."

"I'm not interrupting, am I?"

"What'd you think? What'd you ask me?"

"Was it unusual for Lela not to show up?"

"Yeah. I mean no, but I didn't make much of it. Sometimes she gets . . . you know . . . sidetracked, if you know what I'm sayin'. She has a way of bein' that way."

"Sidetracked?"

"You know. Meets up with a boyfriend along the way."

"Who's she been seeing lately? Is she dating anyone?"

"Dating? Hhhmm. Lela and me never really *date* any one guy. She was seeing this guy that was teaching her skiing, but I forget his name. Tom or Don or somethin' like that. Anyway, she dates around. No one serious. Why?" Sheila said, hushing someone in the background.

"Well, we're at her apartment now. She's not here and her door was left wide open, and her purse and keys are here. We're worried that maybe she left her apartment suddenly. Lela doesn't go anywhere without her purse. And you know how she guards the keys to her truck. So, you don't know where she is?"

"Nope. I gotta go."

"Wait. Do you know of anyone that might have a grudge against her?" There was a considerable pause on the other end of the line.

"A grudge. Hmm. Well, I don't know of no one with a grudge. I mean, there are a few guys around town that she's dumped, so they might be pissed at her. But I don't know of nobody who like hates her or anything, even though she thinks she's smarter than the rest of us." There was another pause. I was about to hang up when Sheila interjected. "But the other day, I was at her apartment after work and the phone rang. I don't know who it was, but she did have a hot conversation with someone. She kept sayin' that she was sorry and that she would fix the problem. When she hung up, I asked her who she was talkin' to and she said, 'nobody.' When Lela says 'nobody' it means 'nobody' and I know to mind my own fuckin' business, if you know what I mean."

"When was that, do you remember?"

"Must have been Wednesday, because that's the day I get off work early. We watched TV together and did our nails. Yeah. Wednesday."

"She wouldn't tell you who called?"

"Nope. And I ain't one to pry."

"Has anyone ever threatened her? Like an old boyfriend?"

"I don't know nothin' about the threats. Ask John–he's the one who follows her all around town."

"Harry's son?"

"Yeah. He's been followin' her around forever. Like since high school. It's creepy. I tell him to get a life all the time. Lela's nice to him on account of his dad being her boss and all, but the guy gives me the fuckin' creeps. I don't give a shit that he was the high school quarterback or whatever. He's fat and ugly. The idiot stopped by on Wednesday and brought her a six pack. As if we can't buy ourselves beer for shit sakes. Lela don't even drink beer. Anyway -"

"Anyone else?"

"Jimmy Lonewolf."

"Who?"

"Like the *whole town* knows about Jimmy Lonewolf."

"That name rings a bell. Who's he?"

"Jimmy Lonewolf is this stupid kid that grew up near Lela on the reservation. He's short and really skinny. He's got a silver front tooth. He always wears his hair in a ponytail with a baseball cap on backwards. He's an idiot. A real fuckin' moron. Lela says that he doesn't got both oars in the water. He's always showin' up around her apartment. She's nice to him because his dad is a friend of her dad's, I guess, but he bugs the hell out of me."

"Anyone else?"

"Nope. That ski guy, but I can't remember his name. He was pissed off that she didn't sleep with him, that I know for sure. He taught her to ski and paid for her ski ticket. She stood him up for happy hour one night. He tracked us down at the Stagecoach and bitched her out. He's an asshole. California pretty boy freak."

"When was that?"

"Don't know. A few months back, I think."

"What's with all of the expensive cosmetics and skin care creams in Lela's bathroom?" There was another pause on Sheila's end of the line. "Sheila?"

"Uh, well, we went to this dermatologist doctor and he gave us some samples. It's no big deal. You know, free samples to try. Listen, I need to go. Call me when you find her." The phone went dead.

Chapter 2

The red light on Lela's answering machine was blinking the number three. "She has caller ID," I said to Tim Marshall. He nodded, as if he already knew, and yanked a latex glove from his front pocket and slipped it on his right hand. He picked up the phone and started to touch the caller ID button, and then realized that his left hand was glove-free. He set the phone back on the charger and put a glove on his left hand and repeated the procedure. I looked over his shoulder at the names and phone numbers of the previous callers.

"Two calls from Samuel Silver?" Tim said. "Why would he be callin' Lela?"

Samuel Silver was an actor who lived on the outskirts of Jackson Hole in a large ranch-style log home. He hadn't been in many blockbuster films lately, so his name wasn't as hot as some of the other celebrities about town. He'd been a client of Harry's for years, and we were currently representing him in a palimony lawsuit. I met him at his deposition and found him to be a nice man, but the tabloids claimed that his drug problem made him abusive on the sets and that directors hated working with him.

"What would he be doin' callin' Lela? He's one of the most famous people livin' around here. I heard that he goes for the younger ones. Has she ever mentioned him?" I shrugged my shoulders and explained to Tim that he was a client, but couldn't imagine why he'd be calling her at home. Tim continued to scroll through the caller I.D. "Looks like Dr. Miller's called quite a few times. Who's he?"

"His name sounds familiar," I said, remembering that I'd seen his name recently. After thinking about it for a minute, I realized that it was his name on one of the skin care products in the bathroom. "He must be the dermatologist that Lela goes to."

"Did she have some kind of medical procedure?"

"Not that I know of. Why?"

"A dermatologist who calls his patients at home?" Tim made another notation in his spiral. "I need to get the records from the phone company to identify the rest of these numbers."

"Can the phone company identify the private caller numbers?" I knew that they could identify any number. We'd subpoenaed the phone company records many times in other cases.

"You bet they can," Tim said, about to go into a long dissertation on phone records. "Oh, excuse me. Camille's here."

A large-breasted woman walked through the front door carrying what looked like a metal toolbox in her right hand. A young man was at her side carrying a similar looking box. Tim walked over to Camille and whispered to her. She nodded.

"Good morning everyone," Camille said, as if she was addressing a large crowd. "My name's Camille and I'm in charge of forensics. I'm sure that Deputy Marshall already told you this, but please don't touch or move anything. We'll ask questions if we need answers. Thanks for your cooperation."

Camille looked like a woman in charge of her life. Her command of the room was like that of a three-star general. She slid her hands into latex gloves and pulled out a wad of plastic bags, shoving a black marker and a pair of small scissors into her shirt pocket. Her colleague pulled out a jar of black powder and a large brush and while he dusted for fingerprints, Camille clipped carpet samples from the stained area and placed them in baggies, intermittently snapping pictures from the camera draped around her neck.

"What's that?" I asked, as she pulled a black wand out of her toolbox.

"It's an alternative light source, which is a fluorescent light that helps reveal prints and stains." She sprayed the carpet with a bottle marked

"Luminol" and then held the light to it. Her assistant nodded. "Take a large swatch," she said to him.

I followed Camille back to Lela's bedroom, where she put the fluorescent light over Lela's unmade bed. A spot appeared in the middle of the sheets. I watched as Camille removed the sheets from Lela's bed and placed them in a paper grocery bag. She then cut out a swatch of the mattress and bagged it as evidence.

*   *   *

When Ed Washakie Duran arrived, the forensic team was just finishing. Ed, a short Shoshone Indian in his early fifties, wore a light brown western shirt that barely covered his girth. The cuffs of his faded blue jeans were tucked loosely into his work boots, which were dusted with dried mud. His high, pronounced cheekbones and almond-shaped eyes reminded me of Lela. He reached out to shake Harry's hand.

"I'd like to introduce you to Deputy Sheriff Tim Marshall. He's in charge of the investigation," Harry said to Ed.

"When was the last time you heard from your daughter?" Tim asked in a tone so strong that it sounded like a horsewhip. Ed took a step back.

"She c-c-called yesterday to tell us about the O'Connor case. We'd been following it c-c-closely." Ed took a deep breath, then wiped a bead of sweat from his brow. "It's h-h-hot in here. Did someone turn up the heat?"

"Did she say whether she had weekend plans or anythin' like that?"

"N-n-no. She comes out to the ranch on Sundays to visit–," Ed paused and sucked in his breath. He looked around the room, taking inventory of the people staring at him, and then continued. "I asked if she was gonna make it this weekend and she said that she wasn't sure yet. She usually calls Sunday m-m-morning and lets us know her plans." His lower lip trembled as he talked.

"It's okay. She's going to be okay," Harry said, giving Ed a pat on the back.

"Did Lela have any enemies?" Tim asked rather abruptly.

I wasn't sure if he was talking to me, Harry or Ed, so I waited in uncomfortable silence for someone else to answer. Ed looked at Harry and shrugged his shoulders. Harry glanced at me and I did the same.

"I don't know of any *enemies*," Harry finally said, sounding unsure of his answer.

Tim looked in Ed's direction and raised an eyebrow, inviting a response.

"Well, I don't know of any *enemies* either." Ed rubbed his chin with his index finger and thumb and took a deep breath before continuing. "There's this k-k-kid named Jimmy Lonewolf who gave Lela a real hard time when they were growing up, but I don't know if I'd call him an *enemy*. Jimmy's a bully and liked to pick on Lela. She was the type of k-k-kid that didn't back d-d-down."

Jimmy Lonewolf's reputation preceded him and I was fairly sure that he was the reason that Lela didn't finish high school. I decided to chime in. "Sheila said that he followed her around town and threatened her." Ed stepped forward after I spoke.

"He's not quite right in the head. He got himself b-b-bucked off a horse when he was a kid and he hit his head on a rock." I sensed that Ed was a bit defensive of Jimmy.

"Do you think he's capable of harming Lela?"

"I hope not," Ed started out, cautiously. Jimmy Lonewolf was protected by the shield of a bad reputation, and it appeared that Ed was not about to stir up any trouble. It was no secret that Lonewolf was a member of the Arapaho tribe, and the Shoshone and Arapaho had never gotten along well. Lela told me how the Arapaho forced the Shoshone west of the Laramie Mountains in the late eighteenth century.

"I've never heard of him being in any kind of t-t-trouble, other than petty stuff. He's been kicked out of school for fighting. That sort of thing. You might know him if you saw him. He's got long, black hair that's usually pulled back in a ponytail and he's got this silver front t-t-tooth. Kids around these parts call him 'Hi Ho Silver' on account of that tooth."

"Sounds familiar. I might have given him a ticket for speedin'. Anyone else?"

"Not that I know of." I sensed that Ed was uncomfortable with the interrogation and was offering as little information as possible.

"What about boyfriends? Does Lela have a boyfriend?" Ed looked at Harry with a sly glance, as if to say, "Do you want to field this one, or should I?"

"I don't know much about her boyfriends. She never brings anyone out to the ranch with her and she doesn't talk much about her personal life. My wife frets about her not being married. But if the Missus brings it up, Lela doesn't like it, so we stopped asking her about it a while back." Ed took a handkerchief from his front pocket and wiped his forehead. "Harry's son has always been interested."

"John's never made it a secret that he cares for Lela, but he'd never hurt her!" Harry said. I could feel the mounting tension between Harry and Ed–some unresolved dispute lingered between them.

"I didn't mean it *that* way. I just meant that J-J-John has been interested in Lela for many moons."

Harry took a step back and folded his arms across his chest, as if to say, "Don't go any further with this one." Ed titled his head to the right, looking directly into Harry's eyes. Communication was unspoken yet understood. Ed did not elaborate any further. Tim broke the silence again.

"Did she owe anyone money?"

"She had a monthly payment on her t-t-truck and she paid rent for this apartment, but that's all I know of. Lela took care of her own finances and she never asked for money. Hasn't asked for a dime since she was fifteen."

Harry cleared his throat and said, "She did ask for an advance on her bonus around Christmas this past year for the first time ever. She said that she needed some money to make a down payment on her truck. And she did ask for an advance recently on a paycheck for April. She'd never done that before either. Maybe she was in over her head on that expensive truck. I tried to talk her into a less expensive model and then I tried to talk her out of getting that stereo put in there. And she clearly didn't need the leather bucket seats. She insisted on every bell and whistle -"

"I'm sure that J-J-John didn't mind selling it to her."

"John threw in half of her upgrades for free. I don't think he made a commission off that sale because he gave her such a good deal."

"Okay. Okay. You've made your point," I said to Harry. "Let's focus on the issue at hand." Tim nodded in agreement.

"Do you know if she borrowed money from anyone else?" Tim asked.

"I don't know. Like I said, she took care of her own money."

"What about clients? Are there any clients that have taken a particular interest in her?"

"All of our clients have taken an interest in her," Harry said in a much more pleasant tone. "She knows all of their names and their children's and spouse's names. She makes them feel well taken care of. The holiday gifts we get are usually addressed to her."

"Have any of your clients asked her out?"

"Probably a lot of them, but I don't know who. I try to stay out of that sort of thing. She's always kept her personal life personal and her professional life professional, as far as I know. Mac knows more about that kind of thing." Tim turned my way for elaboration. I shook my head.

"Not really. Like Harry said, Lela kept her personal life private," I said. On Monday mornings, Harry and I often discussed the weekend, sharing stories of outdoor adventures or social events. Lela, despite her warmth and charm, rarely discussed her personal life. We knew that she went to the ranch most weekends, and if pressed about what she did on the ranch, she usually said that she just hung around with her mom. Not having the opportunity to spend much time with my own mother, I wanted Lela to elaborate, mostly to live out a mother-daughter relationship vicariously through her. But Lela was protective of her family time.

"Have any clients disliked her?"

"No," Harry and I both shouted at the same time.

"Maybe you've gotten someone off from a crime and the victim held a grudge. Or maybe someone's had to do time and they're mad about it?"

"Whoa. You're getting ahead of yourself. This might have nothing to do with my law practice."

"Anything's possible. It's possible that Lela's out there somewhere just partyin' down and you'll see her red eyes Monday mornin' at work. But it's also possible that somethin's wrong. It's better to look at it from all sides," Tim said.

"It might help if I go to the office and look through our client list to see if anything comes to mind," I said. "Hey, that reminds me of something. Remember when I was attacked at the office last December? Whoever it was that attacked me rummaged through Lela's desk and booted up her computer before I got to the office that morning. I wonder what he was looking for?"

"I forgot about that. Lela's desk *was* torn apart," Harry said.

"I never heard about th-th-that. Someone broke into the office? Did you catch the g-g-guy?"

"No," I said. Tim glanced over my way and then took notes in his spiral. He knew that I was upset that the perpetrator hadn't been caught and that the police department hadn't done more to investigate the case. I couldn't get over the fact that I had been sexually assaulted at gunpoint in broad daylight in our office, which sits above a busy bank in downtown Jackson. I felt like either the police didn't believe me, or that they didn't pursue it more vigorously because I hadn't been raped or killed. Since the case hadn't been assigned to Tim and the perpetrator didn't leave much evidence behind for the police to go on, I had to move on and not hold a grudge against Tim.

"Does anyone know if Lela keeps a diary or journal?" Tim asked, changing the subject. Harry looked at me for an answer.

"I've never seen her writing in a diary, but I can't be sure. Maybe Sheila knows," I said.

"She kept one as a little girl," Ed said. "I don't know what happened to it or if she still keeps one. I can ask the Missus."

"Ask and let me know. If any of you can think of anthin' that might be important, anythin' at all, call me," Tim said. He handed out his business card to each of us. As he struggled to get his wallet back into the pocket of his snug uniform, Camille whispered something to him. "It'll take forensics some time to work up the fingerprints and other evidence. We've put an APB out on her. If anyone hears anythin', call the police department and have me paged."

"Come with me, Harry. Let's take a drive. We *have* to find her today because she's supposed to perform the fire dance during the Mother Earth ceremony t-t-tomorrow. Lela's the *only* member of our tribe with the gift of fire." Harry put his arm around Ed's shoulder and they walked out the door. *Gift of fire?*

* * *

Just after Harry and Ed left, Camille held up a pink cotton swap. "We've got blood!"

"Rope it off," Tim said. "This is now officially a crime scene. I need to ask everyone who's not a member of the police department to leave." I ran out the door to catch Ed and Harry.

Chapter 3

"C-c-come with us," Ed said to me from the window of his pickup truck. His voice cracked like etched glass from the news that Camille detected blood in Lela's apartment. His hands were shaking like a freshly caught trout as he reached for the steering wheel. He grabbed tightly and bore down on his intentions. "I'm taking Harry to my sweat lodge."

"Your *what?*"

Ed's chest rose with conviction as he explained. "Whenever I have troubles, I go to my sweat lodge for spiritual guidance and clarity. A good sweat will help us find Lela." I climbed into Ed's truck and rode between Harry and Ed in silence for what seemed like an eternity. We drove south out of Jackson, zig-zagging across the backroads of sprawling ranches outside town. As we continued to climb the plateau, the foliage changed from greenery and pine to drier earth and sagebrush. After driving for a half hour, Ed took an abrupt right turn. "Our ranch is one of the l-l-largest around. It starts here at the fork in the road and goes for thousands of acres. We will s-s- stop and pick up my two nephews to help us with our ceremony."

We stopped at a small rectangular house about a half-mile up the road. Ed summoned his nephews, who jumped in the back end of the truck, holding on to the roll bar as we traversed the rocky and winding road to the top of the plateau. "Here is sacred Shoshone ground. You are invited here as Shoshone guests. You will speak to no one of these practices, for they are sacred to our people."

We emerged from the truck and followed Ed to what looked to be a campfire pit. "This is Flying Cloud," Ed said, pointing to his nephew on the left, "and this is White Buffalo." Both nephews were busy gathering large logs and placing them into the fire pit. "The sweat lodge is like the white man's church. It is built of earth and it is here that natives worship."

Flying Cloud placed the longest planks of wood in the middle of the three-foot wide pit while White Buffalo scattered pinecones, kindling and pine nettles on top of the solid layer of logs. "Use the wood Lela g-g-gave me last week," Ed said. Flying Cloud nodded. Ed turned to Harry and said, "Lela hauled that huge pile of wood out here last weekend. She said it was from some crate business she was involved in. Since Lela t-t-touched this wood, it will bring us close to her spirit." Harry nodded as we watched as Flying Cloud piled large, round rocks in an upside down v-shaped dome over the wood, forming a teepee in the fire pit. After the rocks were carefully placed, they were covered with another layer of smaller logs making the pile about five feet high. Flying Cloud set the kindling on fire and within a few minutes, the enormous blaze erupted before us. After time, it started shrinking down to campfire size. Meanwhile, White Buffalo was busy helping Ed tie together long branches from nearby aspen trees into criss-cross patterns, which eventually were set into a dome shape. As the fire continued to burn down, the men dragged the dome on top of the pit and then covered the dome with large tarps.

"Scrub your b-b-body with these before you enter," Ed said, handing Harry and me a handful of kindling. "Sage and cedar cleanse your skin, opening your spirit for purification." Ed, Flying Cloud and White Buffalo removed their shirts and started rubbing their chests with the sage and cedar chips. Harry watched them for a moment, and then followed along. I was unsure whether I was expected to take my shirt off in front of these men, so I waited and watched. "You may go to the trees and scrub. Some tribes require that you s-s-sweat naked. Shoshone are modest. You may leave on your undergarments." Relieved, I ducked behind a tree and removed my running shirt. Leaving on my jog bra, I scrubbed myself with the sage before returning to the sweat lodge, where all of the men were now inside. I opened the small flap and entered into the pitch-black dome.

After I closed the flap behind me, I couldn't even see my own hands in front of my face. The heat was stifling and sweat immediately formed on my forehead. I could smell the sage permeating my skin as the dry heat embraced me. Fighting the feeling of suffocation, I struggled at first to catch my breath, feeling as if I were in a sauna. It was easier to take small breaths through my nose than to breath through my mouth. I could hear the faint crackling of the firewood at our center and as my eyes adjusted to the dark, I could focus on the dim hew from the burning rocks.

"Chanting is our way of c-c-communicating with the spirits. We chant to summon the spirits of earth, air, fire and water to come to us to help us c-c- connect with the spirit of Lela."

Silence overwhelmed us for a minute, and then Flying Cloud and White Buffalo started a rhythmic humming. A few seconds later, Ed started in, chanting phrases in a foreign tongue. The chant grew louder and then softer, like the peaks and valleys of the Tetons. As the first chant grew quiet, White Buffalo doused the fire with a bowl of water, causing an eruption of steam and heat from the fire pit. The rocks hissed in protest, releasing a fury of intense humidity, making a simple breath a great struggle. Flying Cloud opened the flap for a second, allowing a blast of cool air to redeem our lungs. I gasped for more of the fresh air, cooling the burning sensation in my nostrils. Then White Buffalo doused the fire again with water and the heat intensified to an even greater degree. This heating and cooling process was repeated six times, all the while, Ed continued his chanting. When the chanting stopped, there was a moment of complete silence where even the fire refrained from hissing.

"We splash water on the rocks six times–for grandfather, grandmother, father, mother, the earth, and now for our Lela. We summon the spirit to guide us to her. We give thanks to our sweat, for it has served us well. You will leave now and let me alone with the spirits."

I followed Flying Cloud out of our cramped quarters, shocked by the brightness of the mid-day sun. My shirt was soaking wet from sweat and I could feel the chill of the evening air overwhelming my goose-pimpled skin. Harry climbed out after me, his bare chest glistening in sweat and his damp hair matted to his head. I reached over and grabbed my sweatshirt and put it on.

Ed emerged from the sweat lodge about five minutes later in a complete daze. His eyes were rolled back and he held his hands to the sky. He fell to the ground before us and let out a loud scream. Flying Cloud rushed to his side and knelt before him. I thought he was going to give him CPR, but instead he pulled a sharp knife from the strap around his leg and held it to the sky. The blade of the knife shown brightly, reflecting the moon's glare. He held the blade up high and flicked it in a jerky circular manner and then, to my horror, plunged it into the Chief's chest. Instinctively, I dashed to stop him, grabbing for the knife. White Buffalo grabbed my arm and held it steady, as he gently guided my face in his direction. When he had my full attention, he held up his other hand to me. White Buffalo gently steered my body in Ed's direction and whispered in my ear. "It is okay. Chief is okay. He must be cut open to release Lela's spirit to Mother Earth. She will guide Lela back to us." I looked back at White Buffalo, seeing the wisdom and belief in his young and expressive eyes.

I watched as Flying Cloud took the sharp blade and sliced two more slits above the Chief's nipples. Blood dripped from the slits as Flying Cloud pulled the skin away, slipping some kind of a clasp beneath the skin of each slit. He joined the two clasps together with a horse-hair rope in the form of a "Y" and then tied the conjoined ropes to a tree about twenty yards away. Flying Cloud heaved the rope taught to the tree and then vanished into the thick forest.

Chief Ed Washakie Duran started chanting again, but this time the chants were loud, like the howling of a coyote after a kill. As the howling increased, the Chief pulled back away from the tree, cinching the rope tighter. The slits in his chest ripped wider, causing blood to flow like wine from a barrel. Ed howled and yanked back again, until finally the clasps ripped free from underneath his skin. As blood gushed from his wounds, he shook his head violently and yelled out "Lela!"

For the first time in minutes, the Chief appeared lucid, as if he'd been freed from captivity. White Buffalo handed him a rawhide blanket and the Chief wrapped himself tight, like a newborn. He rocked back and forth for a time, humming a faint rhythmic tune. In time he spoke.

"The p-p-piercing released my spirit in submission to the Great Spirit, which is in charge of all other spirits. The Great Spirit will guide Lela's spirit b-b-back to me. I had many visions on my journey, thanks to the

Great Spirit. I saw water rushing." And then Ed turned toward Harry and narrowed his eyes. "J-J-John was in my vision. He was standing next to Lela."

Harry turned pallid; as if he'd been awaken from his own trance. "What does *that* mean?"

"It means that the Great Spirit connected John to Lela. John must know where she is."

"How would John –" Harry started and then stopped himself. "John would *never* hurt Lela. Tell the Great Spirit that it is wrong!"

"The Great Spirit is n-n-never wrong."

* * *

Chief Ed Duran drove us back to town in silence. When we arrived at Harry's house his wife, Jane, and John were waiting for us in the living room. When Harry explained that Lela was officially missing and that her apartment had been declared a crime scene, John was visibly shaken, like a child left out in a storm. He paced back and forth in the living room, his six foot five inch frame pounding the floor with each step, and with each pounding step, his formerly firm belly giggled like Jell-O. John had been a physical specimen in high school–leading the football team to a state championship. He'd been crowned Homecoming King, but his glory days were just that–his past. Despair was the only crown he wore now.

"When was the last time you saw her?" Harry asked in an accusatory tone. John looked at Harry in surprise, fumbling over words to defend himself. Just as John was about to respond, Jane stepped between them. Her rail thin body seemed larger as she wedged in to diffuse what looked to be another fight starting between her husband and her son.

"Leave him alone, Harry," Jane said, brushing her short brown hair back behind her ears.

"I have reason to believe that he had something to do with her disappearance."

"Reason to believe? How lawyerly of you. What makes you think he had anything to do with Lela alleged disappearance? Hell, she's only been missing for a day, Harry. Maybe she's out on one of her wild weekends, for God's sake." Jane crossed her arms across her chest and glared at Harry, waiting for his next move. Her two-carat emerald-cut diamond glistened in the overhead spotlight, drawing my attention to her recently manicured nails. Jane's disrepute for Lela was not cautiously guarded. Lela's grasp on her son's heart left a scar only a mother could savor.

"I went to the sweat lodge with Ed Washakie Duran. He had visions of John with Lela -"

"A sweat lodge? Visions? You've got to be kidding me, Harry! You'd accuse our son of being involved in something based on Ed Duran's *visions* in a sweat lodge. That's what you've been doing all day? Smoking God knows what and hanging out in a teepee conjuring up ways to further drive a wedge in between you and your son? Are you out of your mind?"

"We weren't smoking anything! How dare you even suggest such a thing? This is serious, Jane. We think that something terrible has happened to Lela."

"We? Who's we? You, Mac and Ed? Now that's a threesome –"

"Mom. Dad. Stop it. Please stop fighting over me. That's all you two ever do. Please stop," John said, stepping out from behind Jane. He shoved his hands deep into his faded Levi's, shuffling his feet back and forth in his tattered Nikes.

I took John's interruption as an opportunity to quietly excuse myself from the family discussion.

* * *

I headed back to the office and sat down at Lela's secretarial cubicle. Lela had two large, gray metal desks: one with her computer, printer and fax machine, the other with stacks of files, papers, binders, pens, and post-it notes. I picked up the photograph of Lela's parents holding a little girl on their lap–a little girl who looked similar to Lela. The picture next to it was of Lela and the same little girl–a few years older, perhaps. And the final picture was Lela with Sheila, arm in arm, sitting on a campground picnic table each holding a bottle of Budweiser with wide smiles that only drunken friendship stirs. Lela had changed since she hooked up with Sheila–that was for sure. Before Sheila stepped into the picture, Lela was the most dependable employee imaginable. But since she started partying with her long-lost high school friend, Lela started showing up late for work and often misplaced or misfiled things.

I set down the photographs and continued searching. Lela kept track of our master calendar by using a giant blotter that covered most of the surface area on her desk. The master calendar contained all of our deadlines and court appearances, as well as Lela's personal appointments. I looked at this past week's appointments, noting that Lela had a "movies with T" on Tuesday; "dinner @ B's" on Wednesday followed by "S after work"; "drinks @ SDB with girls" on Thursday; and "lunch with Dr. M" on Friday. I wasn't sure whom the initials belonged, but I figured that Tim Marshall might be interested, so I made a photocopy of the calendar and our client list for Tim and headed through Town Square toward the police station.

* * *

Jackson's Town Square is the most unique city block I've ever seen. Centered in a quintessential western downtown, it is flanked on all four corners with four giant arches made from hundreds of elk antlers. I watched the children running in the grass and climbing century old trees, while laughing and signing. As the front door to the police station closed behind me, the children's' voices were replaced with ringing telephones. A dispatcher was talking into a microphone, fielding the constant barrage of calls. Focused on the sounds before me, I didn't hear Tim Marshall saunter behind me. When he tapped me on the shoulder, I almost jumped out of my skin.

"Mind if we step outside a minute?" Tim asked, holding up a cigarette. "I'm overdue." I followed him out.

"I brought you a copy of our client list. Maybe you can run the list through the system and see if you can find something."

Tim inhaled deeply while staring at the list of names. "Thanks," he managed, while exhaling a stream of smoke out of the side of his mouth. I dodged to the left to avoid the smell.

"I also photocopied our master calendar because Lela kept track of her personal appointments on here. I'm not sure to whom the initials belong, but I have my guesses. Sheila could probably help us out."

"What about 'Dr. M'?" Tim asked, pointing to Friday's note.

"Probably Dr. Miller, the dermatologist that Sheila mentioned. Now that I think back on it, Lela was often gone during her lunch hour on Fridays. She usually worked through lunch or ate in our break room the rest of the week, but thinking back, she was usually out on Fridays. Again, Sheila would know."

"What's Sheila's number?"

I pulled out my Blackberry and gave it to him. "Is there anything else I can do on this end to help with the investigation? I am so worried about her, Tim. She is more than just a secretary to me–she is my friend."

"I can tell that you care about her a lot and we are going to do everything possible to find her quickly. I'll let you know if there's anything else I need. Right now, it's just a waitin' game," he said, smoke billowing out his nose and mouth.

"Waiting for -?"

"Waitin' for forensics to come back. Waitin' for Lela to show up somewhere. Waitin' for a phone call. I doubt anythin's gonna happen today. You should get some rest. You look beat. Let me drive you home."

"Oh, thanks for the offer, but I'm okay. I feel like I should be doing something -"

"The best thing to do now is get some rest and pray that she's safe."

That night, I wanted to pray. I even tried to pray, but I had prayed for twelve years for God to bring my daddy back, and it didn't work, so I wasn't confident that my prayers were heard. Therefore, I fell asleep that night the way I did most nights–with my head propped on pillows and a book folded on my chest. But was differentiated this night from most others was that within minutes of falling asleep, I wok up with a start. The book felt like it was made of stone–compressing my chest like an anchor on the bottom of the sea. I felt like I was drowning in the heaviness of words.

I set the book on my nightstand and turned to sleep on my side. However, the heaviness in my chest did not go away.

Chapter 4

My alarm clock jolted me from a terrible nightmare about the office assault last December. I hadn't recalled that day so vividly before, but maybe my anxiety was heightened from Lela's disappearance. I pulled the covers up over my shoulders and reached over to pet my cat, Ted, who was sleeping comfortably through my nightmare. As I scratched Ted's cheeks, he started to purr and stretch. I got out of bed and put on my jogging outfit, thinking about Lela.

As I was gearing up for a morning jog, the phone rang. It was Greg, the CNN investigative reporter that I'd dated during the O'Connor trial.

"Turn on channel nine. It's about Lela," he said.

I flipped on the TV. The local broadcaster was standing in front of Lela's apartment describing the scene. The camera panned out to the parking lot where the police were impounding Lela's truck. I watched in disbelief. "Hold on, I've got another call," Greg said. He clicked off, and then returned in a minute. "Breaking news. Someone found a bloody jacket this morning at a campground near the Snake River."

"Oh my God."

The broadcaster then interrupted coverage and repeated Greg's breaking news. Another broadcaster was at the campground panning in on the bloody jacket.

"I need to call Harry."

"I'll drive you to the campground."

* * *

May in Wyoming is anybody's guess when it comes to weather. Yesterday, the day started off brisk, yet ended up sunny and warm–around sixty degrees. Today, clouds were threatening and the temperature was hovering around forty. I pulled a fleece jacket over my jogging suit and waited for Greg on the curb.

Greg, a Montana native who was formerly employed by National Geographic, had been on CNN assignment in Jackson to cover the O'Connor trial. He was the opposite of any guy I'd ever dated before: artistic, nature lover, thoughtful, and altruistic. He pulled up in his rental car wearing his winter fleece and a baseball cap over his thick, disheveled blond hair. He stepped out of the car and opened the passenger door, giving me a kiss on the cheek on my way into the car. His grayish eyes looked blue from the reflection of the collar of his coat, which hugged his two-day old beard.

"Any more information about the campground?" I asked while fastening my seat belt.

"My CNN contact said that a hiker found what looks like a bloody denim jacket at a campground near the Snake River. I don't know much else."

We drove south on Highway 89 past Hoback Junction. The rain started sprinkling, so Greg turned on the wipers, smearing dirt in the shape of an 'M' on the windshield. He pushed on the wiper button for cleaning fluid, but nothing came out. "Damn rental." He reached over and put his hand on mine and said, "How are you doing?"

"Okay. Scared. I have that feeling in my stomach that something bad is about to happen." Greg nodded.

"It might not be her jacket."

"It might not be. I wish I could be more hopeful, but I ended last night with a heavy feeling in my chest and I started the day with a bad omen." I told him about my dream.

"They never did catch the guy that attacked you, did they?"

"No. They dusted for fingerprints, but he was wearing gloves and -"

"The campground is just around the next corner," Greg interrupted, making a hard right. There were news vans scattered along the side of the road. He parked the car and we walked on the dirt road toward the campground. Two sheriff cars were parked nose-to-nose blocking the road at the campground entrance. Yellow crime tape circled the camp. I waved to Tim Marshall and he motioned to his officers to let us pass.

"Harry's waiting for Ed. They're on their way," I said to Tim. Tim nudged me by the elbow and walked me toward the river, leaving Greg back with the blockade force. I watched Tim nod to one of the cops.

"Does it look familiar?" Tim asked, pointing at the denim lump. I looked at the jean jacket wadded up on the ground, heavily soiled and stained. The Navajo inserts along the shoulders of the jacket were distinguishable from any other jacket I'd seen. I remembered when Lela got the jacket as a Christmas present from her parents. She showed it off at work before the New Year, wearing it with a short jean skirt and red high heels.

"Yes. It looks like her jacket," I said, as the bile in my stomach started to churn. The stench of Tim's stale cigarette breath made matters worse and I felt as if I was moving, yet my feet were firmly planted. Tim held my arm a little tighter and tilted his head toward the right.

"The shoe is this way," he said as he directed me toward the river. I was feeling woozy, and I wasn't sure that I could look at the rushing water, so I focused on the treetops, but the clouds rushing overhead made me even dizzier. The rain started creeping its way through the thick foliage of pine trees, so I pulled the hood of my jacket over my head. I could faintly see my breath in the cool morning air as Tim gently separated the bushes in front of me, pointing to the garnet red high heel embedded in mud. Tim signaled to his forensic team.

Greg took Tim's gesture as a green light to come to my side. He pulled me away gently and cradled me in his arms.

"It looks like her shoe," I said. "And her jacket."

"I know. But it doesn't mean the worst. I've reported on hundreds of cases, Mac. I can't tell you how many of those have been mistaken identities."

"That's her jacket, Greg. I know it. It is unique."

"Someone could have stolen it."

"Her shoe too?"

"Who says it's her shoe? It's a red high heel. I've seen dozens like it."

"In Jackson, Wyoming?"

Don't give up on her, Mac. She needs you"

* * *

In the surreal moment, indescribable in the chaos of emotion, I watched Tim take Harry and Ed on the same journey, first to the jean jacket and then to the water's edge. I heard nothing but the rush of water, as Ed confirmed his daughter's belongings, his chest heaving like that of an infant in between screams. I watched Harry comfort Ed and felt Greg's hands on my shoulders and yet, I heard nothing but water rushing, splashing, and calling to me. My inner silence was interrupted by Tim's booming introduction.

"This is Helen Generaux," Tim said. Helen appeared to be in her mid- fifties with graying dark hair and brown eyes. She'd probably spent a good deal of time outdoors, as her face had large sunspots and she had deep creases on her forehead. She was wearing wading boots up to her thighs, latex gloves, and a long-sleeved tan shirt, and her work belt was well equipped with gear. Harry pushed forward to greet her.

"Helen, this is Ed Washakie Duran, Lela's father," Harry said. "I've used Helen as an expert witness in dozens of cases. When it comes to the Snake River, Helen knows it better than most." She shook Ed's hand.

"I hope that we can help find your daughter."

"I hope you don't," Ed said. After a second, he explained himself. "I hope that she's s-s-safe somewhere else."

"So do we, Mr. Duran," Helen said. "The only way to rule out the Snake is to search it. This river is murder this time of year. I've never seen so much volume." Ed winced at the expression. "What I meant to say is that it's unlikely she's here. People tend to steer clear of the Snake in the early spring, especially when there's been late snow."

"I'll go get the dogs," Tim said as he marched over to one of the police vans and opened the back door. He heeled and harnessed two German shepherds, who were barking wildly. A familiar-looking woman rounded the back of the truck to help Tim.

"Camille, I'll need a scent rag," Tim said. Camille was short, maybe five feet tall, and her hips were wide. Her tan blouse bulged at the buttons, especially the ones encasing her chest, and as she bended over to slip on her wading boots, her breasts fell forward. Tim took notice.

"You'll have to use the jean jacket as a scent rag. That's all we have," Camille said to Tim.

"It's already been bagged -"

"Then unbag it and let the dogs have a good whiff. We can't take bagged evidence with us." Tim opened the evidence bag with the jean jacket inside and let the dogs put their noses near it. Both dogs grew excited.

"Let's go!" Helen shouted.

* * *

I followed Tim and his team down river. Harry, Ed and Greg stayed behind. Helen pulled her hydrology map out of a metal cylinder that looked like a fly fishing pole container and gave it a good look. "If she was dumped at the campsite, then she would probably have hugged this side of the river for a bit. The first chute isn't for a mile or so downriver."

The dogs howled and pulled forward entangling Tim in the leashes. Camille, looking irritated, took the dogs from Tim. Taking up the rear of the search and rescue team, I looked back at Ed's face, dismal and discouraged. His eyes silently told me to find his beloved daughter. I waved at him, only to turn around a second too late. A pine branch snapped me on the shoulder, tearing my shirt.

The foliage near the river was thick, with willow bushes, trees and vines trapping our legs with every step. The limbs of the pine trees were stiff and sprung back like a slingshot as we passed. The aspen trees were just beginning to sprout new leaves and, like the willows, were pliable and soft. When there was a clearing in the foliage, the ground was slippery. Each time my foot slipped in the mud, I slid backward, grasping for a branch to stop my momentum. My shoes gathered thick heaps of mud up to my ankles, making me feel like I was wearing leg weights.

After an hour of crawling, ducking, climbing, and sliding, the dogs started getting frenzied about something, pulling forward, like a dogsled team mushing to the finish line. The dogs stood on point at a fallen pine tree, the trunk of which remained ashore, with its roots dangling like tinsel from a Christmas tree.

"What is it?" Tim asked. Helen took her binoculars from her belt and squinted through them, crinkling her nose as she focused the lens.

"I don't know," she said. She looked up and down the river and then back at the tree. She stopped. "Something's hooked on a branch."

"Let me see," Camille said, borrowing the binoculars before Helen acquiesced. "It's red. Maybe another shoe."

Helen pulled the rope from her belt and tied it to her waist. She handed me her keys and said to Tim, "Tie this around your waist and get good footing." Helen climbed on top of the fallen tree trunk and inched her way into the river. Her wading boots were splashed with the frigid winter run-off that rushed over the tree with torrent speed. "Whew. Cold. Don't let go," she yelled back at Tim. "If I go in, I'm dead."

"I got you," Tim said, as he wrapped the rope tightly around his fist and spread his legs apart. He used his free hand to swat at the flock of flies that were hovering over his head.

Helen inched her way to the branch and reached in the water. The current dragged her arm down quickly. She jerked her arm back and repositions herself. "The current is wicked." I watched as she moved in a little closer and then she reached in again, this time keeping her arm above water. She grabbed the red object and tucked it into her belt. With her back toward us, she started inching her way back to shore.

Chapter 5

"It's not a shoe," Helen said as she untied the rope from her waist. She pulled the red object from her belt and handed it to Camille. "It looks like it's part of a blanket or shirt or something. It's wool."

"Lela had two matching Navajo blankets in her living room," I said. "One's over the coffee table, but the other one that used to be draped over the chair is missing."

"Bag it," Tim commanded. After Camille put the evidence bag into her backpack, she rewarded the dogs with a treat.

"We can't follow the river any further on foot. Too much foliage. We'll have to raft it," Helen said.

"I thought you said that the river is a killer this time of year?" Camille said, looking sideways over shoulder.

"It is, but with professionals, it's doable. We run it year-round, with a dry suit this time of year. We'll face frigid waters and perilous rapids, but if you want to find this gal, then we'll need to run it—and the sooner the better."

"What makes you think she's in the river?" I asked.

Helen looked into my eyes with a cold stare. "Nothing. Nothing makes me think she's in the river. For all we know, someone stole her jacket and left it at the campground. Or, someone has a coat just like hers. Hell, this time of year –" she continued, then stopped herself. "The point is, I don't know anything more than you do. Ms. MacIntosh. But the only way that I can rule out the river is by investigating it. It's like taking a deposition in your line of work. Sometimes you're trying to get information. Sometimes you're trying to rule out information."

I thought about what Helen said on our hike back to the campground. She was right. We were only ruling out possibilities.

"Let's head back to the campground and finish our sweep there first," Tim said.

As we approached the campground, both dogs started barking wildly again and charged toward the garbage cans near the picnic tables. The larger of the two dogs jumped up on the garbage can, resting his front paws on the lid and howled in excitement. Tim and Camille rushed over to the can, pulled the dog off and hauled out the green garbage bag from inside.

I went to Harry's side and whispered, "We found a part of a blanket on a branch in the river." Harry tucked his hands deep into his camel hair Polo overcoat. His brown wool scarf flapped in the breeze. "We couldn't go any further down the banks. The foliage is too thick. Helen wants to search the river with a raft."

"This time of year? Is she crazy?" He paused for a moment. "I'm going with them."

"Harry, that's not a good idea. Helen said that the water is unusually fast right now from the late spring storms. She said that it's a job for the professionals."

"I don't care. I'm going."

"So am I," Ed said, pushing into our conversation. "She's my d-d-daughter. I'm going down that river come hell or high water." It made no sense to argue with them. Two grown men, hell bent on risking their lives on a raft. They could take it up with Helen. She'd talk sense into them.

"Helen, when are you planning on floating it?" Harry asked.

"Today. The rain is letting up. The sooner, the better."

"We're going with you," Harry said, patting Ed on the shoulder.

"Like hell you are. A few miles downstream is the Big Kahuna followed by Lunch Counter. They're the biggest rapids around here–Class V plus. It's May. With the high run-off, the rapids are going to be treacherous. You're not going."

"I'm going," Ed said, stepping forward. "My p-p-people have been on this river for a great many years -"

Harry was about to chime in, but was interrupted by Tim's loud whistle. "Check this out," Tim said, holding up a stark-white towel tightly wound. Tim unrolled the towel, which was streaked with a reddish-brown stain. Camille scurried over to the towel and swiped it with a solution. She held the cotton swab up and watched it turn pink.

"Blood."

Tim bagged the towel and continued his search. He pulled out a rubber floor mat and a wad of dark green large garbage bags, like ones you might filled with piles of leaves in the fall. Camille sprayed the rubber mat with a solution and suddenly all sorts of spots showed up. "We're gonna need to vaporize the garbage bags with superglue for latent prints."

"What do you mean by vaporize?" I asked.

Camille put the cap back on her permanent marker and said, "Forensics heats the object to about one hundred degrees Celsius, which seals prints to objects. Then we use a superglue vapor that affixes to latent prints and with the use of a florescent dye, the prints show up under ultraviolet light." Camille shined her flashlight on the dirt for a few seconds and then she pulled her two-way radio from her waistband. "We're at the Cabin Creek Campground, about nineteen miles south of town. I need plaster."

"What do you need plaster for?" I asked.

"See here where these tire tracks are?" she said, pointing to the muddy ground. "These might be the tire tracks to the car that could have transported a body here. There aren't any other tire tracks around and these look to be fairly fresh. It's still muddy from the winter melt. We can take plaster and pour it into the tire grooves and let it dry. Then we pull it up and we have a cast of the tire. The lab can usually pinpoint what kind of tire leaves a certain kind of tread. It's like a fingerprint. It could help narrow suspects."

While Camille continued her investigation, I noticed that Ed and Harry were talking to Tim. Harry looked angry, so I eased over toward them to find out what was going on.

"It was a sweat lodge, for Christ's sake. He claims he had a vision of John," Harry said, his face growing a darker shade of crimson. "That doesn't mean that John had *anything* to do with Lela's disappearance! It's not scientifically reliable evidence, that's for sure. It wouldn't be allowed in a court of law -"

"I'm not t-t-testifying in a court of law. I'm just t-t-telling Deputy Tim about what I saw in my vision. Shoshone have relied on v-v-visions for centuries -"

"Gentlemen, please. I'm tryin' to collect evidence here. If you want to talk to me later, fine. I'll listen to anythin' you have to say, Ed. I know how much you love your daughter and I understand that this ordeal is stressful. Don't let it get between you guys. If we work together, we'll find Lela."

"Not if he's going to falsely accuse my son of being involved."

"I'm not accusing J-J-John of anything. I'm j-j-just t-t-telling what I saw."

I walked away from the argument and over toward Helen, who was standing by the river's edge. "Do you think she's in the river?" I asked.

"You're jumping to conclusions. We don't know anything, yet. Lela's missing, but that doesn't mean that something bad has happened to her. It could be anyone's blood. Who knows how long it's been here."

"But the jacket -"

"Maybe someone stole it. Or maybe someone has one like hers. It's way too early to start assuming the worst." Helen's eyes looked wise and perceptive as she continued to canvas the riverbank, but even so, I couldn't help assuming the worst. My father died when I was little and something about losing a parent at a young age deprives a person of a certain level of hope. I followed Helen along the riverbank.

"Well, let's assume the worst, just for argument sake. If something bad did happen, do you think it happened here?"

"Most of the time when people are dumped in bodies of water, they've been injured or killed somewhere else. I don't remember exactly what the statistics are, but a high percentage of all bodies recovered have been transported after death to the dumping ground."

"Over here," Camille yelled, pointing to some broken branches on a bush near the river. "There are spots on the leaves." She shoved the ultraviolet light into Tim's hands and grabbed her camera from around her neck, snapping several frames before cutting the branches and marking them for evidence.

As I turning around to see where Harry and Ed were, my knit scarf got caught on a branch. While pulling my scarf free, I noticed a cigarette butt stuck on a branch extending over the water. As I inched closer, I noticed that the butt had bright red lipstick on it. I showed it to Camille. She photographed the butt before snagging it with her tweezers and bagging it into evidence.

"What can you determine from a cigarette butt?" Helen asked Camille.

Camille leaned in closer to Helen, obviously pleased to talk shop between experts. "DNA. We can get saliva from the butt of a cigarette, and sometimes when we're really lucky, we can even get a print. Denver has a new fingerprint expert that uses IAI qualifiers and can do great ridge comparisons on fingerprints from cigarette butts and other objects that tend not to have full fingerprints. On cigarette butts, people usually handle them with only part of their finger, leaving only a part of a fingerprint, making it difficult to lift a full print for analysis. But there is an expert in Colorado who can use just the ridge of fingerprints to make matches. She's the best in the country for fingerprint analysis. The FBI uses her all of the time on their toughest cases. Cigarette butts have linked many criminals to the crime scene. Who knows? This cigarette butt could have a secret to tell."

* * *

"We'll need two rafts, two guides and a couple of dry bags for our equipment," Helen said into her cell phone, talking to the white water outfitter that she used for hydrology exploration. "Throw in some extra life jackets and meet us at Hoback Junction. We'll put in near Coburn

Creek. By the way, the lawyers that I work for want to run the river with us, so bring extra dry gear . . . and your patience."

While waiting for the rafting guides to show up, I walked down the dirt road toward the highway to find Greg and the rest of his CNN camera crew. He had a headset on and was talking into a tiny microphone. I tapped him on the shoulder and he motioned for me to wait a minute. When he finished talking, I told him about the rafting expedition and he asked if he could join us. Although Greg was experienced with white water, Helen would not allow the media to join us. She didn't want to compromise the integrity of her investigation and she felt that the circus-like environment of the O'Connor trial would pour over into this investigation. But she couldn't stop CNN from hiring a local helicopter crew to scan the river from the sky.

* * *

"Listen up everyone. We've talked about eddy turns, peel-outs and back ferries. Let's refresh ourselves on what to do if we get stuck in a hole," Dan Sansen, the owner of the rafting company, said. He looked to be in his late forties with graying hair and a three-day-old beard. His arms and legs were well defined and tan, sheltered from the elements by only a t-shirt and hiking shorts. His toenails jetted out from his mountaineering sandals. "If you fall in, remember to figure out which way is downstream and then position yourself to float on your back with your feet downstream and your heels at the surface of the water. Don't try to sit or stand up in moving water. You'll end up trapped in a crack. The best thing to do is float downstream and try to backferry your body to the bank. We have rescue ropes on board. If we are close enough to throw you a rope, paddle like hell toward it and grab hold."

Dan loaded the last equipment bag in his raft and then turned to his assistant and whispered. His assistant nodded and then spoke up. "Hi, mates, I'm Jerry," he said, with a thick Australian accent. "Helen and Camille will be in my raft." Jerry was in his early twenties with reddish hair and a full beard. His oversized unbuttoned flannel shirt made him look even shorter than he was.

"The rest of you are with me," Dan said. "You'll need dry suits. It's damn cold in the river this time of year. Hypothermia sets in less than ten minutes after you're in the drink, so zip up and secure yourselves in your assigned raft. I ain't gonna lie to you, this will be a dangerous run. You'll need to do what you're told when you're told. Understood?"

Jerry handed each of us a waiver of liability form. Harry and I signed it without reading. The others read the form.

"When we first enter, we'll practice some nice, safe eddy turns." Dan said. "The water here is swift but calm. Once the canyon narrows, things will heat up in a hurry. We'll have to boat scout some rapids, others we'll have to get out and take a look-see. We'll be relying on your eyes to spot strainers. Strainers are trees that have fallen in the water. They're like a tea strainer, liquids flow through them and solids get caught. Yell out if you see one."

We put on our gear and secured our life vests before climbing into the neon yellow inflatable. Jerry used his oar to nudge his raft off the bank. Dan made us wade through knee-deep water to embark. Dan positioned us downstream and within a few minutes, we caught up with Jerry's raft.

"Mac, are you sure you're stoked for this?" Jerry asked, as we passed their raft. "You're lookin' a bit ashen. If you're in over your head, now's the time to get out. We're about to hit our first set of ripples, and then it's target eddy or stuck in the hole. I don't want to be pulling bloody blokes out of the drink all day."

I held up my right hand, as if I was being sworn in as a witness. "I'm fine. Really." The truth was that the tight dry suit, coupled with the snug life vest made me feel claustrophobic. I was having a panic attack, but I didn't want to jump ship.

"Sssssssssss," Jerry hissed as his raft edged ours. "The Snake has a lot of curves—that's how it got its bloody name."

Up until now, Ed hadn't spoken a word. "Actually, the r-r-river got its name by mistake. Many years ago, before the white men owned the land, the Shoshone people used a snake hand m-m-movement as our tribal symbol. White man named the river the 'Snake' because of Shoshone sign language."

Jerry rolled his eyes at Ed, jabbing his oar hard into the rippling water, propelling his raft ahead.

"The next bend is gentle, but there is a hole dead center," Dan shouted ahead to Jerry. Jerry gave a thumbs up signal while Dan continued his lecture. "Where frothy, recirculating water meets smooth water flowing downstream, a visible depression or hole is apparent. Holes can be impossible to dig a raft out of because the two opposing currents, compounded by the force of gravity, tend to hold the raft in the hole in what rafters call being 'maytagged,' meaning being stuck spinning like in a washing machine.

As we rippled over the water, I looked to my right and left frequently, trying to find any sign of Lela. The cottonwoods that lined the river showed signs of spring. The late winter storms had forced retreat on budding leaves, but the warmth of the past week had proven fertile.

"Hold on," Dan warned. Our raft spun sideways as he maneuvered around a boulder. "Undercut," he yelled. A splash of freezing water sprayed my face, stealing my breath with its bitter chill.

"Boat scouting ahead, mate," Jerry yelled back. "I've got a horizon line, but the fang is forked. I can't see on either side of my target eddy."

"Stay right," Dan said, leaning heavily over the left side of the raft and paddling as fast as he could. We veered right, around an outcropping that was invisible three seconds prior. We flew down a chute. A mist of wetness squirted my face as Dan hollered, "Maytag, Maytag. Everyone to the front of the raft. We're stuck in a hole. The current is circling backwards and we can't move forward. Everyone bounce forward." Harry, Ed and I pushed our momentum forward, rocking the raft enough to break us free from the recirculating current. "Good job. Now get back in position," Dan said, as we bolted forward toward Jerry's raft.

"Look!" Helen yelled. She pointed toward a tree in the water.

"Object in the strainer," Jerry yelled back at us. He'd already shot passed the tree. Dan backpaddled hard and turned the raft around. We inched toward the resting pine with its bristles tickling the water. Ed leaned out and grabbed a branch, bending it toward him. He tilted left and grabbed the object, hauling it into the raft.

"Fishing net," Harry said. "It's just an old net." Relief overwhelmed Ed's face.

"Hang on to your hats, mates. The Big Kahuna's coming," Jerry yelled. I could hear the water growing louder; the pulse of the percolation was increasing. At first, I saw white water boiling over, but looking ahead, the ripples disappeared into plunging waves of torrent water. I looked back to make sure that Harry was securely holding on to the raft. He was sitting in a near squat, holding on to the edge rope with both hands. I secured my feet to the front of the raft, brushed my hair from my eyes and double-wrapped my grip on the rope.

"Peel-out!" Jerry said. He paddled hard to the right and then to the left. His silver helmet flashed in the sunlight, like a meteor.

"Pull back. You're position's off," Dan yelled. Helen looked back at Dan, and then whisked her head forward before she disappeared over the rapids in front of us. We chased them over the Big Kahuna, falling forward as we jettisoned over the first rock outcropping. Momentarily airborne, I felt the raft come to terms with gravity, pounding us forcefully downward and then underwater. Upon re-entry, I heard Ed gasp for air as the wave of water overtook us.

Chapter 6

Still wrestling with the adrenaline rush from the Big Kahuna, Ed excitedly pointed to the cottonwood that stretched halfway across the river. "What's that? I see s-s-s-something shimmering." Jerry inched his raft as close as he could.

"Closer," Camille said. "It's still out of reach." Camille reached over the side of the yellow raft, still holding on the to safety rope. Jerry backpaddled closer and she snagged the shining object, and then she flopped back in the raft, holding the object high in the air.

"That looks like Lela's belt," I said. Lela usually wore a similar two-inch-wide white belt with a large square buckle with her jean mini-skirt.

"She probably got snagged," Jerry said, sounding overly excited by the find. Ed drew back. Jerry must have realized the curtness of his comment. "Sorry, mate. I didn't mean for it to sound that way."

"Lunch Counter's heating up," Dan said, interrupting the discomfort of the face-off. Jerry backpaddled as quickly as he could, but our rafts crashed together. "Keep your arms inside." The rafts jettisoned forward, picking up speed.

"Holy Moly," Harry said as we rumbled over the white water, which turned into plunging dips of coasters. We plummeted into the depths of mist, splattering squarely on the surface, and then we twisted sideways. The raft high-sided against a large rock, throwing us to the left and then spinning around backwards.

"Man in the drink!" Dan roared. I looked back at Dan, wondering what he meant, and then I realized that Harry was missing. *Man in the drink?* Man overboard. I looked downstream but I couldn't see Harry. "Son of a . . ."

"Throw him a rope," Jerry yelled. Harry swished passed us, head first. Without thought, I dove in after him.

The rush of the freezing water filled my dry suit where I hadn't zipped it up entirely. The spray of icy water on my face stole my breath, as I tried to think about Dan's safety instructions, but my mind drew a blank. Harry was floating away at an alarming speed, bobbing in and out of sight. At times, I could only see his vest.

"Grab the rope," someone yelled, but I was pulled under before I could turn to see who yelled or where the rope was. I surfaced again and heard, "rope" again before being sucked back under. I struggled back to the surface, trying desperately to get my feet downstream, but I was not in control. The rushing water was churning me so fast that I felt like I was in the middle of a cyclone. A rock scraped my back, and in trying to bend away from the sharp rock, another boulder grazed my leg and then my shoulder. I spun away from one boulder, only to crack the side of my head on another rock. The bash reverberated through my skull, making me dizzy and nauseous. I spun around again, trying to catch sight of the raft or Harry, but I could find neither. All I could see was white bubbling water around me.

"Rope falls," the voice yelled again. I poked my head up as far as I could and tried desperately to get my feet in front of me, but the force of the water was incredibly hard to fight. The minute I got myself turned around feet first, the water spun me backwards again, making it impossible to grab hold of anything. I tried desperately to keep my focus on Harry, but I'd completely lost sight of him.

My body felt like it was in suspension between heaven and earth as I cascaded over the falls. It was like a long plunge on a roller coaster, but much louder and without the faintest hint of oxygen. When gravity took hold and I hit bottom, I felt the weight of my body pulling me under.

I didn't notice the water entering my lungs at first–it was more like a slow leak in a faucet. But within seconds, I felt peacefully calm as the water came rushing in with tidal force. My lungs felt heavy, yet my body felt light and free. As water bubbled past my face, I could hear the whisper of my father's voice assuring me that it was going to be okay. "You're a survivor," I heard him say over and over. Suddenly, I saw a sharp ray of light shine through the water like a lifeline to safety. I could feel rocks on the muddy river bottom and I reached forward toward them, feeling my way around. As I dragged myself forward, my body felt lighter, as if it was floating free from the current, and I could see the bubbles above me turning white. My long, auburn hair drifted upward toward the rays of light, and I no longer felt the chill of the water or any pain. I heard my father's voice telling me to sit up and breathe. So I did.

When I emerged again, I was gasping for air, catching a sputtering breath, spitting out fluid. I coughed the water out of my lungs and then threw up. At first, I thought I was near the banks of the river and felt hopeful that I could climb out to safety. But as I flung my legs in front of me in hopes of feeling the muddy earth below my feet, I bobbed up and down again. I caught sight of Harry's bright orange life vest, stealing away down river. I swung my legs back behind me and started swimming the crawl stroke in his direction with renewed power and energy. I forgot about backferries and holes, eddies and currents as I stroked as hard as I could to save him.

As I got sucked under again, I snagged my ankle into the crag of a rock. I had to rip my foot out of my hiking boot in order to free myself. I could no longer see either raft or hear any voices, other than my own because the volume of water around me had grown in intensity. I could feel the water picking up speed beneath me again and as I looked downstream, I saw Harry flip over Rope Falls. I was only seconds behind and there was nothing I could do to save Harry–or myself.

* * *

The free-fall was longer than I expected, but the impact was softer. I popped up without losing my breath this time, and was able to sidestroke away from the boulder that was beckoning my way. As the force of the water diminished, I spotted Harry face down, near the bank.

After dragging him ashore, I flopped him over on his back like a dead fish. His face was bluish and his eyes were closed. I thought about starting CPR, but I was afraid that he'd swallowed such a volume of water. I checked for a pulse, but couldn't find one. My hands were shaking so much that it was hard to feel anything. I plugged his nose and blew hard into his mouth, then pumped his chest repeatedly. He didn't respond. I pushed him over on his side and slid my arm underneath him, reaching for my other hand. I clasped my hands together around his midsection and heaved inward, expelling what seemed like a gallon of water from his chest. Finally, after five or six heaves, he sputtered foam from his mouth. I pushed him onto his stomach and pounded on his back, hoping to hammer the rest of water out of his lungs. He coughed and then vomited, gasping for air.

* * *

"Over here," Dan yelled, as he maneuvered his raft in our direction. He backed in, secured the raft and then rushed to Harry's side.

"You all right, man?" Harry rolled over, nodded and coughed again. "Hell of a ride."

"Uh huh," Harry muttered, still coughing up water.

"Grab the emergency bag," Dan said to Ed. Ed threw the bag to Dan. Dan pulled out a fleece blanket and wrapped Harry in it. "We need the other bag too. She's freezing." Dan handed the other blanket to me, without making eye contact. "That was the stupidest thing I've ever seen," he said to me in a loathing tone of voice. "You're lucky you're not dead."

"Hellofa bump you got. A bit bloody back there. We'd better take you and Joan of Arc to the hospital. Her forehead is bleeding too." I reached up and touched the sore spot near my temple. When I looked at my hand, I saw the blood.

Dan reached toward Harry, pulling him to his feet. As I helped Harry steady himself, we heard the whistle echo through the canyon.

"Over here mates," Jerry yelled.

Chapter 7

Her lifeless body rested face down in the river, stuck between the crags of two large boulders, her hair swimming freely. One arm was caught under her and out of sight, but the other was floating back and forth, like a flagman on the highway during construction. Her feet were bare and she was wearing only the jean skirt that she had on at the office on Friday. She looked plump, probably bloated.

"Is it her?" Dan asked. I nodded, as tears came streaming down my face. "Can you be sure?"

I nodded again. I was certain. "She has a tattoo of an eagle on her . . . lower back. I can see the eagle's wings."

I could hear Ed Washakie Duran moaning in a low-pitched cry - more of a yowl, like an animal caught in the snap-jaws of a metal trap, crying for help. I couldn't bear to look at him, so I stared at her eagle wings, praying that they'd somehow taken her out of her misery quickly, so that she hadn't suffered long.

"She's gone. My baby's gone," Ed yelled over and over, until his voice was barely a whisper. Ed wailed so loudly that his cries echoed through the canyon.

Harry waded through the rushing water behind where Ed stood over Lela's lifeless remains and reached out with his right hand, holding him squarely on the right shoulder. "Leave me alone!" Ed shouted, pushing Harry's hand away. "This is J-J-John's doing."

"Ed, come on now. You know that John would never have hurt Lela. He loved her." Harry put his left hand back on Ed's left shoulder, practically holding him up. "I'm so very sorry for you. I understand how you must feel-"

Ed ripped Harry's hands from his shoulders and blurted, "You can't understand how I f-f-feel. Your son isn't dead. What will I tell our little Lynette? Her mommy's gone . . . her mommy's gone." Ed reached down for Lela's hand, which was floating free in the water. Camille was about to say something to Ed, probably something about crime scene investigation and moving the victim, but she caught herself. Harry moved in closer and squatted down in the freezing water.

"But I lost a daughter once too, Ed. Our baby girl died in the hospital. I do understand." Harry had never mentioned that he had a daughter or that she had died. He'd hinted that he and Jane longed for a daughter and I had always taken this as the rationale behind Jane treating me like the daughter she'd never had. And Harry, likewise, treated Lela like the daughter he'd never had. I'd just assumed that this was their way of making peace with not being able to have more children. It never occurred to me that they could have lost a child. Ed looked at Harry with his deeply wounded eyes, and then he buried his face in his hands and began to cry the kind of tears that can only form in the crevice of a wounded soul. Harry grabbed a hold of Ed and held him tight as he gently guided him to the banks of the Snake River. "I'm so sorry," Harry whispered. "I am so sorry."

My eyes were so flooded that I could hardly see the rushing water at my feet as I scrambled over the boulders and up the muddy bank, seeking solitude near the edge of the trees. I could hear Camille calling headquarters, issuing orders and directives. I could smell the damp earth—wet from recent rain. I could see the tops of the pine trees swaying in the breeze. I touched the rough bark, gooey with sap. But nothing felt real. My senses were alive, yet dead.

I watched as Harry guided Ed out of the water. The guides put warm blankets on them and helped them up the river bank.

I was freezing, yet I didn't care. I didn't want to be warm. I didn't want to be safe.

A gust of wind stirred an overwhelmingly pungent smell of sage. Lela loved sage. She said that it was the scent of her people because her ancestors used sage for many purposes. I looked out on the plain, taking in the sagebrush and pine trees and the vibrant spring bouquet of wildflowers, and prayed for her soul to be free.

* * *

Lela often told me tales of her ancestors and complained of how the West was lost, forever marred by mining and railroads and development. She told me of times when millions of bison roamed freely; when elk, wolves, and grizzlies owned the land, in unison with the natives. Lela said that it was difficult to maintain loyalty to Shoshone heritage while living in town. Ed did not want her to leave the ranch but instead wanted her to marry a Shoshone man and raise their children on the ranch, like Ed and his wife had done. But Lela was a typical teenager and wanted her freedom, dropping out of school at age sixteen and landing a job with Harry. Ed tried everything to win her back, but after years of fighting her desire to live on her own, they made a truce of sorts. Ed and Harry had learned to become friends, deciding that maybe two father figures were better than none at all.

I thought about what Ed said when he discovered Lela's body. Something about Lynette's mommy being gone. I didn't know what Ed was referring to because Lela's mother wasn't named Lynette, and that didn't make sense anyway. Who was Lynette? I made a mental note to ask Harry about it later.

My thoughts were interrupted by the County Coroner's van. Dust billowed as the van skidded to an abrupt halt and two men jumped out. The first to approach Camille was Vern Smith, a fit, tall, fifty-year-old who had the looks of a man who works outdoors. A renowned forensic entomologist, he had worked crime scenes in the County for decades specializing in the study of bugs on decomposing corpses to determine time of death. He was a stickler for details and insisted on collecting data at the scene itself, and then again during the autopsy. He's helped crack many "unsolvable crimes" simply by collecting insects that inhabit decomposing remains, researching blood spatter patterns, and analyzing time since death intervals to determine postmortem movement of a corpse.

Vern sidestepped down the embankment wearing his flannel shirt and blue jeans, holding his toolbox cluttered with nets, vials, forceps, and containers. He held his thermometer in the air and noted the ambient temperature before submerging it in the freezing water. He grabbed a net from his kit and started waving it madly, trapping insects flying around Lela's body. I wandered closer to watch him. "These go into my 'killing jar,' which immobilizes the insects so that they can be transferred to a vial of ethyl alcohol," Vern said to Camille. She nodded with great interest.

When Vern was finished, he hollered to the coroner, Grady Martin, a short, pudgy middle-aged man with a crew cut. "Grab a bag and your wader boots," Grady said to Camille, as she scurried to the van to collect the necessities. "Don't forget a rope."

Camille secured the rope to a large pine tree and slowly made her way down the slippery banks into the freezing, swift water. She tied the rope around Lela's waist, trying to pry Lela loose from the crag. Camille yanked again hard, losing her footing and falling backwards into the freezing water. She quickly scrambled to her feet.

"You're going to have to get to the other side," Grady shouted. "Be careful. The current is swift. There's a hole on the other side of those rocks. If you step over, you're going to get sucked down."

Camille waded waist-deep into the water and tied ropes around Lela's legs and torso, then signaled to Grady and Vern to yank hard. After several tries, they finally dislodged her, allowing Lela's body to float free, releasing her long dark hair into the current.

"Reel her in," Grady said, as if she was a salmon fighting for freedom. The thud of her body making contact with mud was vivid. I watched as Ed squeezed his eyes tight, turning in the opposite direction to avoid looking at her bloated, bluish face. Her body was covered with scrapes and scratches, like she'd been in a vicious catfight. As Grady aimed his camera at her lifeless figure, a helicopter whirred overhead. A telephoto lens peered over the scene, snapping shots for the evening news.

After Grady had her on the gurney, about ready to zip the body bag, Ed shouted for him to stop. "Wait," Ed said, his eyes swollen and red. He removed his necklace, examined the arrowhead strung onto a thin black rope, and asked, "May I?" Grady nodded and allowed Ed to fasten the arrowhead to the bag's zipper. As they loaded her into the van, Ed chanted in rhythmic tones similar to the ones he chanted in the sweat lodge, as he made hand motions to the sky, beckoning for the spirits to welcome his beloved among them.

Chapter 8

Lela's death set off a wrongness about me that I knew would never be right. I was sure that the answers of her death would only beget more questions.

After we were discharged from the hospital, I took a long, hot bath. I tried to take a nap, but sleeplessness plagued me on the best of days. The walls of my apartment were closing in on me, and even Ted's meows sounded like cries for help. I couldn't take my mind off Lela's last moments of torment. Her body had been beaten and bruised and her clothes stripped. Who could possibly have wanted her dead? And why? I couldn't stand it any longer. My crazed mind was not going to allow my exhausted body to sleep, so I decided to bury myself with busywork at the office.

Our office is located on the upper floor of the Bank of Jackson Hole. The Bank has a façade that makes it look like a cabin built with knotty pine and river rock. The roof is cantilevered in the front in two tiers–the second tier housing a clock tower lookout, yet the roof over our part of the building has a flat line that gives the office a low industrial ceiling. Harry's decorator made up for the low ceilings with high archways and tall plants in every corner, but today, the ceiling felt lower than ever. I wandered around the office, looking at Lela's workstation, thinking that she'd never be there again. I picked up the photograph of her parents from her desk and looked into their eyes. I imagined the despair that they must be feeling at the moment. I stared at the little girl on their lap in the picture. She didn't look like Lela to me. Her hair was light brown and her skin was fair, unlike Lela who had dark skin and black hair. The little girl was wearing a mouse hat that said "Lynette" on it.

I set the picture down and wandered into Harry's office, which was decorated in Stanford red and white with a beautiful cherry-stained

U-shaped desk which was kept clear of paperwork. His college and law degrees were framed on the walls, and his many scholastic and athletic awards were displayed in a tasteful hutch. I stepped in his office, thinking back on all of the times I'd seen Lela in there, making sure that everything was in its proper place. She kept Harry's life organized and predictable, the way he liked it. I thought of the confrontation between Harry and Ed, and how gracefully Harry handled Ed's anger.

In trial, Harry was personal and professorial toward the jury, as if he was trying to help them solve a jigsaw puzzle in the dark. He talked to them in a very natural, caressing tone, smiling at them often and even making light of a situation during an overly tense moment. Conversely, when he was driving a point home, or aggressively objecting to a line of questioning, Harry was demonstrative and imposing. Juries responded. He gained their respect, nourished their desire to do what's right, urged them to do their civic duty, and inspired them to confer justice. The juries that Harry empanelled usually ruled in his favor and justice, according to Harry's clients, was served. I wondered whether we would find justice for Lela.

I was lost in my thoughts when the phone jolted me to reality. I answered Greg's call. "I heard the news. I'm very sorry." I knew that he was being truthful in his condolences, but all I could imagine was the CNN helicopter flying over the Snake River, panning in on the rocks where Lela's body was recovered. Anything for a gory cover shot.

"We found her in the river."

"I know."

"It was so cold."

"I know."

"She's dead."

"I'm so sorry, Mac. Are you okay?"

"I don't know. I don't feel well. I couldn't sleep, so I came here. I was going to call you in a while, I just needed a little time to myself."

"I understand. I tried to call you at your apartment, but when I didn't get an answer, I figured that you'd holed yourself up in the office. I can't imagine how you are feeling right now. You probably want to crawl into bed and hide under the covers, but on the off chance you need or want company, I'm here for you."

"Thanks. I appreciate it." I wasn't sure what I wanted at the moment. I wanted to be alone. I wanted to be with Greg. I wanted my mom to call so that I could cry on her shoulder. I wanted to see Lela's face walk through the front door. I wanted to wake up and realize that this was just another one of my ugly nightmares and that everything would be okay. But things weren't okay. I was not okay.

A few hours later, I called Greg back. I needed company.

"Have you had anything to eat today?" I hadn't. "Would you have dinner with me? I'm leaving tomorrow for New York. And like I said, I can't imagine how you're feeling, and I'm so very sorry. I just thought that if you wanted company, a shoulder to cry on, I'm here. Nothing heavy. Nothing romantic. Just a friend to listen to you and support you." I thought about it for a minute. I hadn't eaten a thing all day and my stomach was churning. I didn't want to be in the office or at home, so I agreed.

"I'm not good company right now."

"That's okay. How about a light dinner or some coffee or a drink?

You don't have to talk if you don't want to. If you do, I'll listen. I'll pick you up at your apartment in an hour."

* * *

I rent an apartment in the basement of a house that belongs to Mrs. Duncan, a woman somewhere in her seventies, slight, five-foot-two with white hair and creased skin. Her creases look smooth, as if each one has loving significance. I found her ad for the apartment in the paper the same week I interviewed with Harry, and I signed the rental agreement as soon as I saw the place. The neighborhood was nice and the apartment had all the charm of living in your own home, without the worries and headaches of owning a place. I often had dinner with Mrs. Duncan on Sundays because it was the day she missed Mr. Duncan the most.

Black seemed to be appropriate for my mood, so I put on black slacks and a leopard-pattern blouse, black leather boots and the tiger's eye earrings I inherited from my grandmother's estate. I waved to Mrs. Duncan on the way to Greg's rental car and she waved back, and then ducked back behind the curtain in her living room.

* * *

We arrived at the Pines Restaurant, which was situated in the newly remodeled, gorgeous Teton Pines resort west of Jackson. By this time of year, the snow had melted away, revealing the lush fairways that yearned for the summer tourists sporting golf clubs instead of skis. The view from the resort revealed the rugged and wild peaks of the Tetons - the deep grooves and crags of each peak promising danger and excitement to those brave enough to cross the threshold. Just beyond the peaks lies the Jedidiah Smith Wilderness with canyons so steep that hell was sure to lie below.

The reception area of the restaurant was flanked with an elegant flagstone fireplace on the right and a cozy bar on the left. The most exquisite feature of the restaurant was the nineteen-foot, etched glass wall created by local artists. I followed Greg in his chocolate-brown chinos and his cream cable-knit sweater as he walked over to admire the glass wall while we wait to be seated.

"Good evening. I'm Justin and I'll be your server this evening. May I offer you something from our exclusive wine collection?" Justin's dark hair was tied back in a ponytail and neatly tucked under the collar of his crisp white shirt. I wondered what wine Harry would choose if he was here. Harry had one of the most envied wine collections in Jackson Hole. He'd converted the basement of his remodeled Victorian into his own private cellar, hosting labels to some of the finest wines. He served as a wine advisor to several restaurants in the area, offering his opinion to anyone who'd listen.

"We'll try your Stag's Leap cabernet sauvignon," Greg said as he closed the leather-bound wine list and handed it back to Justin. Justin made a note, nodding in approval. "You'll love the plum, cedar and sage flavors of this wine and it has a long finish with elegant tannins." Little did I know that Harry and Greg were both wine connoisseurs. At last I'd found something that the two men in my life had in common. Grinning at Greg, I realized that Justin was staring at me, wanting to take my dinner order. I quickly picked up my menu when he spoke up.

"Aren't you the lawyer that defended Michael O'Connor?" I nodded. "This must be a popular place to come for lawyers on his case."

"What do you mean?" Greg asked.

"Because the other lawyer was here Friday night with the movie star's daughter."

"What lawyer?" I asked.

"What movie star?" Greg asked.

"You know, Samuel Silver. His daughter Amanda is in town and she was here the other night with Christopher Bain. I remembered his name because he was the lawyer who was always on the news."

"Did you wait on them?"

"Yes, at this same table. They brought their own wine and asked me what our corkage fee was. The bartender said that the bottle they drank cost nine hundred dollars."

I nodded at Justin. I really didn't care how much their wine cost. In fact, I really didn't want to be there anymore. I didn't feel like being social and I was having a hard time acting the part.

"She's amazing," Justin continued. "She had on this pink top and it was so low cut that -," Justin stopped himself from further description. "Anyway, I'll get your wine." He backed away slowly as if he'd stepped over the invisible line of decency.

"Bain gets around," I said.

"I didn't know that Amanda Silver was out."

"Out where?"

"Out of jail. She served time for possession of narcotics with intent to sell. It was a big story a few years ago."

"I must have missed it. She sounds like a real class act. Her daddy must be proud."

"Daddy's probably the one she was selling it to," Greg said with a smirk. "She's not the sharpest tool in the shed. She brought the drugs with her on the plane in her carry-on bag–stuffed into the center of tennis balls. The dogs sniffed her out at the Salt Lake airport. Utah is apparently not a good place to be caught with cocaine. I heard that Samuel Silver was trying to pull some strings with a Senator to get her out. Must've worked."

"You know that Samuel Silver is one of our clients," I said. Greg was unaware. I explained the palimony case to him. "I wonder how Bain hooked up with Amanda? Maybe he got a referral from Salt Lake's district attorney's office." Greg laughed.

"I doubt he needed one. She comes with all of the bells and whistles, if one likes that sort of thing. She apparently has an inflated opinion of her good looks and goes out of her way to be noticed. At her sentencing hearing, she wore black leather pants and a white see-through halter-top. She looked like she was on her way to either a Vogue photo shoot or a nightclub. Instead, she got to trade in her designer clothes for a bright orange jumpsuit."

Justin returned with the wine, opened the bottle, and handed Greg the cork while offering a sample. Greg nodded while Justin filled our glasses. Not having much of an appetite, we decided to share the salmon entrée and a Caesar salad.

"You've had a rough weekend," Greg said, as he reached over and grabbed my hands. "How's your head feeling?" I reached up to touch the bump on my temple. The Tylenol was doing its job, keeping the throbbing at bay.

"Rough doesn't even begin to describe it. I'm still in shock. Today seemed surreal–like a nightmare in slow motion. It hasn't even sunk in yet." As I took a sip of wine, I felt my nerve endings releasing, setting my tension free, and yet allowing my feelings to flow through me like a storm. Greg's gray eyes drew me in, but I couldn't focus for long. My mind wandered back and forth, in and out of Ed Washakie Duran's sweat lodge and his accusations about John. I could hear Ed chanting, howling, crying for his daughter and I could feel the wings of her spirit fluttering free, like a Chinook wind in winter.

"Do you like living here?" Greg asked, apparently for the second time. I apologized for drifting off.

"Most of the time I do. I love being so close to the mountains. The scenery around here is hard to beat. I grew up in Boulder, so it's similar. I love to ski and hike and do outdoorsy stuff. But, having a social life is hard in a small town, especially when one is in her thirties. It's hard to find professional men to date."

"I've been meaning to ask you, how is it that the most beautiful woman in town is single?"

I inched back in my chair and looked out the window again. "I'm certainly not the most beautiful girl in town, but thanks for the compliment. As for being single, I guess I haven't met the right person yet. I can ask you the same question. Why are you still single?"

"My mother asks me that all the time. She keeps reminding me that the closer I get to forty, the harder it is to settle down. She's tells me that I'm going to get to stuck in my ways and no woman will have me. I tell her that I'm waiting for the right one to come along."

Justin dropped warm bread off just in time. I watched Greg unwrap the square of butter and spread it with his large, ruddy hands. We talked openly for hours over a leisurely dinner -- about Lela and how much I was going to miss her. I even told him about hearing my father's voice after I went over the waterfall trying to find Lela. Greg listened patiently and seemed to genuinely care and understand.

On the way home he said, "Did you hear about the security breach at the Wort Hotel?"

"No. What happened?"

"Someone broke into the vault at the hotel."

"The vault? When did this happen?"

"Thursday night. The only thing taken was the master key to the rooms. They didn't touch any of the other valuables in there. It was especially weird in that CNN had a ton of people staying there and most of the people used the vault. No one's stuff was missing. Go figure."

I couldn't get too excited about a hotel burglary at the moment. Lela was haunting me. The thought of sleeping alone in my apartment was isolating and frightening. I decided to invite Greg to stay.

Chapter 9

"Are you sure about that?" Harry shouted into the phone as I entered the office Monday morning. "How do you know that it's his?" I slowly crept into his office, mouthing the word, "What?" He looked up from behind his desk and held up his index finger, signaling that he'd be off the phone in a minute. "The stain on Lela's sheets was semen," Harry said to me with his hand over the receiver.

I stared at Harry for a moment, wanting to say, "Of course the stain was semen. What else would it be?"–but I decided it was best to say nothing. Old school or not, such a stain was customary for a sexually active thirty-something year-old.

"They sent it to the state lab for DNA testing and they've been able to match the DNA," Harry said after he hung up.

"Already?"

"You're never going to believe the match." By the look on Harry's face, my gut reaction was that it was going to be John. John had been infatuated with Lela forever, it seemed. Maybe John had finally allured Lela.

"Christopher Bain. Bain's semen was in Lela's bed. Can you believe it? I wasn't even aware that she was . . . dating him," Harry said.

"What? You've got to be kidding me. Please tell me that you're joking!" Bain was the prosecuting attorney in the O'Connor case. Tall, dark and a fairly handsome single man in his early forties, he's known around town as a ladies' man, but as far as I knew, Lela wasn't one of his ladies. I'd heard rumors that they had a little flirtation going, but Lela always denied that it was anything more than just that. "Bain?" I repeated, not as a question, but as a suspicion. "How would the crime lab have his DNA to begin with?"

"Same question I asked. The state has a voluntary drug screening for all government employees. Bain has voluntarily given urine and blood samples, so his DNA is on file with the Wyoming DNA Identification Record System. Wyoming is a member of CODIS, the Combined DNA Identification System, so when the semen was tested for DNA, Bain was a match."

"I don't believe it." An intimate relationship between Lela and Bain was as undetectable as a landmine. Lela loved to flirt, but from what I knew of her, she was not promiscuous, and she would not have been sleeping with Bain unless the relationship was serious. And I had never known Bain to be serious with anyone. If they were serious, why would they be hiding it? Even worse, if they were serious, Bain certainly didn't seem too distraught over her death. And had they been in a committed relationship, he certainly wouldn't have been on a date with Amanda Silver Friday night–the night Lela disappeared. I shook my head in disbelief.

"What?"

"I went to dinner with Greg on Sunday night," I said. "I didn't feel like going out, but I didn't feel like being alone either." I felt the need to explain myself. "Anyway, Greg took me to The Pines and our waiter told us that he served Bain and Amanda Silver on Friday night."

"Who?"

"Samuel Silver's daughter. Apparently, she just got out of jail after serving time for possession of narcotics with intent to sell."

"Bain has interesting taste in women."

"The waiter at The Pines said that they were at the same table as we had. If Bain was intimate with Lela, why was he taking Amanda out?

"It wouldn't surprise me if Bain was two-timing Lela, but what does shock me is that he's dating a felon. I've always said that Bain was as bold as brass and twice as thick." Harry had a million little quips to describe people. He claimed to have picked them up from his fifth grade teacher in parochial school.

"What are the police going to do about the DNA?"

"I don't know. They're still evaluating fingerprints and the carpet stain and some other evidence they gathered on a rush basis. I promised the department that I wouldn't say a word to anyone about the DNA–it is not a matter of public record yet, so please don't say anything."

"I won't say a word, but what if Lela and Bain were an item? What if Lela caught wind that Bain was out with Amanda Silver? What if she invited Bain over for a drink, had him in the sack, and then he came up with an excuse to leave because he had another date. Maybe there was a fight -"

"Whoa. You're getting ahead of yourself -"

"I'm just thinking out loud."

"Any coffee around here?" Harry asked. I took this as a hint and headed for the break room. I could have used a cup of coffee myself.

"While you're up, do you think you could cut a check for a motion fee? I have to file the change of venue motion in the Pilcher case this morning," Harry said. Lela had been in charge of the office expense account. I'd never seen the check register before and I wasn't sure where to begin looking.

"Anything else?" I said, a bit sarcastically.

"Yes. The motion needs a blue back stapled on it." Harry was serious.

"Should I call the temp agency and see if they have someone available?" It was the most polite way I could think of to tell Harry that I was not his new secretary.

"That might be a good idea."

I opened the cabinets in the break room searching for the coffee stash–and a stash is exactly what I found. Several fifty-pound burlap sacks of coffee beans were jammed in the sink cabinet. I knew that Harry was a caffeine connoisseur, but this was ridiculous. I poked my head around the corner and yelled, "What did you do, Harry? Buy the entire supply of Costa Rican coffee?" Harry inspected the contents of the cabinet, completely bewildered by the stock.

"Lela bought the break room supplies with firm petty cash. Maybe she got a good deal on java in bulk quantities? I don't know what to tell you. She made good, strong coffee, that's all I know."

After I got Harry caffeinated and off to his hearing, I checked e-mails and then toggled to my word processing screen, but in the back of my mind, all I could think about was Bain. Did he drop by and pay Lela a quick "visit" before meeting with Amanda? Maybe he told her that he had to go because he had a dinner date and she got mad. Did they get into an argument and she ran out of her place without her purse and keys? Even if she did, where would she go? Maybe she ran into trouble. There are some gang bangers in town. I thought about the wine bottle. It had been nagging at me all weekend. Lela teased me for drinking wine. She wouldn't choose a nice bottle of German wine.

I logged into the Internet and typed in "German wine" in the search category, bringing up numerous wineries in Germany. I toggled through the articles and found an interesting editorial on www.deutscheweine about the Wine Law 1971, where vintners in Germany found themselves obligated by law to keep numerous records of where, when, how much and which varieties grapes were harvested and the degree of ripeness of the grapes. Germany required that this information be documented in the Herbstbuch (Harvest Book), which guaranteed that a wine's contents comply with threshold values, such as sulfur content not exceeding the legal maximum. Each bottle of German wine must apply for a quality control number and in order to get one, must submit a chemical analysis of the wine and three sample bottles from the same lot. The quality control number was referred to as the "A.P.Nr." Once a wine passes inspection, the individual wine bottle must have the quality category, wine origin, appellation of region, quality control number, producer, and alcohol by percentage of volume indicated on each label.

If this were true, then every single bottle of German wine would have to have a quality control number on it. It was worth a trip to the outskirts of town to Teton Liquors, one of the few places in town selling imported wine, to see what a German wine label looked like. In Wyoming, liquor isn't sold in grocery stores–it is sold in liquor stores. I was once told that this was so that the liquor dealers could ensure that minors weren't given the opportunity to get booze under the age. But the truth of the matter is that most towns in Wyoming have "drive-up liquors" where you can drive up in your car and order your beverages of choice, like fast food.

I went to Teton Liquors and asked the clerk to direct me to the German wine selection. "We keep the fancy stuff over this way," the clerk said.

There were only a few bottles of German wines, but each had a distinctive A.P.Nr. on them. I made note of the numbers.

"Are you required to keep track of the A.P.Nr. numbers on the German wines that you import and sell?" The clerk, a silver-haired man in his mid to late fifties, had a ruddy complexion and a bulbous belly. He introduced himself as the owner of the store and gave me a fifteen-minute dissertation on how wines were imported and sold in America.

"To make a short story long," he said, "the answer is no. Wine importers and distributors have to keep track of the numbers, but retailers don't. You can find out if a certain type of German wine is sold by a local retailer, but you would have to go to the importer to track the number of the bottle." I thanked him for his time and information.

After leaving Teton Liquors, I drove to the police station and asked to see Tim Marshall. Tim and I talked about the wine bottle and although the bottle was in the evidence locker, he agreed to give me the name of the wine and the A.P.Nr. number so that I could try to trace it. Tim was not allowed to take the bottle out of the evidence locker because he would have been breaking the chain of evidence, meaning that the evidence must be in the custody of the police at all times once collected from a crime scene. So he traced a replica of the wine label on a sheet of paper and handed it to me. The diagram of the wine bottle label was in the shape of a bell curve and read:

A.P.Nr. 3 561 303-07-02
Qualitatswein Mit Pradikat - 1997er
Reisling Gutsabfuulung Kirchendtuck - Forst D-54292 Trier-Eitelsbach

I drove back to Teton Liquors with the wine label information, but the owner told me that he didn't sell that particular type of wine. He informed me that there weren't many retailers in Jackson that sold German wine, but recommended a few stores to check out.

The woman behind the counter at Westside Wine had a foreign accent and appeared to be of French or Spanish decent. She had beautiful, thick dark hair pulled back into a chignon at the nape of her neck and wore a taupe silk blouse with chocolate wool slacks. She studied the label through her reading glasses.

"Are you familiar with German wines?" she asked.

"Not really."

"Germany has thirteen regions of wines. This particular label is from the Pfalz region, which produces the richest, fullest wines. I was raised in Paris myself and prefer French labels, but I can tell you that this wine is highly rated and expensive."

"Is it sold around here?"

"Let me see." She logged into her computer and clicked on the keyboard. "The distribution website should tell us where this label is sold." She printed out her search results and handed me the paper. "The wine is only sold in San Francisco, Chicago, New York, and Boston. The printout showed the name of the retail stores where the wine was sold. I hope this is of some assistance."

"Do you have a suggestion as to how I can find out where this particular wine was sold?"

"Yes, madam. I would be happy to e-mail these four retailers and inquire about their import log. I will call or e-mail any information I can get for you. Which is your preference?" I handed her my business card and circled my e-mail address on the bottom of the card. She handed me her business card in kind, and I noted her name - Nicole Trudeau.

"Thank you, Nicole. I appreciate your help."

"I hope you catch her killer." I stopped dead in my tracks and turned around.

"What did you say?"

"I hope you catch the person who killed your secretary."

"How did you know?" Nicole turned around and pointed to the television behind the counter.

"It's a pretty boring job. I watch the news when the soap operas are over. Terrible thing that happened to that girl. I hope you catch the idiot that did that to her."

Chapter 10

The temp agency sent over a gum popping post-adolescent to occupy Lela' cubicle. The clasp on the girl's pants didn't surpass her pubic bone while her midriff started somewhere north of her rib cage. I had to yell her name three times before she removed her portable CD headset from her ears. I closed myself in my office to avoid further irritation and logged into my e- mail. The first entry was from Nicole Trudeau, the French lady at the liquor store. She found where the wine had been purchased: a liquor store in downtown Boston called Boston Proper Liquors. How would a fine German bottle of wine get from Boston to Jackson and into Lela's apartment? Michael O'Connor lived in Boston and was in town recently for his trial and he knew Lela from high school, but they saw each other almost daily in our office during the two-week trial and there was no hint of friendship, much less an erotic tension between them.

I emailed the Boston Proper liquor store and explained the situation, informing them that I could issue a business records subpoena for the sales receipt relating to that particular bottle of wine, but preferred a more cooperative and informal relationship, asking that they voluntarily supply me with the information.

Next, I focused on the Snake River. Harry and I agreed that we needed to talk to Helen to determine where Lela's body was dumped in the river and we also needed to talk to our forensic anthropologists, Grady Martin, about his analysis of the decay rate of human tissue to help ascertain when her body was dumped in the water. If we could answer the when and where questions, it might help us figure out who was responsible for her murder. Just as I was about to log off the Internet, I heard the familiar tune of "You've Got Mail." I double-clicked on my mailbox and read

Boston Proper Liquor's response to my inquiry regarding the bottle of wine. The manager of the liquor store, Abe Cohen, informed me that he would comply with any subpoena sent, but preferred to voluntarily supply the information about the wine. According to Abe, the Riesling had, in fact, been imported from the Pfalz region of Germany in 1998 and was purchased in March of this year. He didn't know who purchased it yet because the credit card receipts were in storage, but he promised to look into it and get back to me. I emailed back, thanking him for his efforts.

Just as I was about to grab the documents off the printer, I looked over my computer screen, and saw a Tiger Swallowtail fluttering outside the window to my office. The butterfly seemed to look right at me, as if it was trying to tell me something. It darted up and down and side-to-side, slowing its wings for a split second and then fluttering like mad to regain altitude. The yellow and black striped pattern on its wings looked like a tiger's eye and her sheer beauty mesmerized me, causing me to think about Lela. Lela knew the name of every butterfly in the western hemisphere and is the reason that I can identify a tiger swallowtail. As a Shoshone girl, she said that she wandered the riverbanks catching moths and butterflies. She took them back to her ranch and studied them, categorizing them and drawing pictures before setting them free. I wondered whether Lela had returned to us in the form of a butterfly, flying gracefully and freely in the crisp spring air. I reached over to the window, as if to beckon the creature, but it flew away as quickly as a gust of wind.

The peacefulness of the moment was shattered by Harry's booming voice. "The autopsy will be conducted tomorrow. Make sure that Vern is there when they do it. Deputy Tim Marshall met us at the morgue to report that the preliminary analysis has John's fingerprints on the wine bottle." The words rang loudly in my ears, as if the reverberation might make them escape without notice.

"Oh my God. Have you told John yet?" Harry shook his head.

John was a chip of the ol' block growing up, excelling in every sport, just like Harry. Nowadays, John was lucky to make a sale on a used car down at the Chevy dealership. John was everything in high school—handsome, athletic and popular. These days, he's a balding, overweight couch potato.

Harry and Jane gave John everything, but John shortchanged himself by flunking out of his football scholarship during the second year of college.

"I traced the bottle of wine to a liquor store in Boston. The manager of the store is searching now to find out who purchased the bottle. He thinks that it was purchased in March of this year. John has never been to Boston, has he?"

"Boston?" Harry said. "How would John get a hold of a bottle of wine purchased in Boston? That doesn't make any sense." Harry shrugged his shoulders and headed for the door, but as he was about to exit, he did an about face and slammed his hand down on my desk, knocking a stack of files to the floor. I jumped. "The gift basket from Michael O'Connor."

"What are you talking about?"

"Michael sent me a gift basket right before the end of the trial with a thank-you note for our hard work on his case. The basket had some wine and cheese and chocolates—all expensive and foreign. Maybe John took a bottle of wine from the basket! That damn kid. It's not the first time he's taken liquor from my home. He probably stole a bottle of wine from the basket and took it over there, trying to impress her. John wouldn't know good wine from grape juice."

"We need to talk to John right away and ask him about the bottle and remind him not to talk to the police or anyone else without a lawyer present," I said.

"That puts him at the scene!" Harry shouted, pounding his fist on my desk again.

"Harry, calm down. We don't know that he was there. We need to talk with him. There are all kinds of possible explanations. Let's not jump to conclusions." I turned to pick up the phone to call John's work number when Harry reached over and slammed the receiver back in place. I'm stunned by his sudden move. "You don't want me to call him?"

"Tim Marshall told me the information in the strictest confidence. He went out on a limb, Mac. If I jump the gun and tell John confidential investigative information, Tim won't trust me, and he won't help me on this one. I need to handle this information carefully. I'll go and see John on my way home, and talk to him in person about his relationship with Lela. I'm not going to mention the wine bottle. I'm just going to ask him general questions, and then caution him not to talk to the police unless I'm present. I don't want to say too much at this point. God, Mac, my head is spinning. Jane is going to have a nervous breakdown when I tell her."

* * *

I don't know when day turned into night, but it was sometime around when the thunderstorms hit. The window in my office was cracked open, allowing a crisp, gentle breeze to permeate. Somewhere in the midst of the two motions that I'd been working on, the light breeze grew still. The air intensified and the sky drew in darkness like a cloak. In the still of the night, a flash of thunderbolt shocked me from the confines of my mind and about three seconds later, raucous clamor belted through me like a gunshot. My mother told me when I was little that the number of seconds between the lightening bolt and the thunder boomer indicated how many miles away the thunderstorm was. I used to sit up for hours in the late of the Colorado night trying to figure out when the storms would pass.

One thousand one, one thousand two, one thousand three. Boom! It was nearly nine o'clock and the storm was three miles away. Normally, my stomach reminded me of the time of day, but today I felt no hunger. Ironically, Harry, too, was back at the office working. Missing dinner, for Harry, was a first. He seemed so defeated - like a vessel taking on water and I felt like the lifeboat rowing away.

I tried to settle back into my work after the storm passed, but I couldn't help but think that John might have had something to do with Lela's death. He had been obsessed with her since high school and she rebuffed his advances at every turn.

John's roommate, Duane Towns, was a career criminal. Duane started out with petty stuff, like shoplifting, but in recent years, his larceny crimes had escalated with his rumored methamphetamine habit. Maybe Duane's bad influence had rubbed off on John. Perhaps John went to Lela's place to show off with expensive German wine that he swiped from Harry's house, and when she turned him down once again, he snapped. Maybe he felt that if he couldn't have her, then no one would. I hated to think of Harry's son in those terms, but it was an obvious possibility.

At home that evening, after a cup of chamomile tea, I slept deeply, but dreamt vividly. I dreamt of an avalanche racing toward me at breakneck speed. I tried to outrun it, but I couldn't. It buried me alive. As I lay suffocating in the snow, I felt a rush of warmth like a ray of sunshine beaming out from behind a cloud. Then I heard voices: voices of rescue workers trudging through the crunchy snow, piercing their sticks deep into snow pack searching for my remains. When the stick struck me in the leg, I bolted from sleep to the voices of my radio alarm clock and the ray of light from my bedroom window. Ted, my cat, nudged my hand, urging me to feed him breakfast and as I did, I wondered what the symbolism of the avalanche meant. For some reason, my subconscious was fixated on suffocation.

In need of air, I strapped on my running shoes and headed out for a morning jog. The blue skies of Wyoming framed the earth, so much so, that the landscape took back stage. The aspen trees were gaining buds, giving life to each branch soured by winter arrest. The sounds of spring filled the air with meadowlarks singing love songs to one another. As daylight crested, the sky transformed from periwinkle to cornflower to turquoise to indigo, especially following such a wicked rainstorm. The fresh air blew my hair back, lifting my spirits as I focused on my breathing.

As I arrived at the office, I noticed that a local news van was parked out front. I climbed the steps to the foyer, to find Harry berating some investigative reporter regarding Lela's case. "The autopsy report hasn't been issued by the coroner. You'll have to wait. I don't know anything more than you do," Harry said to the young man wearing a three-piece tan suit. "Now, if you'll excuse me. I've got work to do."

A few seconds later, Harry poked his head in my office and said, "I'm on my way to meet with the coroner. His preliminary findings are bewildering."

"Wait! What do you mean?" I shouted after him, but Harry did not respond. The only thing I heard was the office door slamming behind him.

Chapter 11

I needed to tab some exhibits for the motions that I was filing, so I rummaged through Lela's desk to find where she kept the tabs. For such an organized woman, she kept things in strange places. When I finally found what I was looking for, I noticed a peculiar file inside a Pendaflex. The file didn't have a label on it, which was odd since every other file in the drawer was labeled. I opened the file and found a stack of invoices for beauty products. Most of the invoice entries had check marks next to each invoiced item, with the retail price for the product is in one column and the discount price in the other. At the bottom of every invoice was a commission entry and a reference when the commission was paid *in cash*. I thumbed through the two-inch stack of invoices trying to find a name of a business or some other way of identifying what the invoices were for, but the only identifying mark was a fax number at the top and a date when each fax was sent. The fax number was local, but it wasn't a number that I recognized, so I logged on the Internet and checked the white pages site. The website pulled up "Targhee Day Spa" as a match, listing its address and telephone number. I looked it up in the Yellow Pages and found an ad listing Dr. Miller as the cosmetic surgeon performing the newest age-defying procedures at the day spa. After thinking about it for a moment, I realized where I'd seen his name before. Lela had a ton of prescription-type facial creams in her medicine cabinet prescribed by him, but why would she have a stack of invoices from him? To find out, I booked an appointment for a facial.

* * *

"Hydrogen cyanide," Harry said as he came bounding in the office after meeting with the medical examiner. "Lela had hydrogen cyanide in her blood, and get this: it was also found in the wine." Harry handed me a copy of the toxicology report.

"How'd you get this?"

"Don't ask."

I read the report out loud. "Hydrogen cyanide is an extremely poisonous, colorless liquid with a bitter-almond odor. It causes asphyxiation in humans if given in high doses. Acute exposure causes weakness, headache, confusion, vertigo, nausea and/or vomiting, among other symptoms. "Was that the cause of death?"

"No. Only trace amounts were found in her bloodstream, but possibly enough to make her confused or make her pass-out for a short time. Maybe enough time to transport her from her apartment to somewhere else."

I thought about it for a second. John's prints were on the wine, and he wanted Lela like nobody's business. Did he slip her the drug to relax her so that he could get her into bed? Maybe he gave her too much, and then didn't know what to do when she passed out. As if Harry could read my mind, he said, "I don't know if John had anything to do with this, but it's possible that he got a hold of what he thought was one of those 'date-rape' drugs from one of his loser friends. Maybe he was trying to seduce her."

"Good God."

Harry turned and paced the length of our conference table, rubbing his hands through his hair. "I don't think John has it in him to hurt anybody, but he isn't the same kid as he was in high school. I hate to admit this about my own son, but he runs with a group of idiots who only think about the next drinking binge. He could have been anything he wanted to—he had a great scholarship to a good college, but he just couldn't get beyond the glory years of being the high school jock. Selling used cars was easier than applying himself in college. I love him, and always will, but I'm afraid that he's done something terribly wrong. I tried to talk to Jane about it last night but she absolutely came unglued. I don't know what to do." Harry flopped down into one of the black leather conference room chairs and cradled his head in his hands.

The mental image of John pouring Lela a glass of poison and watching in horror as her respiratory system collapsed was vivid and real. John clearly had motive and opportunity. He was in love with Lela, but she loved John as a friend. True, they did hang around together sometimes, and she certainly would have invited him into her apartment, but John wasn't the handsome, tall, star-athlete in high school anymore, and even if he was the father of Lela's child, she didn't appear to want to have anything to do with him romantically. I realized that my mind had drifted when I heard Harry's voice thundering through my skull. "I said, have you heard from John?"

"No. You said that you were going to talk with him, so I haven't contacted him. He hasn't called here, as far as I know."

"Is my son capable of such malevolence?"

I didn't respond to his question. Honestly, I thought that John was capable of date rape if he'd had enough to drink, but I don't think that he would have deliberately harmed her. Desperately wanting to change the subject, I said, "I found something bizarre in Lela's desk. I was looking for exhibit tabs and came across a file with these invoices in them." I slid the stack of invoices to Harry and looked on as he thumbed through them, crinkling up his eyebrows like always when he's trying to figure something out. "They don't identify who the invoices are to. The only identifying mark is the fax number on the top, so I did some investigating, and the fax number belongs to Targhee Day Spa. The dermatologist at that spa is Dr. Miller. I think he's the dermatologist that Lela and Sheila went to."

"Why would she have all of these invoices?" Harry asked.

"I don't know. I can't imagine that she was buying that large of a quantity of stuff for her face. Do you think she could have had a side job?"

"I side job? Like what?"

"Maybe she was doing Dr. Miller's bookkeeping or something for extra money. She did just buy that expensive truck. I've never asked you how much she made, but by the upgrades on that truck, she made a lot more than I do."

"You make more, Mac."

"Look at the bottom of each invoice. Someone was making a hefty commission for each of the sales on these invoices." I grabbed the calculator from the credenza and started punching in numbers. "Just in February alone, the commissions total twelve thousand dollars."

"We don't know if they're commissions or not, or even if Lela had anything to do with these, but it's worth looking into."

"That's why I booked you an appointment tomorrow with Dr. Miller for a facial and a pedicure," I said. Harry scowled at me. "I'm kidding. I scheduled a facial with Dr. Miller for tomorrow during the lunch hour." Harry nodded, giving me a half-smirk.

"Listen, I've got to get to the courthouse for a post-probation evaluation hearing," Harry said. "Then I'm going to pay John a surprise visit. I expect to get the official autopsy results either late this afternoon or early tomorrow morning. Keep a lookout on the fax machine. The medical examiner promised to fax them over. Also, check the message machine and the stack of mail. By the way, what happened to our temp?"

"She can't type and listen to her heavy metal at the same time. I called the agency and asked them to send over someone else, preferably with experience in a law office."

* * *

As I walked into Targhee Day Spa, I was overwhelmed by the scent of lavender, so intense in fact, that it smelled sour instead of sweet. The reception area looked like a Tahitian hut, with bamboo shoots sprouting from every planter and a waterfall streaming down from the ceiling. The receptionist asked my name in a phony European accent while handing me a chilled glass of water, flavored with cucumber and orange.

"It's wise to hydrate before the facial. It enhances purity," she said. I wanted to tell her that no glass of tonic could enhance my purity, but she didn't appear to have a sense of humor. Her black hair was pulled back so tightly into a ponytail that it made her eyes slant and her splotchy cheeks glistened with a thick application of extra heavy moisturizer.

After waiting about ten minutes, a stocky man with a tan face and acne scars introduced himself as Dr. Miller and then escorted me to the facial laboratory. He sat me down in a reclined chaise lounge covered in a white sheet and placed a terrycloth headband around my hairline. He then spritzed my face with a mist.

"Who referred you to the spa?" he asked, as he applied a hot cloth over my face. After he lifted the cloth I said, "Lela Duran." Dr. Miller's eyes widened, and then darted away. He swiveled his chair in the opposite direction so that his back was to me for a minute. I wondered whether he'd heard the news of her death. "She was my secretary."

"Terrible tragedy. I saw it on the news last night."

"Yes, it is terrible. We miss her very much. You knew her pretty well didn't you?"

"I wouldn't go that far. She was a client. Lovely young lady. She came in for treatments on her Friday lunch hour." He turned back in my direction and swabbed my face with a moistened pad. It stung.

"Oh. That's where she went on Fridays. I thought she was having an affair," I said, hoping to provoke a response. An uncomfortable silence filled the air in that moment and I noticed Dr. Miller's upper lip was twitching. He broke the silence by smearing my face with an apricot scrub.

"So she came in here for facials?" I said, trying to pin him down, but careful in my tone.

"Her treatments are confidential, as are all of my clients."

"I see. She just spoke so highly of you. She called your office a lot, so I just assumed that the two of you had something going on." I had no basis in fact for making such a bold statement, but his reaction to my audaciousness was amusing. His lip started twitching again as he applied some stringent that stung like rubbing alcohol in a wound. Paybacks, I wondered?

"We were . . . acquaintances. Nothing more." He applied something hot to my face that smelled like chamomile and then wrapped my whole face in a towel, covering my mouth. He then placed cucumber slices over my eyes.

"Relax for a minute. The cucumbers should help the swelling under your eyes. I'll be back to check on you." He knew how to shut me up. I honestly didn't know much about him or his relationship with Lela, but something about him clearly gave me the creeps. The minute I mentioned Lela's name, his demeanor changed.

He returned a few minutes later and removed the cucumbers from my eyes. Standing over me with a mask over his face and latex gloves on his hands, he lowered the lights and removed the towel, adjusting the light so that it shown blindly into my eyes. Centering a well-lighted magnifying glass above me and hovering over my face, he offered the following advice:

"Here's my opinion of your skin portfolio. Your pores are oversized, meaning that you need a daily regime of cleansing and self-applied light dermabrasion. Your eyebrows are beautiful and full, but could using a waxing treatment for better overall shaping. I strongly recommend a laser facial to get rid of the aging spots on your nose and forehead, and I practically insist on Botox injections around your eyes and on your forehead to slow down the aging process. Your upper lip is quite small in comparison to the size of your mouth, meaning that you should strongly consider a filler. Plumaze injections in your upper lip and crow's feet would add volume and permanently get rid of the tiny lines. I'm the only doc in town that administers Plumaze, and let me tell you, it's a real miracle worker. I have movie stars flocking in here from all over the place to get it because no one else is injecting it. Pretty soon, it'll put Botox out of market. It is the only filler that permanently fills wrinkles. You won't believe your eyes. I'll have Victoria out front give you a pamphlet. Let's get you signed on for a treatment plan."

"Thank you for your recommendations, Dr. Miller. I'll think it over," I said, slightly offended by his brazen description of my skin. I've been told all of my life that I hade flawless, silky skin and I've never had acne. I do have freckles, but nothing that a light dose of make-up can't cover. No one has ever complained about the fullness of my lips or the creases in my forehead, and I've never even heard of Plumaze.

"Before you leave, I'll print you out a copy of my skin care recommendations and a schedule to follow for cleansing and refurbishing your skin."

As I sat up, he handed me some sample products. "These will get you started. I *highly* recommended that you purchase a month's supply of these products from the front desk."

When I went to the front desk to pay for the services, I picked up a pamphlet on Plumaze. On the front page, a woman in her fifties was pictured sitting on the beach with the sun shining on her face. Her skin looked flawless. *Plumaze* was typed in large, bold fancy italic print and underneath it said, "Natural beauty made in Sweden." I opened the pamphlet and learned that Plumaze was a long-lasting gel for filling out lips, facial wrinkles and folds. Its claim to fame was that the hyaluronic acid was nearly identical to that naturally found in the human body—only slightly modified. Its product base was a yeast enzyme found in thermal water, making it biologically degradable. "It is naturally integrated into the tissue, allowing nutritive agents to pass through the implant and cells to pass between fragments of the gel. It is the first and only *true* permanent wrinkle filler."

I kept reading. This gel was injected into the skin like collagen, but the product was hyped to be better than collagen because it was made from a sugar-based, natural molecular enzyme, but the effects were similar, in that it filled out the lips or lines wherever it was put under the skin. The results looked good and the testimonials claimed that the results were permanent. Most fillers had to be re-touched every so often, but not Plumaze. Once a wrinkle was filled, it was gone. Most actresses and models with the huge lips look to me like they've had a fight with a suction cup and lost, but the women in the pamphlet looked natural and normal. At the very bottom of the pamphlet I noticed an asterisk with a notation that Plumaze was not FDA approved.

I turned to Valerie at the front desk of the spa and asked, "Is it safe to use Plumaze if it's not approved by the FDA?"

She look up at me in utter annoyance and said, "It's *supposed* to be approved very soon," in her fake European accent.

"Can you sell something that's not FDA approved?"

"Yes. Of course. The patient must sign an additional consent form, but it is perfectly legal to sell it."

I wasn't sure that her statement was accurate. During the O'Connor trial, Michael O'Connor spent a good deal of time explaining the FDA approval process to me. Some of the drugs that his company manufactured needed FDA approval, and some didn't. The ones that needed the approval had to have it before they could be sold in the United States. I paid for the facial and left. Valerie bid me good-bye with a "ciao." By her vernacular, she couldn't decide whether she was Swedish, English or French.

I picked the copies of Lela's invoices off the passenger seat of my car and sure enough, Plumaze was one of the products listed on the invoices. Lot numbers were listed next to the products, and then various abbreviations were noted in the description column. I took the top invoice back into the spa and showed it to Valerie. "I found this in my secretary's desk. It has your fax number at the top. Do you know what this is for?"

She looked at it for a minute and then stared at me. "I don't know what this is." She quickly handed it back to me.

I pushed the invoice back at her and showed her the fax number. "Whose fax number is this?"

"It's Dr. Miller's personal fax number. Our fax number at the front desk is different," she said in an American accent.

"Why would Dr. Miller be faxing these invoices to my secretary?" She looked me up and down and leaned forward toward me. I don't know whether she was sizing me up to punch me out, or going to tell me a secret. Her furrowed brow concerned me.

"I think he had a thing going with Lela for months," she whispered. *So the receptionist knew Lela by name.* She leaned in even closer. "Lela came here during the lunch hour all the time. She went in his private entrance. He locked his office door during lunch and we were not allowed to bother him. I could hear them in there. She arrived at nearly the same time every Friday, and left at the same time too. He told us that if we ever breathed a word of it, we would get fired, so you didn't hear it from me." She leaned back and put her index finger to her lips, giving me a shush and then a slight wave–a signal for me to leave. I took the hint.

Chapter 12

I knew the minute I crested the bluff overlooking the Duran family ranch that this would be no ordinary funeral. Not that I was a funeral expert–I hadn't been to one since my father's and I don't remember much about that horrible day. But I do recall an overwhelming sense of reverence that day. Today, however, I felt an overwhelming sense of sorrow–a sorrow as deep as the Grand Canyon. When Harry and I arrived, I noticed that Jane was consoling Ed's wife, and that John was hugging a young woman next to Ed. I asked Harry who the young woman was, but he hushed me, motioning that the ceremony was about to begin. Ed, in full ancestral dress, began chanting in the low moan of an injured wolf. His chanting grew louder and then quieter and louder once more in a sequence denoting Lela's birth, death and afterlife. He spoke in his native tongue but cried like any father who has lost a child.

Lela remains were displayed in ancestral dress on a table made of pine, covered with wild flowers, the roots of which were still attached. Ed took three sticks that had been tied together in the shape of a six-point star. He reached for a long piece of twine and wrapped the end of the twine in the center of the star, and then he slowly wove the twine around the sticks, creating what looked like a large spider's web. He placed the web on her chest and spoke in a commanding voice, "You were born connected and you remain connected, to your past and to our people's future. This web is a symbol of our connection. You were our Gaea–Mother Earth."

The ceremony continued for the better party of an hour, and while most of my attention was toward Lela, I couldn't help but stare at the young woman next to John. She looked more like Ed than anybody, and I guessed her to be around sixteen. *Was she Lela's daughter?*

Near the end of the service, Jimmy Lonewolf appeared over the crest of the high bluff, and the crowd turned in unison and glared his way. John quickly put his arm around the young woman next to him, and Ed made clear his desire that Jimmy leave. Jimmy took note of Ed's gesture, tipped his hat and disappeared over the horizon.

"Who was that girl next to John?" I asked Harry as we drove back to the office after the ceremony. Harry looked out the driver's window and shook his head before taking a big breath.

"Lynette is Lela's daughter. After she had Lynette, Lela dropped out of school and tried to be a mother, but she wasn't ready to raise a daughter, and she knew it. She left Lynette on the ranch with Ed and his wife, and that's when Ed asked me if I'd give Lela a job. She refused to go back to high school, and Ed said that she was like a caged lioness on the ranch, so I did him a favor and hired her."

"John seems well acquainted with Lynette," I suggested, more of a probing question than I had intended. Harry, uncomfortable with the direction of our conversation, nodded and quickly changed the subject to a work- related topic. My mind drifted to the funeral service–to the connection that Ed spoke of when referring to the web of life. How was John *connected* to Lela? To Lynette? Did this *connection* lead to her death? And if so, why were Jane and John allowed to stand with Lela's family at the funeral? Ed had made it clear that he thought John was involved in Lela's death. Why the change of heart at the service?

When I got back to the office, I headed straight to our conference room, where Lela's autopsy results were posted to the easel, page by page, explaining how the medical examiner believed that she met her death. "An acute exposure to hydrogen cyanide caused a rapid increase in her respiratory rate, which later turned to a slowing and gasping due to inadequate respiration. The cause of death, however, was a gunshot wound to her larynx that flooded her lungs with blood. The weapon used was a .38 special. The bullet was lodged in the spine. The shot ripped open her throat, opening a gateway of blood to her lungs, liver and stomach."

According to the autopsy, her lungs had filled with blood long before she was disposed of in the Snake River, making the official immediate cause of death "asphyxiation from blood caused by gunshot to the larynx. Contributing conditions: hydrogen cyanide." Further details described the gunshot wound as a contact wound, meaning that the muzzle of the gun was likely held at close range to Lela's throat. "Contact would produce a stellate pattern on the victim due to the close range explosion of gases tearing the skin in a star-like pattern."

"The autopsy pictures were not delivered to us because the report itself is not yet official," Harry said to me from the doorway of the conference room. "I had to pull strings to get it early." I nodded. "I have no idea why anyone would shoot her in the throat, unless she said something to anger someone. People don't shoot people at close range in the throat, Harry. If they wanted her dead, they would have aimed for her head or heart. The throat tells me that whoever did this, likely shot her there deliberately, maybe to silence her." Our momentary silence was broken by a ringing telephone. I picked up the receiver.

"Could you and Harry meet me over here at the station? I've got some interestin' news on Lela's case," Tim Marshall said. We agreed to meet with him right away. Harry dumped his stale coffee into the trash and we headed out the door.

* * *

"Have a seat," Tim said, as he opened a file and sat down. "We got the autopsy report back on Lela. It's lookin' like she was drugged and shot and then dumped in the river." Tim looked over his reading glasses at us, gauging our reaction to his news. Since we weren't supposed to have known about the report, I tried to look surprised. Tim passed over the autopsy report for Harry to look at while he opened another file from the stack on his overloaded desk.

"The hair, fluid and fiber samples taken from Lela's apartment have been analyzed by our crime lab. We found three different hair samples: one is from Lela; the other two are from two other individuals. The semen on the sheets matches Christopher Bain's DNA."

Of course, Harry and I already knew about the DNA match. Small town leaks are only as good as the small town theatrics that cover them up.

84

"Bain has agreed to be questioned with counsel present, but that's not why I've asked you here. I figure that you already knew everythin' I've just told you. I asked you to come here to tell you that we're gonna need an exemplar from John."

"What kind of exemplar?" Harry asked, surprised.

"We'll need a hair sample as well as a swab from his mouth. We're plannin' on goin' down to the car lot today to get it. You can come with us if you like. This isn't standard operatin' procedure, just professional courtesy."

As a criminal defense attorney, Harry wasn't a favorite of some of the local cops because it was Harry's job to find where they may have screwed up in order to avoid a conviction for his clients. But Harry hadn't always been a defense attorney. In fact, in the early years of his practice, he was a civil litigator, often representing cops and other government officials accused of wrongdoing in and out of the scope of official duties. Even though Harry's practice these days consisted mostly of criminal defense work, he was still on the good side of most of law enforcement.

"Thanks, Tim. I definitely want to be there when you collect samples from John. Let me call him at the dealership first so that he can make arrangements to excuse himself for a few minutes and meet you somewhere discreetly. I don't want to cause a scene or cause him undue embarrassment. You know how upset he gets when he's embarrassed. He's trying really hard to gain back his reputation around town. Is it all right with you if I give him a call?"

"You bet. Tell him to meet us in the back lot by the 'Used tar' banner in ten minutes. I'll get Camille to come with me for collection."

* * *

Just as Tim had promised, we met John by the Used Car sign. John approached cautiously, wearing tan cords and a white collared shirt with the dealership logo on the chest pocket. John's belly protruded over his belt. I detected a strong stench of body odor.

"Hey Tim," John said, in a tone reminiscent of their high school days.

"Sorry to do this to you buddy, but I gotta do my job." John nodded and shook Tim's extended hand.

Camille approached John and quickly swabbed the inside cheek of his mouth, placing the cotton swab in a small labeled plastic bag. "You'll need to remove your cap," Camille said, then she tugged a few pieces of hair remaining from the crown of John's balding head and placed them in another evidence bag. "That's all I need," Camille said, backing away from John with a friendly smile on her face. She winked at Tim, then gathered her collection kit and headed toward the police van.

"John, we'd like to call you down to the station later for questionin'. When do you get off work?"

"Today's Monday Madness. I have to work to nine o'clock. I have my lunch hour from five to six."

"Can you meet us at the station around say five fifteen?" Tim asked, looking at John and then at Harry.

"We'll be there," Harry said.

* * *

Tim Marshall pushed down the play button on the tape recorder and said, "Good afternoon. I'm Deputy Tim Marshall of the Teton County Police Department. I've asked John Harrison here today for questionin' regardin' the murder of Lela Duran. Mr. Harrison is being represented by counsel who are both present at this interrogation. This conversation is being recorded. Please identify yourself for the record."

John cleared his throat before beginning. "John Harrison."

"John, where were you last Friday, May seventeenth?"

"Well, I went to work at eight thirty in the morning. I worked through lunch that day because I was trying to sell a Chevy Cheyenne pickup. The deal finally closed around four in the afternoon. I did some paperwork and waited on the lot until around five, and then I drove to my apartment and had a shower."

"Do you live alone?"

"Uh, well, yes and no. My roommate is Duane Towns, but he's in jail right now. So, his stuff is still there and he still pays rent somehow, but he doesn't live there at the moment, but he's supposed to be -"

"So no one can verify that you went to your apartment at five?"

"I guess not."

What did you do after your shower?"

"I called my mom and asked her about my dad's trial and she told me that Lela was coming over to have a drink with them, so I figured that I would join them," John said, stroking his goatee.

Tim looked up from his file for the first time. "So you knew that Lela was supposed to be going to your folks' house for a drink?"

"Yeah."

"So what did you do next?"

John's face turned a lighter shade of rose while tiny beads of sweat started forming near his receding hairline. He unbuttoned the top button of his collared shirt and switched positions in his chair. Harry noticed John's fidgeting and said, "Would you like a glass of water? It's a little stuffy in here."

"Yes, sir," John answered. Tim slid the pitcher of water and a glass toward John. After drinking half of the glass, John resumed. "I went by Lela's."

"What do you mean that you went by Lela's? Tell us exactly what you did from the time you left your apartment."

"Like I said, I took a shower and called my mom. When she said that Lela was coming over, I put on a nice shirt and some jeans. I drove from my apartment to hers, which is only a few blocks away."

"Did you take anything with you to her apartment?"

"Uh, yes."

"What did you bring?"

"A bottle of wine."

"Are you a wine drinker, John?"

"No, sir. Beer. I sort of borrowed a bottle from my folks," John said sheepishly, glancing over at Harry, an apology in his eyes.

"What do you mean that you borrowed a bottle of wine?"

"Well, there was this basket at my parents' house. It had all this fancy stuff in it from Germany. My dad is a wine collector, but I've never seen any German wine in his cellar, so I didn't think they'd mind too much if I took the bottle."

"Where did you park when you got to Lela's apartment?"

"On the street out front."

"So you used the front entrance to get in, right?"

"Yes."

"Doesn't the front entrance require a key?"

"Yes, but I just punched Lela's code in and told her I was there. She buzzed me in."

"So, Lela knew that you were coming up to see her?"

"Yes, well, I mean, I wasn't really invited or nothing. But she said I could come up for a minute, so I did."

"When you got to Lela's door, was it opened or closed?"

"It was closed, so I knocked and she answered the door."

"What was Lela wearing when she answered the door?"

John closes his eyes momentarily, as if he is imagining back to that moment, trying to remember what she was wearing. "I think she was wearing a lacy top with a skirt and high heels."

"What happened after Lela answered the door to her apartment?"

"I went in and handed her the bottle of wine. She thanked me and set it on the kitchen counter. She said that she was in a hurry to go over to my folks' house and that she was gonna change her clothes and stuff. I asked her if she wanted to have a drink, but she said that she didn't. She told me that I could meet her at my folks' for a drink in a few minutes and basically asked me to go, I guess."

"You didn't open the bottle of wine?"

"No."

"Are you sure?"

"Yes."

"You just handed her the bottle and she put it on the table? Neither of you opened it?"

"Objection. You asked him two different questions. He must answer one question at a time for the record to be straight," Harry said.

"Sorry. I'll re-ask the question. Neither you or Lela opened the bottle of wine?"

"No."

"What time was it when you got to Lela's?"

"Around five thirty or so."

"Were you dating Lela?"

"No."

"Would you like to have been dating her?"

"Yes."

"Had you ever asked her out on a date?"

"Many times. She met me at the bar a few times and stuff."

"Were you ever boyfriend and girlfriend?"

"Briefly. In high school. But not after that. Lela dated other guys," John said, gnawing at the inside of his cheek.

"Do you date other girls?"

"No, not really. I mean, I could. But I don't. "

"So you were waiting for Lela?"

Harry looked at Tim with fierce eyes, like a lion protecting his young. It was his signal to move on in the questioning. Tim was well aware of John's love for Lela. As it is with a first love, John was obviously willing to endure the agony of watching Lela out on dates with other men on the off chance that he might just be there for her when the chips fell.

"Did you leave, as Lela suggested?"

"Yes, I left. I told her that I would meet her at my parents' house."

"What time did you leave Lela's apartment?"

"Around five forty-five or so."

"So you were there for fifteen minutes?"

"I guess. Maybe not that long."

"How long do you think you were there?"

"Maybe closer to five or ten minutes. Not that long."

"What did you do in that five or ten minutes other than hand her a bottle of wine and agree to meet at your folks' house?"

"Nothing. That's all that happened."

"What you're describin' takes about one minute. What else did you do?"

"Nothing. I just sat there on her couch."

"Where was she?" "In her bedroom."

"Did you go back to her bedroom to talk to her or anything like that?" "No."

"So, you sat on the couch the entire five or ten minutes you were there?"

"Yes."

"What were you talking about?"

"The O'Connor trial, mostly."

"Have you ever been in Lela's bedroom?"

"Yes."

"When?"

"When I helped Lela move into her apartment."

"Any other time?"

No," John said, in a defeated tone. Tim got the message and moved on with his questioning.

"Did you leave Lela's door to her apartment open or closed when you left?" Tim asked.

"Hmm. I think I pulled it half closed, 'cuz I knew she was leaving right behind me, but I'm not sure. I might have closed it all the way. I don't remember. She was gonna change her clothes, so I probably closed it."

"But you're not sure?"

"No. Honestly, I'm not sure."

"You didn't open or drink the wine that you brought for Lela?"

"No. It was a gift to her. I don't drink that stuff. I just brought it for her."

"Did Lela drink wine?"

"Sometimes."

"How do you know?"

John elbowed Harry and whispered in his ear. "Tim, we need to take a minute outside. We'll be back," Harry said. He escorted John out of the interrogation room, while Tim turned off the tape recorder and made notes in his three-ring binder.

I didn't know whether to join Harry and John in the hallway or to stay put in the interrogation room. The air in the room was thick and had the lingering smell of stale cigarette smoke. I looked for an ashtray, spotting one on the windowsill, blackened with old soot, but free of butts. I looked around the rest of the room, noticing that there were no pictures on the walls, or lamps, or pens and paper. The room was naked, perhaps to keep the witnesses' mind from wandering.

The door opened within a minute and John followed Harry back in, like a sheep following the herder to the butcher block.

"Are we ready to continue?" Tim asked. Harry nodded, so Tim turned the tape recorder back on. "How do you know that Lela drank wine?" Tim repeated, even before Harry and John had assembled back into their seats.

"Because I've seen her drink wine," John said with an inflection that suggested that he wasn't sure of his answer.

"Where have you seen her drink wine?"

"Out on dates."

"Dates with you?"

"No. Dates with other guys."

Tim looked at John with the burning eyes of a leopard zoning in on a gazelle. He leaned forward over the table and asked, "Have you ever spied on Lela when she's been out on a date with another guy?"

"I sometimes end up at the same place she is, so I notice her."

"Have you ever followed her? Let me clarify. Have you ever waited near her apartment for her to leave on a date and then followed her while she was on a date?"

"Like I said, we've ended up at the same places. Jackson's a small town. There's only so many bars."

"So your testimony is that you've never followed her?"

"Objection. Asked and answered," Harry said.

"This isn't a deposition, Harry. I can ask John the same question over and over if I want. He hasn't squarely answered my question. I want to know if he's followed her."

"Let's move on," Harry said, looking at his watch. "He needs to be back at work shortly."

"I'm not movin' on. This is an interrogation. It will take as long as it takes, Harry." Tim said, turning his attention back, "Have you followed Lela?"

"Yes."

"Yes, meanin' that you've waited outside her apartment and followed her and her date to where they were goin?"

"Yes."

Satisfied with his answer, Tim looked down at his notes. "Do you know of anyone that Lela was datin' whose name started with a 'T'?"

"Tom," John blurted out. Harry nudged John under the table.

"Who's Tom?"

"The ski instructor. He thought he was hot shit 'cuz he's from California. He's not even that great a skier. He taught Lela to ski this year."

"Was he the guy that you saw Lela drinkin' wine with?"

"No. Tom drinks *martinis*. Pink martinis. What a fuckin' wuss. She was drinking the wine with a doctor." Harry held his hand up, signaling to John to take it easy.

"What doctor?"

"Dr. Miller. He is a pimple-popping doctor. Lela goes out with him and they drink *wine*."

"So you thought that if you brought her some wine like she drinks with the doctor, that maybe she'd be interested in you, right?"

John shrugged his shoulders.

"But it didn't work, did it? She shunned you like she always has and that made you really angry, didn't it?"

"I wasn't angry!" John shouted, pounding his fist on the table. Harry grabbed his arm.

"Have you and Lela ever had sexual relations?" Tim pressed.

"Objection," Harry said. "Come on now, Tim. This is an invasion of privacy. John's sexual history isn't relevant and you know it. You're just trying to incite him."

"I'm not pryin' into his past for the sake of it, Harry. His past history with Lela is relevant to this investigation, and I'm askin' a valid question. John needs to answer me square."

John looked to Harry for an out, but Harry nodded in Tim's direction. "Yes. We had sex in high school."

"Did your sexual relationship with Lela result in her getting pregnant?" Tim asked, leaning on John even harder.

"I don't know," John said, looking down at his lap. He fought back the tears by squeezing his eyes shut. "I don't know who Lynette's father is. Lela would never tell me. I've always wanted to be the father. I offered to pay support. Lela refused to take money and told me that I wasn't the father." John's voice trailed off as tears rolled down his cheeks.

"I think we're done here," Harry said, "unless you need anything further. If so, why don't we continue this another time," he said as he stood and helped John from his seat. Harry's imposing figure made his intentions clear.

"Just one last thing, John. Did you go to your parents' house last Friday after you left Lela's?"

John glanced at Harry with his tear-stained face.

"We're going to step out for a minute," Harry said. "We'll be back." This time I followed them into the hallway.

"Can you cover for me, dad?" John asked, like a little boy caught stealing bubble gum at the drug store.

"Cover for you? No, goddamit. I can't cover for you. This testimony is under penalty of perjury. I'm an officer of the court, John. I can't cover for you. Why in the hell do I need to?"

John bit his lower lip to stop it from quivering.

"Oh Jesus, John, don't tell me that you did this!" Harry turned, as if he was going to walk out. John reached out and grabbed him by the arm.

"No. No. I didn't do it! I swear!" he shouted. "I would *never* hurt her, dad. I loved her," he cried, his eyes wet with tears.

"John, you've got to tell the truth. But tell it to me first."

* * *

John's large hands were folded tightly on the conference table. I could see the tips of his fingers growing purple from pressure, while his knuckles turned white. "No."

"No, you didn't go to your parents' house?" Tim repeated.

"No, I didn't."

"Where did you go then?"

"I went for a drive and then down to the Cowboy for a drink," John said, exhaling loudly.

"Where'd you drive to?"

"Just around. I was bummed out that Lela wouldn't have a drink with me and I just needed to clear my head, that's all."

"You mean that you were upset that she wouldn't drink the bottle of wine with you?"

"Yeah."

"But I thought you said that you don't drink wine."

"I would have if she would have had some with me," John said, unclenching his hands.

"So you would have drank wine with her, even though you don't like the stuff, as long as it meant that you could be with her?"

"Objection. Asked and answered," Harry said.

"How long did you drive around?"

"I don't know. Maybe an hour or so. Not longer than that because I got to the Cowboy before happy hour was over and that ends at seven o'clock on Fridays."

"You said that you left Lela's around five forty-five, right?"

"Right."

"Then you drove around from that time until sometime before seven o'clock?"

"Right."

"Can anyone verify this?"

"Uh. No, not really."

"We're gonna need to see that truck of yours," Tim said. "Is it in the parking lot?"

"No. My dad picked me up from work. My rig is at the dealership."

"Camille will be down to take a look. Any objections?"

I watched as Harry rubbed his temples. John had no alibi and was the last person known to have seen Lela alive. "Give me a minute," Harry said. He took John back out into the hallway. I followed. "Is there anything in your truck that could incriminate you?"

"No."

"No drugs? No beer? No girl's lingerie?" Harry asked.

"No."

"Nothing that belongs to Lela?"

"No."

"Any notes to her? A diary? A gun?"

"No, dad. None of that. My rig's clean."

"Has Lela ever been in your truck?"

"Yeah. I've given her a ride home from the bars when she's been too drunk to drive."

"So her DNA could be in there."

"Her DNA? No. We've never done it in the truck or anything like that."

"John, DNA isn't just body fluid. It can be hair, fiber, and things like that. My concern is that they're going to find Lela's DNA in your truck and assume that you took her involuntarily from her apartment."

"Well, I didn't."

"I believe you, but can't you see what the police will try to do? And if we don't agree for them to comb your truck for evidence, they'll think we're hiding something. If we do agree and they find Lela's hair or something in your truck, then they'll have means to prove that she was a passenger in your vehicle. We're screwed either way. If I make them get a warrant to search the truck, then the seed will be planted that you're a suspect."

"I'm sorry," is all that John could manage to say. Harry said nothing as he walked back into the interrogation room.

"You can have Camille take a look at the truck tonight on the lot. John's working late for Monday Madness. But let's go back on the record." Tim turned the recorder back on. "John has given Lela rides in his truck on numerous occasions, so finding hair or fiber consistent with Lela's DNA is not conclusive."

Tim was about to say something when Harry interrupted. "That's a wrap. John needs to get back to the lot. His lunch hour is up."

"Sure, fine, we're finished. Thank you, John, for meetin' with me. If we need a followin', I'll give your old man a call."

Harry shook Tim's hand and escorted John out to the car. "Remember, don't talk with anyone about Lela or the police interview. Any inconsistent statements can be used against you in court."

"Court?"

"Yes. Court. If the police find evidence in your truck, or anywhere else that links you to Lela, you could be in court for her murder," Harry said.

"Shit."

"By the way, you don't own a handgun do you?"

"A handgun? No. I have a few hunting rifles—the ones you gave me."

"Have you ever had access to a handgun?"

John looked down at the ground for a moment before responding. "Yes, I've fired Duane's handgun."

"When?"

"Recently."

"Last Friday night?"

Chapter 13

I dropped in on Dr. Calvin Rudolph, Chief Medical Examiner for Teton County. Rudy, as everyone referred to him, had been in the business a long time, and at retirement age, he'd refused to step down. His work was everything. He was standing over a half-draped corpse when I approached from behind and tapped his shoulder lightly. Without even turning in my direction he said, "Evening, Mac. What brings you down to the bowels of justice?" I wondered whether he had ESP, until I noticed an overhead mirror.

"Hey Rudy. I'm here about Lela Duran."

"Of course. My condolences."

"She'll be missed by a lot of people." Rudy and Harry were old-time friends—the kind of kinship that didn't allow a differing opinion to interfere. It was no secret that Harry had taken Rudy to task on the witness stand a time or two, but Harry told me that Calvin Rudolph was so meticulous with his work that even Harry could hardly catch him off guard with a discrepancy.

"Have you been able to determine when Lela died?"

"We're doing the analysis on that right now. I've got my forensic entomologist looking at the bluebottle flies to determine whether any of the female flies laid eggs. I'm also testing for mayflies, too. I'm not sure how quickly her body was dumped into the water after she was murdered. From the tissue analysis and the entomologist, we should be able to narrow it down shortly, my dear." By the look on my face, Rudy could tell that I didn't understand why he was telling me about bugs. He put his scalpel down on the metal tray and removed his mask.

"The first insects to arrive on a corpse, a few hours after death when the body starts to release fluids and gases, are the flies–bluebottle and house flies seem to have the best radar and get there the quickest. According to my entomologist, within two days, the female flies lay eggs on the body, particularly near the orifices like the eyes, nose, mouth, ears and genitalia. If the victim was beaten or shot, then the flies are also expected to lay eggs in those types of open wounds. Generally speaking, about a week later, the eggs hatch into small larvae that live on the dead tissue." Rudy removed his glasses, cleaned them with a square cloth, and then puts them back on.

"The next flies to congregate on the dead body are the greenbottle and grey flesh flies. They arrive after the body emits the foul odor of decay. If we don't detect any flesh flies on the corpse, then we often know how recently the person was killed." Rudy slipped his mask back over his nose and mouth, signaling that he was about to continue with official business, but just then he leaned in close to me and said in a whisper, "My guess is that she was drugged and taken somewhere and killed, then transported to the river and dumped some time later, but that's only a hypothesis. We'll see if I'm right by tomorrow." He moved away from my ear. "I'll call you with the results."

As I walked toward the door, I turned and asked, "Was there any sign of sexual abuse or trauma?"

"It's hard to say. The body was in water for some time, so we were not able to obtain fluids. The flesh was saturated to the point where swelling was no longer detectable. We did not notice any bruising to the genitalia. Our results remain inconclusive regarding penetration, whether voluntary or involuntary."

He affixed his mask and started making an incision into the chest of the cadaver lying on the gurney in front of him. Quickly, I thanked him and bolted out the door. Emerging into the dusk sky, I noticed that Christopher Bain's car was parked out in front of the police station. Curious about what Bain was up to, I told the receptionist of the police station that I'd left something in the interrogation room earlier in the day. She buzzed me in. I slinked my way through the hallway, trying not to be noticed. I tiptoed near Tim's office and leaned in as close as I could, and overheard him talking to Bain.

"I don't know how my semen got in her bed, Tim. I swear, I've never slept with Lela. Never. Not once," Bain said.

"Well, it didn't just walk there. Come on, man. I wasn't born yesterday," Tim said. "Word around town is that you were seein' her. Rumor has it that you're quite a ladies' man and that you've been known to brag about how many women you've bagged. Don't sit here and try to tell me that you didn't have sex with Lela. I don't buy it, and I won't believe another word you say if that's your story. The department is givin' you a courtesy talk here. The next talk we have will be an official interrogation."

"Is that a threat?"

"More like a promise. And before you come up with another lie, we want to know what you were doin' last Friday night havin' dinner with Amanda Silver at The Pines," Tim said. I couldn't see Bain, but I heard something slam down.

"Now, what? You're having me followed? Am I under surveillance, Tim? Am I a suspect here?"

"Just because you're some hotshot lawyer doesn't mean nothin' to me. The fact that your semen puts you at the scene of the crime puts you on the suspect list. So yes, you're a possible suspect. That's all I'm tellin' you."

"I had dinner with Amanda Silver. Big deal."

"Tell me exactly what you did last Friday."

"I went back to the office right after the verdict was read. I dropped off my trial notebook and briefcase. Some of the people at the office invited me out for a drink at the Silver Dollar, so I went. When I was there, Amanda Silver came in. Of course, every head in the bar turned her way. She was wearing a low cut blouse and tight jeans. You know what I'm saying. I wasn't the first guy to buy her a drink. But when I did, she came over to my table and introduced herself. After a few drinks, she asked me to dinner. I was a little surprised by her offer, to be honest, but I agreed. She told me to pick her up at The Wort at seven o'clock. So, I went home and showered and waited for her in the hotel lobby. She showed up about seven fifteen or so and we went to The Pines and had dinner."

"What did you do after dinner?"

"I invited her to my place to have a night cap."

"What time was that?"

"Around nine thirty or ten, I guess."

"Did she agree to have a drink at your place?"

"Yes."

"How long did she stay?"

"Well, let's see. I guess she left pretty late. Maybe around midnight."

What did you do from ten to midnight?"

"We had a drink or two."

"What else?"

"None of your business."

"Was that the first time that you'd had sexual relations with Amanda Silver?"

"No," Bain said.

"When was the first time that you had sex with Amanda?"

"The night before," Bain answered.

"I thought you just said that she *introduced* herself to you for the first time on Friday night. Are you changing your story?"

"No, she introduced herself to our table on Friday. That's what I meant to say. She acted like she didn't know me when she came up to our table, but I think she just likes to play games."

"So, you had sex with Amanda the night before the closin' statements of the O'Connor trial? Where did this take place?"

"It's not a sin to have sex during a trial, Tim. To answer your question, it was in her hotel room, if it's any of your business. We're getting off the subject, which, at this point, I'm not even sure what the subject is. Whatever it is, I'm not answering any more questions about Amanda."

"Do you have an alibi for your whereabouts from six to seven p.m. last Friday night?"

"Like I said, I was at the Silver Dollar with my office staff and then went home to shower."

"Did you stop anywhere along the way from the Silver Dollar to your place?"

"I stopped by the liquor store to pick up a bottle of wine."

"Which liquor store?"

"Teton Liquors."

"Got a receipt for your purchase?"

"I probably do somewhere."

"I'd like to see it," Tim said.

"Why?"

"Why do you think?"

"You tell me."

"Because I want to see what time it was when you made the wine purchase."

"You think I went to Lela's, don't you?"

"I think you could have," Tim said.

"What in the hell is this? I've never dated her. Never slept with her. You're accusing me of not only sleeping with her, but also *killing* her? Are you out of your fucking mind? Is the department so desperate to figure this out that you're stooping to this?"

Without warning, the door swung open and Bain charged out. "I'm not answering any further questions without counsel present," he yelled over his shoulder. "This interview is over."

As Bain turned to leave, he saw me standing around the corner from Tim's office. There was no time to hide. I stammered for a second, trying to think of an excuse for being there. "Uh, Tim, sorry to interrupt," I said. "Harry left his reading glasses somewhere. He thinks he might have left them in the interrogation room. Have you seen them?" Bain rolled his eyes at me–his face beet red and his forehead laden with beads of sweat. Tim looked around his office and shook his head. "Well, thanks anyway. I'll keep retracing his steps. If you see them, please call." I tried to scamper away quickly, but Bain caught my arm as I headed down the hall.

"You were eavesdropping, Mac. Don't try to lie to me," Bain said. I eased my arm out of his grasp.

"Sounds like the pot is calling the kettle black."

* * *

After making an ungraceful exit from Tim's office, my next stop was a visit to Helen Generaux's office. She'd done some testing since we found Lela's body in the Snake River and had some information for us. Helen's office was located on the second story of an office building about three blocks from Town Square. The sign on the door read, "Helen Generaux, Ph.D., Hydrogeology." I walked into the waiting room, which had two chairs centered in front of a gigantic picture of Lower Falls in Yellowstone National Park. "Ms. Generaux?"

"Come on in," she said. "Harry said you'd be right over. By the way, call me Helen." I entered her office. Helen was wearing a chestnut brown sweater that matched her eyes. She reached out to shake my hand and offered me a seat. "Hell of a rafting ride, wasn't it?" she said. Before I responded, she continued talking. "Your bruise is getting better. I can't believe that you don't have pneumonia. Or at least bronchitis. You were in that water several minutes."

I started to respond, but she kept on talking.

"Listen, Harry asked me to determine where Lela Duran's body was dumped in the Snake. I've done some hydrology tests and I'm fairly certain that I can pinpoint the area within a few hundred feet of the put-in point."

She took the diagram from her desk and tacked it to the blank white wall, which had so many tiny holes in it that it looked like a beer can that had been pelted by a teenager's B.B. gun. "Here is where Lela's body was discovered, as you know," she said, placing a red thumbtack on the spot. "Here's Cabin Creek Campground." She placed a yellow tack there. "Here's where we found a piece of the Navajo blanket when we went for a walk south of the campground." She placed a blue tack there. "This is the range where I believe she was dumped, based on surface-water hydrology."

"How can you tell where she was put in?"

"We analyze the flow of current and water volume using complicated geomorphology. It would take too long to explain, but suffice it to say, we are able to narrow the possibilities of where an object enters the water. But this is not a precise science by any means. It is impossible to tell exactly where her body was put in, but I think I'm pretty close."

"You're pretty sure that she was dumped in the river somewhere south of the campground?"

"Yes. I'm no criminologist, but when we were at the campground, remember we saw snapped branches near the river?" Helen said. "And you even found a cigarette butt there, didn't you?" I nodded. "I think that the killer had her stashed in a car and drove to the campground, looking for a place to dump her. He probably walked to the riverbank and saw that the water wasn't moving very fast there. Remember the fallen tree just a few feet south of the campground? It was causing the water to pool by the bank. The killer probably noticed that the water was slow and didn't want to risk putting her in there because she would be discovered easily. He decided to carry her down the trail a bit. He shoved her body in, knowing that the rapids would pull her apart or send her a long way down river."

"Do you think she was dead when she was put in?"

"That's for forensics to decide. My guess, though, is yes. Or she was heavily sedated. When we searched the banks, I didn't see signs of struggle."

"Meaning?"

"Meaning broken shrubbery or drag marks in the mud. And the dogs didn't get hot on her scent until we found the blanket. If she was struggling, grabbing at trees and bushes, the dogs would have picked up on it."

"Will you be issuing a report?" I asked

"Not unless I'm asked and compensated."

"I'm sure that Harry plans on paying you for your time," I reminded her.

"That's not what I meant. I'll issue a report for the prosecution or defense if I'm hired as a witness for a murder trial." I nodded, appreciating he keen business sense and the fact that she was not biased in making her scientific evaluations. I thanked her for her time and said, "I'll let Harry know your preliminary findings." She untacked the diagram from the wall and handed it to me.

"Keep it. I have the original in my safe."

* * *

It was getting late when I got back to the office, and I was surprised to see that Harry was in his office with his door closed. I could hear him yelling and I could see someone sitting in the chair near his desk and someone else standing near the window. The low ceilings and poor acoustics of our office made it easy to eavesdrop. I slipped into my office and listened.

"It isn't mine," a voice said. The arguing carried on for a bit. I decided to poke my head in Harry's office to let him know that I was back from Helen's.

When I peeked in, I saw John sitting in the chair and Jane, standing near the window wearing a red cashmere sweater with black silk pants and a Louis Vuitton belt. She looked like she could use a cigarette.

"I'm back from Helen's," I said, breaking an uncomfortable silence. "Looks like you're busy. I'll fill you in later." Harry nodded.

"I swear, it's not mine," I heard John say again.

"Then how in the hell did it get on Lela's carpet?" Harry asked.

"Don't yell at him, Harry. It doesn't help," Jane said.

"I'm not yelling," Harry bellowed. "I'm just trying to figure out how our son's blood ended up on Lela's carpet. If we don't find a rational explanation, Jane, he's going to be convicted of murder. Is that what you want?"

"Dad! It's not mom's fault. Don't be so mean to her."

"I'm not being mean. She's babying you, as usual. She still does your laundry and cooks for you. It's about time you stand on your own two feet."

"I do *not* baby him. I simply help him out. I do your laundry and cook for you too. I don't see you complaining about that."

"You're my wife, not my mommy."

"Same difference."

"What's that supposed to mean, Jane?"

"You know exactly what it means."

"Come on. Stop arguing," John begged.

"How did your blood end up on Lela's carpet?"

"I'd been in a fight."

"A what?"

"When I went to Lela's place on Friday, I'd been in a fight," John said.

"Who'd you get in fight with?"

"Jimmy Lonewolf."

"Again? The two of you have been fighting since high school, John. When are you going to get it through your thick skull that –"

"I taught him a lesson."

"If you taught *him* a lesson, why were *you* bleeding?"

"The jerk pulled a knife. See?" John said, pulling up his shirtsleeve.

"Oh my God!" Jane said. "You need to go to the doctor. That looks terrible. I think it's infected. It certainly needs stitches. It's going to leave a horrible scar –"

"It's nothin', Mom. It's scabbed over."

"No, it's not. You need to see the doctor," Harry said. "How did your blood get on Lela's carpet? You just walked up to her place with a bottle of my wine, dripping blood all over the place?"

"It wasn't like that. It wasn't like blood was gushing out or anything."

"I thought you said that you went home and took a shower and then went to Lela's?" Harry asked. The silence in the room was deafening "Well?" Harry said, breaking the silence.

"Well, I really didn't go home first. I went straight to Lela's after I got in the fight."

"So you lied to the police?"

"I guess."

"Why in the hell would you do that? For Christ's sake, John, this is a *murder* investigation. It's not like high school when you have to sit out a football game for playing hooky. This is the real deal. You get tripped up in lies during a murder investigation, then the cops are going to stick to you like glue."

"Harry, don't be so hard on him. He was probably nervous when they questioned him. You know how tricky the police can be. You say so yourself."

"I'm not being hard on him! He's making it hard on himself, as usual. Stop defending him. Don't you get it? His fingerprints and blood are at the scene of a crime. And it's not like his criminal record is squeaky clean."

"Oh, not that again. Every time he has a problem, you have to bring *that* up."

"*That* criminal record is relevant. The prosecutor could use it against him, Jane."

"It was a stupid prank, dad."

"Stupid, yes. Prank, no. It was vandalism. And let's not forget about the felony drunk driving."

"Here we go again."

"So you get in a fight after work and go straight to Lela's, hoping that she'd take pity on you?"

"Sort of, I guess."

"Let's take it from the top. This time, tell us exactly what happened Friday. The truth, John."

"Like I said, Lonewolf dissed me at dealership. We got into a fight. He stabbed me in the arm with his knife. I drove to Lela's house. I gave her the wine then I showed her what happened to my arm. She took a look at my arm and went to her bathroom to get some bandages. I waited for her on the couch. She gave me a gauze thing to put on it to stop the bleeding. She told me to go to the emergency room. I asked her to come with me, but she said that she had plans. So I left."

"I thought she told you that she was going to meet us for a drink at our house?"

"That's what she said. That's what I meant by plans. She said she was going over to your place for a drink and then out later."

"So you just left? You didn't try to get her to have wine with you?"

"I would have, but she was hinting that she was running late and that I should go to the hospital."

"Why didn't you go to the hospital?"

"I didn't want to report it. If I squealed on Lonewolf, he'd send his gang to beat the shit out of me."

"He's a gang member?" Jane said.

"Why didn't you come to our house? Didn't you tell the police that you told Lela you were going to meet her at our house?"

"I didn't want you to see my arm either. I knew you'd get mad or make me go to the hospital."

"So what did you do?"

"Like I told Tim Marshall, I just drove around."

"For how long?

"A couple of hours."

"Did you see anyone during that time that can provide you with an alibi?"

"I drove out Highway 22 toward Teton Pass. I stopped in Wilson for a beer at the brewery. Maybe someone there could give me an alibi."

"I'm going to have to tell Tim Marshall that you didn't tell him the whole truth. He's going to want to question you further."

"You're going to tell the police that he lied?" Jane said. "You defend countless criminals day in and day out, probably hiding the truth from the prosecutor at every turn, but the minute your son misspeaks, you become the town Samaritan?"

The ringing phone interrupted my eavesdropping. I hesitantly answered, not wanting to miss out on the conversation in Harry's office. It was Sheila on the line. After exchanging pleasantries, I said, "I didn't see you at Lela's memorial service."

"That son of a bitch that I work for wouldn't let me have the day off. I even got someone to cover for me, but he wouldn't allow us to switch. He said that it was against store policy. Anyway, I called because my friend, Patty, who works at the courthouse in record keeping, you know, you met her that one night at happy hour, anyway, Patty said that the cops got a search warrant for Christopher Bain's house. Patty lives with her mom a few doors down from Bain. Anyhow, Patty said that the cops just searched his house and they found long black hairs in his bed. You think it could be Lela's?"

After witnessing the exchange between Bain and Tim Marshall, I was shocked to learn that the police had already secured a search warrant for his house. Tim was obviously quite serious about his threat. I didn't dare discuss the matter with Sheila because anything I said would be directly repeated to Patty, or someone else in Sheila's gossip chain. "I don't know. Listen, the other line's ringing. I need to go. Thanks for the information."

"I'll call you if I hear any more scoop," Sheila promised.

I hung up and answered the other line (which really was ringing). "Mac, it's Tim Marshall. I need to talk with Harry. It's important."

"He's in a conference at the moment. Can I help you with something or do you want him to call you back?"

"I'm going to need to talk with John again. Under oath."

Chapter 14

"Camille took a metal detector back to Cabin Creek Campground and she found a few bullet casings," Tim Marshall said to Harry and me the next day at the police station. Tim reached around his desk to show us the ballistics report when Camille and Helen walked past Tim's office. Camille poked her head in.

"I was just showing Helen the lab," Camille said in a giddy tone. I noticed that Helen was standing very close to her.

"Come on in. We're just discussin' the bullet casings you found at the campground," Tim said. Camille brought us up to speed on her campground search.

"How can you tell if the casing matches a bullet?" Helen asked. "It's fascinating to me. Camille and I were just talking about forensics over lunch." Helen had no idea of the magnitude of the can of worms she's just opened. I looked at Tim. He stared back, beckoning me to engage him in a battle of forensic science.

About a year ago, Harry defended a local rancher who was accused of murdering his wife and burying her body in a shallow grave near the southern border of his ranch. The bullet came from a .22 caliber handgun and our client owned many guns, including a .22. The investigator confiscated all of the rancher's guns and conducted bullet-lead analysis to compare lead trace elements in the bullets found in his .22 to the bullet found in his wife's body. It was a knockdown drag-out battle in court regarding the chemical analysis of the bullets. Harry discredited the prosecution's bullet expert and proved through his own expert that the bullet found in the victim did not match the rancher's gun.

Tim, an avid hunter and the son of a former Green Beret, knew a lot about bullets. Helen was about to learn more than she ever needed to know about bullets, guns and forensics. "Well, you see," Tim started, "bullets are made of lead mostly, but they also contain trace amounts of arsenic, tin, and silver. Experts examine the bullet and figure out exactly how much of these other elements are in the bullet and then compare that to the bullets found in the possession of the suspect. Experts are able to link one bullet to others from the same production run or from the same box. So that is one way to link the bullet to the suspect." He was obviously not finished. Helen seemed genuinely interested and turned her good ear towards Tim. "The other way is to examine the grooves carved in the bullets as they scream through the barrel of the gun shaft. Every gun is thought to have its own unique 'rifling mark.' Experts compare the bullet to other bullets shot from that same gun to see if the rifling marks are the same."

"That's very interesting," Helen said. She turned toward Camille, as if waiting for Camille to add her two cents.

"But Helen, the bullet analysis is not without flaws," I interjected. Tim rolled his eyes as he walked over to his coffee pot and poured himself the last cup in the pot. He took one sip and scrunched up his nose, dumped the cold coffee out and brewed a fresh pot. I continued talking. "The premise is that each batch of lead used to make bullets is unique. But the truth is that batches of bullets produced years apart have had the same compositions of trace elements such as zinc, iron, silver, copper and tin. And the converse is true. Within the same batch of bullets, the trace elements have a tendency to converge in the middle, making bullets created from the same batch quite different."

From under his breath, Tim uttered, "Bullet analysis has been iron clad in court for years. Leave it to a defense lawyer to muck it up."

After the requisite lawyer jabs, Camille and Helen left and Tim continued questioning Harry. "Does John own a gun?"

"Hunting rifles. He doesn't own a handgun. Is that what you want to question him about?"

"In part. Obviously we need to talk about John's blood bein' in Lela's apartment too. I'm givin' you the heads up. I got a search warrant for John's apartment and his truck. We'll be sendin' the troops to his place today. Have him bring his truck to the meeting' this afternoon. Forensics needs to comb it. Remind him that it's illegal to destroy evidence. I don't want Johnny boy to take that truck of his to the car detailer. The only reason I'm givin' you these forewarnings is that I trust you. I want to keep this as amicable as I can. But in doin' so, I'm puttin' my faith in you that John will cooperate to the fullest extent of the law." Harry concurred.

"I heard that you searched Bain's place last night," I said. The z-shaped scar on Tim's forehead crinkled with his frown.

"How'd you hear about that?"

"Small town gossip. Did they find anything?"

"You know that I can't divulge the results of our investigation to you. I've obviously been too lax as it is."

"I heard that they found long, dark hair in his bed."

"You know what they say about rumors, don't you? They're worth the weight of the source. Who's been feeding you that line of bull?"

* * *

When I returned to the office after my lunch hour, Harry was in the conference room visiting with his old attorney friend, Glen Williams. Harry motioned me in to join them.

"Mac, you know Glen," Harry said. Glen stood and extended his hand. He was a cute little man, about five and a half feet tall, with a shiny bald head and brownish stained teeth.

"Have a seat," Glen said, pulling me into the chair next to him. "Harry and I were just discussing an interesting coincidence. You see, a prospective new client came into my office this morning, asking for assistance in a possible criminal matter. His name was Dr. Miller." Glen, known in the legal community for his theatrics in court, waited for my reaction to his statement before continuing. "After the good doctor told me his story, I told him that I wasn't able to take his case. It seems as though Dr. Miller was served with a subpoena from the county attorney's office and has been asked to meet with the police today for questioning. He showed up in my office because he wanted a lawyer present with him for the questioning. I told him that I may have a conflict of interest, but I listened to his story anyway. He spilled his guts about his relationship with Lela and what they were up to." Glen winked at Harry, signaling that it was Harry's turn to talk.

"I'll fill you in with the details later, but let's just say that Dr. Miller and Lela were more like business partners than lovers, I'm afraid," Harry said.

"Business partners?" I said, certain that I'd misunderstood.

"You were on to something when you found the invoices for Plumaze. Apparently Dr. Miller was worried that Tim Marshall is on to him too. Miller told me that he bought Plumaze from Lela. He said that he has plenty of patients that want Plumaze injected in their wrinkles and are willing to sign waiver forms that the drug is not FDA-approved. He said that Lela dropped off a shipment every Friday at noon."

"I don't get it. How would Lela -?"

"Because she's a Shoshone," Glen interrupted. "The stuff was flown in on a private jet and in order to avoid customs inspections, they landed on the Shoshone airstrip outside of town. Lela was a patient of Dr. Miller's and when he found out that she was Chief Ed Washakie Duran's daughter, he knew that she could access the airstrip without question. Although he didn't admit this to me, I think he offered her a lot of money to make a weekly pickup from the airstrip. His version of the story is that Lela approached him and told him that she had access to the Plumaze. Dr. Miller said that it was all her idea, and that he just got a weekly shipment. My hunch is that he sought her out."

"How much of this does the police know?"

"Not sure," Glen said. "They searched Dr. Miller's office and car this morning. They asked him to come down to the station this afternoon for questioning. Maybe they found something."

"Even if we assume, for argument sake," I said, "that Dr. Miller is telling the truth, where would Lela get a hold of a European-produced cosmetic product? She's never left the State of Wyoming, for God's sake! She couldn't possibly have contacts in Europe to import a non-FDA approved drug. Second, assuming that she had the contacts to import Plumaze, which I highly doubt, she couldn't have done it alone. Someone had to have helped her." Glen nodded in agreement. I continued. "I'm not meaning to discount Lela's resourcefulness, because she was a very smart woman, but she didn't seem to be the type to be able to broker an international business deal. And if she didn't broker the deal, but was somehow involved in the import-side of it, she still would have needed help coordinating such an effort."

"Maybe that's where John comes in," Glen offered. Harry shot him a sharp glance. "I'm just thinking out loud, old friend. Sometimes we get lost in the forest."

Harry looked like a 14-year-old Labrador that was on his last leg. I heard him sniffling as he walked Glen to the door. Tears were rare for Harry, but the past week had been an anomaly. His son was a murder suspect, his secretary was dead and his wife was furious with him. He was lost in the trees.

The ringing phone interrupted my thoughts. I answered. It was Tim Marshall again, calling again for Harry. "Seein' that you like to gossip," Tim started, "pass this along to Harry. We searched John's apartment today and we found a gun. Based on the gun, we're impoundin' John's truck. If there's a ballistics match on the casings, John will be charged with murder."

"Hold on. I'll get Harry on the phone."

Chapter 15

"All rise. The Honorable Sheryl Furmer presiding." A door to the left of the bench opened and Judge Furmer entered. She was still fastening the top button to her black robe. In her mid-fifties, with short, highlighted hair and deeply set brown eyes, she was often described as the "legal fashion model" around town, standing a lean five foot eight, with a narrow nose and high cheekbones. She had an exacting style and presence in and out of the courtroom, being the product of conservative ideals and mores. Her chambers were decorated in deep hues of scarlet and gold, with vivid floral arrangements perfectly placed on each table.

"Please be seated," Judge Furmer said as she whisked her robe around her chair and starting shuffling through the stack of files before her. As the courtroom settled in, Furmer exchanged words with her clerk and files were shuffled and rearranged according to her orders.

John, wearing a brown tweed sport coat and a tie, sat down between Harry and me. His tan slacks were wrinkled and his brown shoes were badly in need of a shine. Harry had already preached his disapproval about the shoes on the courthouse steps, and I noticed after we were seated that John was trying desperately to shine his shoes on the cuff of his tan slacks.

The courthouse in Jackson Hole looked like any other government building from the exterior. The cement blocks showed their age, and the windows were dark and didn't open. The courtroom, however, was modern with slate-blue carpeting and comfortable black canvas bucket-seat chairs. An impressive dark wood partition separated the jury box from the gallery. Above the judge's high-back leather chair was the Wyoming state seal with the inscription:

Great Seal of the State of Wyoming
Equal Rights, Livestock, Mines, Grain, Oil.

I loved this seal because it memorialized that Wyoming was the first state to allow women to vote.

"The People of Wyoming versus John David Harrison," the bailiff announced as he handed Judge Furmer the file. Harry and I escorted John to the defense table. Just as the judge was about to open the file, the courtroom doors burst open and a mob of Indians from Chief Ed Washakie Duran's tribe came bounding in, filling in every vacant chair in the courtroom and spilling out into the aisles until it was standing room only. Ed Duran was the last of the group to arrive, taking a seat behind the prosecution's table. We were not expecting Ed's tribe to attend the hearing, and the newly mounting tension in the courtroom could have been cut with a knife.

"Order in the court," Judge Furmer said, her gavel falling like a hammer on her desk. Civil unrest was not high on her list, and the look on her face told that she was aware of the possibility that the mob of Shoshone Indians seated in her courtroom were looking for a fight. She picked up the file and carefully examined it, taking her time to read every page. "Mr. Harrison, this is a probable cause hearing for an indictment for murder in the second degree. Counsel, identify yourselves for the record."

"Jill St. Clair for the People." Jill St. Clair was Teton County's District Attorney. She headed the prosecution's office with efficiency and purpose. She had short, spiky dark hair with blond highlighted tips. She was a tall, fit and tan woman who could lap you at the track while talking a mile a minute. Her glow-in-the-dark white teeth drew attention to her overstated chin. Rumor has it that her boyfriend was ten years her junior.

"Mary MacIntosh on behalf of the defendant." Judge Furmer looked up.

"Mr. Harrison, are you sitting second chair?" Furmer asked, with a hint of a smile forming an apostrophe on the side of her left cheek.

"Yes, Your Honor," Harry said, with quiet dignity. Harry wanted to represent John, but he'd always said that a lawyer representing himself is a fool. He felt the same way when it came to immediate family. He knew that he was too close to the situation to represent John, but he was too controlling to refer John to another firm. Harry also worried that Ed Duran would think that he'd betrayed their mutual trust if he didn't at least appear somewhat neutral. It was a difficult situation no matter what.

"This is a first," Furmer said. "Ms. St. Clair, present evidence for probable cause."

Jill St. Clair quickly arranged her three-by-five color coordinated note cards in her hand. "Your Honor, the State will easily be able to make probable cause on the following evidence against John Harrison. First of all, his fingerprints were found at Lela Duran's apartment on a bottle of wine. John Harrison admitted to bringing the bottle of wine to the victim on the night that she disappeared. Second, John Harrison's blood was found near the coffee table at the victim's apartment. Third, a .38 special was retrieved from John Harrison's apartment, matching the casings found at the site where our expert believes that the victim was dumped into the Snake River."

"Objection, Your Honor," I said, popping out of my chair with nervous conviction. "My client denies the existence of a gun at his apartment. Furthermore, there is no link between a gun and John Harrison. Mr. Harrison has a roommate and the roommate could have stashed a gun there. There's no evidence that my client's prints are on the gun. And in any event, the search was illegal and any evidence obtained from the illegal search cannot be admitted, not even during a probable cause hearing because -"

"Your Honor," Jill St. Clair interrupted, "ballistics has matched the gun to the casings found at the site where the victim was likely dumped into the Snake River. John Harrison was given due notice that his apartment was a target of a search warrant. The fact that John Harrison's roommate is serving time for various felonies does not bolster his case. The State is not offering to prove that the gun belonged to Mr. Harrison—only that he had had access to it."

"Objection overruled," Judge Furmer stated. She nodded at Jill St. Clair to continue.

"Fourth, the victim's hair was found in the cab of Mr. Harrison's truck. It is well known, and even admitted, that Mr. Harrison had a long- standing obsession with the victim."

"Objection," I said, jumping to my feet again. "Mr. Harrison has acknowledged his long-term friendship with Lela Duran. They've been friends since high school. He has given her a ride home on several occasions. It is of no consequence that a strand of her hair was found in his truck. She's been Andrew Harrison's legal secretary for nearly two decades."

"Objection overruled."

"Your Honor," I continued, "It is crucial to note that -"

"Overruled. Ms. St. Clair, please continue."

"But Your Honor," I said, "the State has -"

"Overruled, counsel. Take your seat before you are placed in contempt."

I sat down, fuming. Harry reached over and thumped my shoulder. Furmer had never liked me. At every Bar Association meeting, she looked me up and down and the times that I've approached her, she's made no effort to converse with me.

"The State offers that Mr. Harrison had motive to kill Lela Duran based on his long-time romantic obsession with her. We have witnesses willing to testify that the victim continuously rejected his advances. In addition, he had opportunity to kill in that he was the last person known to be in her company while she was alive. He admitted going to her apartment on Friday, May seventeenth. He has no alibi. He claimed that after he left her apartment that he drove around for hours. He admitted to taking the bottle of wine to her apartment. His prints were on the bottle. His blood was found on the carpet in her living room, where there was evidence of a struggle. Her hair was found in his truck. In short, Your Honor, the State has met its burden of probable cause in serving up motive, opportunity and forensic evidence linking Mr. Harrison to the murder of Lela Duran."

Jill St. Clair sat down, tucking her note cards into her open briefcase. Judge Furmer turned in my direction. I'd already challenged the evidence on every ground that I could. I knew that no matter what I said, her ruling was a foregone conclusion. "Your Honor, the State has not met its burden regarding probable cause."

"Ms. MacIntosh, do you have anything to add to this probable cause hearing that you haven't offered as rebuttal evidence to the State's prove-up?" Judge Furmer asked, sarcastically.

"Yes, Your Honor. First, there's no evidence to suggest that my client was obsessed with the victim. There is no denying that the victim worked for my client's father for nearly twenty years. So it's natural that Mr. Harrison was acquainted, and even friendly with Lela Duran. To suggest that their friendship somehow paints John Harrison as an obsessed admirer of Lela Duran is absurd and without factual merit."

"You've said as much, Ms. MacIntosh. Do you have anything fresh to add to this discussion?" Her eyes gazed down on me like a hawk on its prey.

"Your Honor, John Harrison was born and raised in this town. He did fine in school and was well known for his athletic contributions to our local teams. He works at a local car dealership where he keeps regular hours and has excelled in his position. He's a reputable citizen with a good explanation for the wine and the blood," I said. I heard Harry groan.

"Your Honor," Jill St. Clair said, bolting to her feet like a lap dog, "the defense has opened the door. The prosecution would like to challenge character evidence."

"Objection, Your Honor."

"Overruled. Defense stated that the accused is a decent citizen. You've opened the door to character evidence, Ms. MacIntosh. The prosecution can either bolster or undermine your character assessment of John Harrison. Proceed, Ms. St. Clair."

"The State offers John Harrison's criminal record as evidence of the fact that he's had several brushes with the law."

"Objection! The State can't offer evidence of prior bad acts."

"We're not offering up prior bad acts to prove that John Harrison did the crime. We're offering up his rap sheet to prove that he's not the model citizen the defense claims him to be."

"Overruled."

"John Harrison was arrested several years ago for misdemeanor vandalism. The nature of the crime was retaliation. According to the police report, John Harrison was working at a local steak house as a waiter. He waited on a table where a wife, husband and their two children were eating. John Harrison took their order and when the wife asked for broccoli and carrots as a substitute for mashed potatoes, John told her that there were no substitutes allowed. When she told him that she was on a special diet, he still declined to make the exception. She then suggested that he allow her to visit the salad bar instead of serving any vegetable with her steak. John told her that she'd have to pay extra for the salad bar. She then asked to see his manager. The manager of the restaurant allowed the substitution and not only gave the customer the broccoli and carrots that she'd asked for, but personally served her a salad from the salad bar.

"That evening, sometime after midnight, John Harrison and his roommate, Duane Towns, a convicted criminal, served their own version of side dishes on the family's front lawn. They smashed eggs on the side of the house, threw toilet paper over the trees, slopped maple syrup on the driveway, and threw several pounds of flour over the grass. When the sprinkler system came on in the early morning, the flour formed what was described as a cement-like mixture. Clean up was complex. Next, -"

"Objection."

"Overruled."

"John Harrison pleaded no contest to a drunk driving arrest five years ago. Three years ago, he was arrested again and pleaded guilty to a felony drunk driving. His driver's license was suspended for six months and he was sentenced to one hundred hours of community time."

"Your Honor, the defense respectfully requests that the Court declare the drunk driving arrest as a wobbler," I said.

"The prosecution objects, Your Honor."

"John Harrison's plea to the felony drunk driving was a wobbler," I continued. "It could have either been charged as a felony or a misdemeanor. The conviction resulted from a plea as opposed to a verdict. Your Honor must determine whether both the conviction and the plea itself are admissible. There are separate considerations. A felony guilty plea or a no contest plea is admissible as a party admission or a prior inconsistent statement. However, although a guilty plea to a misdemeanor is similarly admissible, the judgment of conviction is not because it is considered hearsay.

"John Harrison's plea to the drunk driving arrest is clearly a wobbler. As you know, a wobbler is an offense that may be charged as either a felony or a misdemeanor. A wobbler offense, charged as a felony, can be reduced and declared a misdemeanor for all purposes by the trial judge."

"I decline to rule that the felony drunk driving arrest is a wobbler," Furmer said. "The defendant pleaded guilty to a felony around the time of conviction. He knew the consequences of being marked as a felon. He assumed the risk and it is now part of the record to his murder indictment."

"But Your Honor," I said, "John -"

"Overruled. The prosecution has met it burden of proof in the probable cause hearing of The State of Wyoming versus John David Harrison. The indictment is henceforth issued for murder in the second degree. Court is in recess for fifteen minutes," Judge Furmer said, striking her gavel especially hard. She gathered her files quickly and vanished to her chambers.

The Shoshone mob roared with excitement and as they shuffled out of the courtroom, they started chanting, "Make him pay. Make him pay. Make him pay."

We waited for the Shoshones to clear before attempting to leave. Ed Duran gave me the evil eye for a good ten seconds on his way out. I wanted to explain to him that I was on their side too, that I wanted more than anything to find Lela's killer and make sure that whomever did the crime was put behind bars for life, but I knew that any such conversation would have to wait for another day. Emotions were too raw. Anyhow, I was more afraid of Harry's reaction to my blunder in court than I was of Chief Duran's glare.

We weren't more than five feet out of the courtroom when Harry slammed his briefcase down on the bench. "Why in the hell did you allow character evidence to creep into a probable cause hearing? Where have you been the last seven years? Haven't you learned a damned thing from me?"

"I'm sorry! It was a mistake. It's never happened before. I don't know how I could have done something so stupid. I'm so sorry."

"Now John's prior convictions are part of the record. We might as well have served him up on a silver platter -"

"I know. I know. I'm so sorry -"

"Damn it, Mac. That's a first year gaffe. Do you know the strings I had to pull to keep his record under wraps? I got him that job at the car dealership with the understanding that he'd . . . nevermind. Just wait until Jane gets a hold of me. She begged me to handle the hearing. I'll never hear the end of it."

Chapter 16

"I told you that you should have handled the hearing," Jane said to Harry on the way out of the courthouse, making no effort to conceal her displeasure. She glared at me with the same disdain that the Chief had.

"It's dangerous to represent family, Jane. I explained this to you yesterday. Judgment gets clouded. Anyway, what's done is done. We can't unring the bell. Let's keep our voice down–I don't need the rest of the town to hear about it on the way out of the courthouse."

"Keep it down? Don't you dare hush me, Harry. I'll say what I want, when I want, as loud as I damn well please. And do you know what I think? I think you don't want to represent our son because it's *Lela's* murder trial. You were always overly concerned with her."

"Overly concerned? That's crazy talk. Don't even start that business again. If I didn't want to represent our son, then I would have referred him to another law firm. Instead, I'm working with Mac to give him the best defense possible."

"Is that why he got indicted today? Because you gave him the best defense possible? Now the whole town will know about what kind of trouble he's been in and they'll assume that he's gotten himself into trouble again.

They'll wonder why you aren't representing him. They'll think that you think he's guilty and that's why you're pushing your thirty-two-year-old associate in to defend him."

"We all make mistakes. Mac's a good lawyer–she can handle this. I don't think it mattered one way or the other. The State had sufficient evidence to support the probable cause to indict, regardless of who represented John. We need to focus on what's ahead of us at this point."

"I think it makes John look guilty—you not defending him. It looks like you're embarrassed about your own son. That's what I think."

"Well, if that's what you think, you're wrong."

"Am I, Harry? Am I wrong?"

Jane paused on the sidewalk and took hold of Harry with a cold stare. Harry started to speak, and then he stopped himself. Jane stormed off to her car and screeched the tires of her diesel Mercedes as she left the parking lot. Harry whispered privately to John for a few minutes and then patted his back as he handed him the keys to his Yukon.

"Looks like your truck is going to be impounded for a few days. Mac and I'll walk back to the office. Don't say a *word* to anyone about the indictment. Not a word, John. Do you understand?" John nodded as he sauntered to the Yukon, like a dog with his tail between his legs.

As we started down King Street, we saw the mob storming toward us. It was too late to retreat back into the courthouse. The Chief was surrounded by members of his tribe, all of who were chanting. The odd thing was that Jimmy Lonewolf was among them, and it was well known that he was not well liked by the Shoshone.

"Justice will be served, old friend," Chief Duran said to Harry from the center of his wolf pack. Ed's breathing seemed deep, as if a spark had ignited within him, setting off a craving for justice and retribution, fueled by a father's love. Before Harry could respond, Ed turned and slowly walked away, chanting a low-pitched hum.

On our walk back to the office, I turned to Harry and said, "I'm really sorry. I know I screwed up at the hearing."

"You got a little flustered up there. You can't be lured like that under pressure. Sometimes, less is more. I think she was going to indict him no matter what you said, but it seemed to me that you and Judge Furmer have an oil and water-type of relationship. Has she always treated you with such contempt? You've never said much before now, and you've appeared before her dozens of times."

"She's always been terse with me, but I've heard that she's like that with a lot of female lawyers. But some days are worse than others."

Harry patted me on the shoulder and said, in his fatherly tone, "You need to get along with the judges, Mac. It's imperative to our practice. I've known a lot of judges in my day, and some I've liked, and some I haven't, but I've always maintained a professional relationship with all of them. You must do so also. You must also learn how to think three steps ahead of your adversary in court. Consider it a competitive chess match. You blew it today. You were checkmated. I'm not going to sugarcoat it, but I'm confident that you've learned a lesson and that it won't happen again, but understand that you must be better prepared next time, understood?"

I understood it perfectly. I think Harry was going easy on me because he didn't want any more adversity in his life at the moment, but I clearly understood that I wouldn't get another warning.

"Great. The reporters are lined up at the office. This is the perfect ending to a crappy morning."

* * *

"What'd you make of the search warrant for the Wort Hotel?" one of the reporter's shouted at us.

"Don't know anything about it," Harry said as he pushed by the cameraman.

"What does it have to do with Lela's murder?" another reporter asked. Harry didn't respond.

"Sources say that the police are following up on a lead. Amanda Silver stayed there over the weekend. They searched her room."

"What were they searching for?" Harry asked the reporter, showing more mercy than usual.

"Word has it that they got a tip that Amanda Silver stopped Lela on the street on Friday and grabbed her by the arm. A witness came forward and reported it. The witness said that Lela and Amanda got into a fight."

"Over Bain?" Harry blurted out, obviously shocked by his own slip of the tongue. "I mean, over -"

"Bain? Oh, you mean the county attorney. Why would they be fighting over Bain?" the reporter asked, eyes widening, like a dog staring at a new bone.

"I don't know that they were."

"But you said -"

"I misspoke. Now if you'll excuse me," Harry said as he pushed by. I handed the reporter my business card. She took it. I leaned in close so that the microphone didn't pick up my voice.

"Maybe we can talk more later. It's been a trying morning," I said. I didn't want to burn bridges. The media could be a drivable source of information for John's defense and in a small town like Jackson, where leaks were as common as faucets, we could use all the help we could get. She handed me her card too. Her name was Carly Baumgartner.

* * *

"Bain, Harry here. I think we need to talk," Harry said over the speakerphone.

"What? Sending a heard of reporters to my doorstep wasn't enough?" Bain shouted.

"Sorry about that. I slipped."

"Slipped? Right. Trying to focus the media attention on me and away from John, aren't you? You never *slip*, Harry. The pavement's too arid where you walk for a slip. I know you're tricks—been around you for too long -"

"Listen," Harry interrupted, to change the subject, "What's the story with Amanda Silver?"

"I'm not at liberty to discuss it with you."

"*At liberty?* You sound scared, Bain. I bet Jill St. Clair is breathing down your neck right now, trying to find out how you're involved in this mess. She's probably found out that you and Amanda -"

"No, Harry. Jill St. Clair is preparing pre-trial motions to nail your son for this crime. So far, all the evidence points in his direction."

"So, why are you so worked up about discussing your relationship with Amanda? You sound confident that Jill doesn't suspect anything."

"That's because there's nothing to suspect. I need to go," Bain said, and then speakerphone clicked.

The phone rang again immediately. I answered.

"Carly Baumgartner here. Reporter for the Channel 2 news. You might want to follow up on this. Deputy Sheriff Tim Marshall just brought in a boy by the name of Jimmy Lonewolf for questioning. Lela Duran's neighbor reported that she saw a man that fits his description leaving Lela's apartment last Friday. She said the kid was Indian with a silver front tooth and long hair in a pony tail."

"They're at the police station now?" I asked.

"Yes. But you didn't hear it from me."

"Thanks, Carly. I owe you one."

"I'll hold you to your promise."

After I hung up, I told Harry the news. As Harry was about to comment, the phone rang again.

"Harry, Camille wants to analyze Lela's secretarial space for evidence again," I said, cupping the receiver. He shrugged and nodded. Within minutes, Camille was in the foyer calling out Harry's name.

"Were you in the downstairs lobby when you called?" Harry said, in a slightly sarcastic tone.

"Let's just say that I'm on a mission." She opened her toolbox and spread a cloth down on the carpet.

"What's the rush? Is there something going on?"

"I can't discuss too much with you. We have a few other leads that we're following up on before any more indictment hearings. I was told to keep my mouth shut." Camille turned back to focus on her work. Her curly blond hair bobbed up and down as she dusted Lela's workspace for fingerprints. "Is this Lela's handwriting?" she asked, pointing to a "to do" list on the desk.

"Yes," Harry said. "Why?"

"I need to take a sample of it for handwriting analysis. Can't tell you more than that. Where is the paper she used for the printer?"

"Over here." I showed her the reams of laser-quality printing paper on the shelf above the printer.

"May I?" Camille asked, as she took the remaining paper out of the printer's paper tray and marked it. She also took the opened ream of paper and slipped it in an evidence bag. After writing down the lot number of the paper from the label on the box, she examined the coffee cup full of pens and pencils on the desk. She bagged them also.

"Why do you need her pens?"

"To see if anyone used them to forge her signature. It's hard to get prints from pens because often in an office setting, too many people use other people's pens. But we sometimes get lucky."

"So, you're obviously analyzing something that Lela wrote."

"Like I said, I can't talk about it right now. I'm sure that Tim will call you if we find what we're looking for. Can you boot up her computer for me?" I booted up the system, explaining our file management system and where Lela stored documents. Camille gently moved me aside. She clicked in and out of several programs before she found what she was looking for. She scanned the files and opened a few. Then she printed a copy of the subdirectory and copied a few files to a disk. I peeked over her shoulder to see that she was copying files out of Lela's personal subdirectory. I made a mental note to look through the files myself after Camille left. She closed out the files. "Do you want me to shut down the system?" she asked.

"No thanks. We might need it later."

She gathered the contents of her toolbox and hurried toward the door. I noticed that she left a Q-tip swab in a plastic envelope on Lela's chair.

"I'm going to try to catch her," I said to Harry as I hustled out the door after her.

I ran down the steps in my two-inch navy heels and out to the sidewalk. I didn't see Camille, so I walked quickly toward the police station, crossing

King Street, I headed up the steps of City Hall. In my haste, my heel got caught in a crack in the sidewalk and as I lunged forward, I accidentally ran into a woman walking in my direction, knocking her to the ground. I instinctively reached out to her, apologizing. As I scrambled to my feet to help her up, the beautiful young woman with long, dark hair scowled at me with piercing green eyes. Her skeleton-thin frame was clad in slick black pants that fastened below her navel. Her midriff tank revealed man-made cleavage and three belly rings. She reached for my grip with her red lacquered fingers.

"You should be more careful," she snapped, as she steadied herself on her four-inch high stiletto black leather boots. Her hair swayed from side to side, revealing a tattoo on her mid-back of a large skull with a butterfly for each eye. The skull was outlined in black and the butterflies were bright yellow. I guessed her to be somewhere in her late twenties or early thirties. I was sure that I'd never met her before, but something about her looked familiar. I slipped my navy high heel back on my foot and followed her into City Hall in time to overhear her tell the front desk clerk that she was Amanda Silver, there to see Tim Marshall.

I dilly-dallied in the lobby, hoping to learn more about Amanda Silver, but Tim caught on real fast.

"Slow day for depositions, Mac?" Tim asked. "Harry doesn't have enough work to keep you away from City Hall? Or is this how you guys get new clients?"

I told him why I was there. He asked for the swab and told me that he would make sure that it got to the lab, but cautioned that since the swab had not been properly in the chain of evidence, that Camille would likely need to come back to the office to get another sample.

After dropping off the swab, I headed back to the office and booted into Lela's computer, searching her personal subdirectory files, one by one. I was amazed by how many personal files Lela had on our system. She did her taxes at work. Her Christmas card labels were on the system. She had loads of letters for some warranty claim on her new truck. Disputes with a credit card charge were documented. Medical insurance claims were noted. Class action settlement forms for some diet drug she experimented with were evidenced. The files were endless, it seemed.

I stopped snooping when I found several threatening letters from Lela to Amanda Silver.

Chapter 17

"I saw the headline in this morning's paper. What in the hell is that all about?" Harry yelled into his speakerphone. I inched forward into Harry's office to hear the conversation better.

"I've been given a paid vacation from the prosecutor's office while the case is open," Bain said to Harry, like a defeated warrior charged with treason. "Jill St. Clair felt like she had no choice. The press is making me out to be the prime suspect and she said that she can't afford the negative publicity. That's what I get for nine years of dedication to government service."

"Well, if you've been given some time off, then why not work with me to try to find out who killed Lela and clear your name," Harry said. "I'm working my tail off here trying to clear John's name from the suspect list. If we pool our resources and collaborate on a timeline, then perhaps we can clear both of you and find out who is responsible for this heinous crime." Bain remained silent on the other end of the line, like he'd been issued a Miranda warning. "It'll be probably the only time in our professional lives that we can work together," Harry continued, trying his best pitch. "I don't want you to go down for something you didn't do, nor do I want John to, but you know the system better than anyone. Innocent people get convicted by juries every day."

"And guilty ones go free," Bain said. "But if I associate with you, it'll look like I'm guilty."

"Why? Because I'm a defense lawyer?"

"That's a start."

"Maybe it will and maybe it won't. It's a risk, but I think that it's the only chance we have of keeping each other in the loop. Will anyone at your office be willing to keep you informed?"

"Every office has leaks, Harry. Especially this one. I'll be able to find out what's going on here. That's not my concern. My concern is that I'll know too much of what's going on because I'll be arrested. Then my career will be ruined, all for sleeping with her."

"You mean Lela?"

"No. Amanda Silver. I told you that I've never slept with Lela! When are you going to get that through your head? I'm telling the truth," Bain said much louder. I'm sure that regrets were sprouting like weeds in his mind, based on his tone of voice. "All right, I'll meet with you, but it's got to be in private."

* * *

"The magistrate wasn't goin' to give me the warrant for the Wort, but we talked her into it," Tim Marshall said to me on the courthouse steps. "Those letters to Amanda that you found on Lela's computer were the ticket. Camille also found some evidence at your office that might link Amanda to Lela. Now tell me exactly what you think my team should be lookin' for." I was surprised by the frankness of his request. I wasn't sure what they might find in Amanda's hotel room, but my gut feeling was that Lela might have been in Amanda's room.

"Blood."

"Lela's blood?"

"Have your forensics team test the sink and tub drains in Amanda Silver's room. If she was involved in killing Lela, the most logical place for her to have cleaned up was in her hotel room." I was winging it, really, but I had to listen to my instincts.

"Why was she stayin' there in the first place? Why not stay at her dad's fancy ranch?" Tim asked, swallowing a large gulp of diet soda from a can.

I'd thought of the same thing myself. Her father was a famous movie star and had a huge ranch on the outskirts of town. From what I'd heard, his ranch house was more like a mansion and could sleep upwards of thirty people. Why she wasn't staying with him was a mystery, but perhaps it had something to do with the fact that she'd recently been released from prison and she wanted her freedom. Or maybe her relationship with her father was strained. His most recent girlfriend (the one suing him for palimony) was younger than Amanda. Maybe she was an unwelcome houseguest.

"Maybe she doesn't like to bed men in her father's house. Anyway, she checked out of the hotel last Saturday morning early."

"Obviously, the towels and sheets have been laundered by the maid service," Tim said in a pompous tone, "so we won't be able to gather that kind of evidence. But, if there was blood anywhere else, it'll probably still show up with a few sprays of Luminol."

"Also, check the dumpster behind the Wort. She may have dumped bloody towels or blankets in there."

"I don't have a warrant for the dumpster, only Amanda's room."

"You don't need a warrant for garbage cans."

"Right. I know that. I was just testin' you."

"We need to find out what kind of car Amanda drove. Maybe her daddy had some spare cars around the ranch, or maybe she rented one. Either way, we need to impound the car."

"If I can get her car, I'll have Camille comb it for hair and fiber." Tim removed the pack of cigarettes from the front pocket of his uniform, slid out a cigarette and lit up, pulling a long drag. "The tires should be compared to the tire tracks at the campground," he finished, blowing a thick cloud of smoke to the side.

"How soon can you get on it?"

"I have other cases that I'm investigatin' but Lela's case has been tagged a first priority, so I reckon that the county will keep payin' me overtime to solve this murder. Been workin' nearly twenty hours a day since we found her."

"We appreciate your efforts," I said, patting him on the shoulder. He smiled a toothy grin at me, with cigarette smoke seeping through the gap in his front teeth. As his cowboy drawl drifted through my fatigued brain, it occurred to me that I was talking Tim Marshall into linking Amanda

Silver and Bain as co-conspirators for murder, while Harry was trying to convince Bain to join forces with us to solve the crime. We couldn't have it both ways. Something was bound to give.

* * *

Some men look better in a business suit–the formality of the apparel refines them, making them look powerful. Other men look better in a faded pair of jeans and a wrinkled flannel shirt. Bain, however, looked good in anything. Today, he looked especially good in his crisp Levi's, tan pullover sweatshirt and alligator boots. But as handsome as he was, I never felt that flutter inside. Harry was bemused by my lack on interest in him, especially because he was probably the most eligible bachelor in town. Today, however, he didn't look too eligible. His eyes were bloodshot and he looked very worried. He staggered through the back door of our office carrying a yellow legal pad and quickly took a refuge in the War Room, as if getting down to business was all he could do.

"Here's what we know," Harry started, ready to confide in Bain.

"Harry, I need you for a second," I interrupted, waving hello to Bain. Harry looked annoyed, more by the fact that he was going to have to stand up again, than by the intrusion. He followed me into my office and I shut the door.

"I just left Tim Marshall on the courthouse steps. He's on his way to the Wort to comb the place for evidence and he said that he's going to try to get a warrant to impound Amanda Silver's car. For probable cause, he's using Amanda as a possible co-conspirator with Bain. If Bain finds out, he'll scream bloody hell. He'll think that we set him up. We need to figure this out without Bain's help."

Harry walked over to my window and looked out, leaning forward, allowing his forehead to touch the glass. He rolled his head back and forth. "I guess I'm grabbing at straws here. I'm so terrified that they're going to nab John on this that I'm not thinking straight. Jane is furious with me. She's not even speaking to me. Ed Duran thinks that I've turned against him now that John has been indicted. Half of my neighborhood stares at me when I drive up, as if *I'm* a suspect. Jane won't do any volunteer work at the hospital or the library because she says that people are whispering behind her back. Of course, she blames me for everything. I come to find out after all of these years of marriage that Jane never even liked Lela! Can you imagine? I'm losing it here. Everything that I've known to be true is suddenly false. I'm fighting for my wife, my son, my secretary, my old friend–yet none of them seem to give a damn. I don't know what I should be fighting for anymore, but I don't know how to stop fighting. Fighting for justice is all I know, and I just want to talk with Bain and see what he knows, that's all. I won't give away the farm. He might know something that will help us," Harry said, pulling away from the window and turning in my direction.

I wanted to console Harry, to let him know that I cared about him, but I wasn't sure that he really wanted that right now. He *needed* to talk with Bain, as if two adversaries' minds could somehow bridle the reigns of justice. Without comment, I followed him back to the War Room where Bain was waiting.

"So, the police suspect John, me, Dr. Miller and Jimmy Lonewolf?" Bain asked, scribbling notes on his legal pad.

"What do you know about Jimmy Lonewolf?" Harry asked.

"According to my sources, Jimmy Lonewolf was dating Lela when John first met her in high school. John fell for Lela right away, and that was the beginning of the feud between Jimmy and John. As a new student and because she was a Shoshone, Lela was, of course, infatuated with the idea that the quarterback was smitten with her. Jimmy was very jealous and threatened John. I'm sure you've heard most of this."

"Actually, I haven't," Harry admitted. "John's version is remarkably different. Go on."

"Well, like I said, this is just town gossip, but the way I heard it is that at a party after a homecoming dance, John put the moves on Lela, despite the fact that she was there with Jimmy. Lela and John snuck off for a while and when they returned, Jimmy and John got into a fistfight. John, being twice Jimmy's size, and encouraged by the entire football team who stood in line as back up, beat Jimmy up pretty good. Lonewolf fled the party, dragging Lela out under protest, and returned a few hours later with half the Arapaho tribe. By then, the cops had been called and broke up the party, but they were not able to break up the warfare that would develop between John and Jimmy.

"When Lela ended up pregnant not long after that incident, she dropped out of high school and never returned. You know the rest, I'm sure." Bain stood up after spilling his story and stretched, waiting for Harry's response. Harry stood silently, thinking. Bain walked over to the mini- refrigerator and helped himself to a bottle of cold water. Harry remained silent, so Bain continued. "Lela broke up with Jimmy not long after that, but he never let the flame die. She called the cops on him many times for stalking, but she refused to press charges against him. Apparently the kid isn't playing with a full deck, so the police haven't taken it too seriously, up until now." Bain stepped closer to Harry and continued. "This isn't confirmed, so you can't quote me, but he works down at the feed supply store, where they have industrial cyanide for sale. Some of it has been reported missing this week and the police are looking into it. Apparently, they've questioned Lonewolf in the presence of a public defender and I heard that he has no alibi for last Friday night."

"What about Dr. Miller?" Harry asked.

"Rumor in the office is that Dr. Miller and Lela had been seen out together. He's known to have a very large ego and a loose temper. He claims to have been at home with his *wife* last Friday, but the lady who lives with him is not his *legal* wife, and our office is checking into her true identity. Whoever the lady is, she has yet to verify his whereabouts. The police did get a search warrant for his office and his car this week, and I guess they found numerous hair samples belonging to Lela at his office, but that's to be expected since she was a patient of his. The catch is that Lela's hair was also found in his car, but he claims that he gave her a ride home from a bar once. Right before I left the office yesterday, I heard that the police were going to compare Dr. Miller's tires to the tire prints found at the campground."

"What's the word on John?" Harry asked, biting on the corner of his index finger.

"The biggest deal is that he has no alibi for Friday night."

"He admitted to stopping by her apartment, and then he went for a short drive before meeting up with some friends at the Cowboy. He was supposed to come over to our house for a drink because that's where Lela was heading, but he didn't, but that doesn't make him a murderer."

"Of course it doesn't, but he did have access to Duane Towns' gun and a .38 caliber casing was found at the crime scene."

I watched as Harry's jaw stiffened with mention of the .38. "Anything else?" Harry asked.

"I heard that Lela's skiing instructor had an axe to grind with Lela because she dated him all winter for free ski passes, but since the snow has melted, so has her desire to hang around him. I heard that they got into a shouting match last Thursday night at the Mangy Moose, but he apparently has an iron-clad alibi last Friday night."

Harry leaned in closer, compressing his sizable arms on the table. "Let's get to the heart of the matter. You were out to dinner with Amanda Silver the night Lela was murdered."

"Yeah. So? What does my dinner date have to do with anything?"

"Maybe a lot. Amanda isn't just a pretty face. We both know that she recently got out of jail for a drug conviction." Bain immediately stood and walked over window. The trees, barren from winter, were just showing the promise of spring. Tiny blooms were sprouting from the silken earth. The indigo blue sky was yearning for a cherry hue before darkness set in. Bain turned around and leaned against the windowsill, crossing one leg over the other, shoving his glasses back up the bridge of his nose with his right index finger.

"Look, I know it doesn't look good," Bain said, taking a deep breath. "She approached me last Thursday and things got a little out of hand. I didn't use my better judgment—I guess I was worn out from the stress of the trial. Anyway, it was a mistake to sleep with her. I'm not making excuses for my behavior. But now that I've had time to reflect on it, she seemed to have an agenda that night, and I was too damn tired to care, so, I went to her room at the Wort and she screwed my brains out. She was in control. She told me what to do and how to do it. I've never been with anyone quite so . . . forceful. I insisted on wearing a condom, especially since I knew that she'd been in prison, but when I reached for my wallet to get one, she adamantly demanded that I use one of her special stock. She said that she only likes the abrasive kind. What did I care? A condom is a condom."

"TMI," I interrupted. "Too much information."

Harry shot a disdainful look at me.

"I realize that I'm in a real mess now," Bain continued, "because I slept with her, but sex with Amanda Silver has absolutely nothing to do with Lela, and how my semen ended up at Lela's apartment is a total mystery. But let me tell you something," he said, pointing his index finger at us, "I have *never* had intercourse with Lela. We dated every now and again, more of a flirting thing than anything. But we've never done anything other than kiss goodnight. And not a romantic kiss–more like a peck on the lips. Friendly. No sex. Never. And especially not at Lela's apartment. In fact, I've never set foot in her apartment and I have no idea how my semen got on her sheets, but I can tell you that this: it's a set-up. Someone is trying to frame me for Lela's murder."

"Listen, I'm not one to pry, and this might sound like a ridiculous question, but other than Amanda, who would have access to your semen?" Harry said, half choking on his words.

"*Access* to my semen? It's not like it's lying around my house like some kind of weapon–I mean it's not like it's a gun hidden in my nightstand drawer. Access to my semen? Do you know how absurd that sounds?"

"I know. I know. It is absurd, but help me out here. Sperm doesn't just 'show up.' Have you ever donated sperm or anything like that?"

"No, nothing like that. I've racked my brain trying to figure this one out," Bain said, running his fingers through his wavy hair, "I have no idea how it got there. The only thing that I can think of is that I always use a condom. Maybe someone saved the semen after sex. I generally just tie a knot in the end afterwards and throw them in the trash. Maybe someone saved one and planted it there to frame me. I saw a movie where it happened like that," Bain said. The words hung in the air like a hot air balloon.

"But the semen they collected from Lela's sheets did not show traces of spermicide. Don't all condoms have spermicide in them?" I asked.

"I don't think they all do," Harry said, "But I'm no expert on the subject. What I do know is that semen collected in a condom shows traces of *latex*. The sperm collected from Lela's sheets had no trace elements of latex."

"I don't want to get into the graphics of the night with Amanda, but let's just say that the first time . . . I hadn't penetrated her yet."

"Meaning?"

"Meaning that my semen was on her stomach."

"TMI," I said again. "That's way more than I ever wanted to know about you."

"Likewise. It's more than I wanted to say. Especially in front of you, Mac. But I'm trying to be honest here. After that happened, Amanda got up and went to the bathroom for awhile. She came back to bed with white powder under her nose."

"Maybe she collected some semen in a cup when she was in the bathroom," Harry said.

"But if she did, it would seem like her DNA would be mixed with the semen."

"You honestly think Amanda framed you?" I said.

"I have no other rational explanation for it. But I keep asking myself: Why would she do that? What possibly could be her motive?" Bain asked out loud. I looked at him like he was a child asking why some bully beat him up in the schoolyard.

"Did you ever consider that she might have slept with you because she wanted to be on the good side of the prosecutor? It's no secret that she has a drug rap. Did it ever occur to you that she might have wanted you to deposit semen on her chest so that she could use it against you? She has a criminal mind. And a criminal mind with idle prison time can probably concoct any number of good schemes. Think of the stories that are exchanged behind prison bars."

Bain looked at me and then at Harry. He was shaking his head back and forth. "I feel like I'm stuck in some weird *Twin Peaks* episode and I can't find my way out."

"Hopefully the way out isn't behind bars," Harry said.

Chapter 18

"Just wanted to let you know that they had Jimmy Lonewolf down at the station for questioning today," Sheila gossiped at me over the phone.

"How did you find out?" I didn't want to tell Sheila that a news reporter had already told me about Jimmy Lonewolf. I wanted to hear Sheila's version.

"Well, when I was working at Albertson's today, Janet Ridehouse came through my line, and you know what a town crier she is," Sheila started. About as big of a town crier as you, I thought to myself. I pictured Sheila swirling her two-inch long fake fingernails through her frizzy bleached-blond hair while talking. Sheila continued, "Janet's son, Kevin, is best friends with Jimmy Lonewolf's cousin. It turns out, Jimmy didn't lie to the police when he said that he was in Pinedale ice fishing that night. Kevin and some other guys are willing to alibi him. So, you can think what you want of him, but he didn't have nothin' to do with Lela's killing. Now do you believe him?"

"Anything is possible," I said. "Look, the other line is ringing and I'm expecting an important call. Thanks for the information. I'll talk to you later."

The other line really was ringing. It was Jane. "Listen, I'm sorry for using such harsh words about you at the courthouse. I blame Harry, not you, for this whole mess. You know how much I adore you and I know that Harry has trained you to be a good lawyer. It's just that so much is at stake here and I can't understand for the life of me why Harry wouldn't handle John's hearing. Lord knows, he would never have handed over an important hearing for one of his other clients. It just makes no sense at all that he'd do this to our son. Don't get me wrong, I know that you tried your best, dear, and -"

"Thanks, Jane, but I did make a mistake. Harry and you both had a right to be upset with me. I don't think it affected the outcome of the hearing, but it shouldn't have happened and I'm sorry if it caused you embarrassment."

"This has been very, very difficult and it's not over yet. Hopefully, John's name will be cleared soon and we can resume our lives. When that happens, I'd love to take you to lunch. We're overdue." I agreed.

* * *

When the phone rang for the third time in two minutes, I felt like a receptionist fielding calls. This time, it was Greg.

"Calling to give you the heads up before it hits the news in the morning. A paralegal in her late-twenties was found in the Kennebunk River today in Maine. She was shot close-range in the throat, just like Lela, and she worked for a mid-sized law firm in Portland, Maine. No suspects have been identified."

"Oh my God. What does this girl look like?"

"She has long, dark hair, that's about all I know at this point. Sounds copycat, doesn't it?"

"How long had she been missing before they found her body?"

"I don't know. I just read the headlines of the CNN ticker tape. I've told you everything I know for now. When I learn more, I'll call. Are you going to be at the office late?"

"Looks that way. I've been spending so much time on Lela's case that I'm buried in my other work. Call me if you hear anything."

"Anything new with Lela? Are you getting any closer?"

"We lost John's probable cause hearing. It looks like he's going to be tried for murder. But I think I'm on to something. Do you remember at The Pines restaurant when our waiter said that he'd served Christopher Bain and Amanda Silver? Well, it looks like Amanda and Lela had some kind of standing feud. I don't know the details yet, but they apparently had an argument on the street the other day. You know a lot more about

142

Amanda than I do. Can you snoop around a little bit and see if you can find out anything more about her past?"

"Like I said, she served time in the Utah State Prison for selling drugs. She looks hard, to me. I've seen her interviewed and she comes across as an arrogant, spoiled bitch. From what I've heard, Amanda practically raised herself. She went to a private boarding school in high school, but ran away so many times, that she was finally asked to leave. She flunked out of U.C. Santa Cruz, which is a pass/fail university. She's been a drug user since she was a teenager, flitting through the L.A. bar scene long before she was of legal age. Her dad never had much to do with her, although I heard that he supplied her with drugs as a teen. He's had about four wives and countless mistresses. You get the picture."

"I get it. I saw her at the police station today. She's beautiful all right, but she has attitude to spare."

"How would Amanda be connected to Lela?"

"That, I don't know yet. I went through the personal files that Lela stored on her computer and there were several pretty outrageous letters that Lela wrote to Amanda."

"Outrageous in what way?"

"Threatening letters. Threats, in response to previous threats, like: 'If you expose me, I'll expose you,' kind of threats. It seems like they had something on each other. I don't know what it was, but I'm going to find out. Amanda was staying at the Wort Hotel last weekend. I'm convinced that something went down there."

"Meaning?"

"Meaning that I think she's has something going around here. I don't know, really. I just have this feeling. Anyhow, she seduced Bain -"

"Seducing Bain in her hotel room isn't a crime. From what you told me during the O'Connor trial, seducing Bain is like feeding candy to a baby."

"True. But something about this feels different. I know that I'm on to something."

"Let me know if I can help."

"This crime in Maine is remarkably similar. When you hear more, call me. I'd like to talk to the district attorney in Maine to find out his or her take on the crime. You never know. There could be a copycat out there–or there could be a connection to Lela."

"Get some sleep. You sound exhausted. I miss you. I can't wait to hold you in my arms again."

* * *

"You were right, Mac," Tim said when he called the office the next morning. We found blood in the hotel sink drain. Another thing. No one else has stayed in the room since Amanda checked out last Friday morning, early. When Camille examined the drain in the tub, she collected several hair samples. She thinks that there was hair in the shower drain from two different people. Some hair in the drain was smooth, straight dark hair. But the other hair was wavy and course. She sent it to the lab for analysis too. No sayin' that the shower drain's been cleaned in months, but it's worth a shot."

"I heard that you questioned Jimmy Lonewolf. Did you learn anything new on him?"

"Nothin's sacred in this town, is it?" Tim asked. Nothing was sacred in a small town, but this was especially so when police officers like Tim called people like me to share confidential investigatory information. "His alibi for last Friday night checked out. Earlier that day, he threatened John, but that's nothin' new between those two guys. They've been beatin' each other up for years. We have no other evidence to tie him to the scene of the crime, other than the neighbor sayin' that she spotted him in the apartment building, but when we questioned the neighbor again, she couldn't remember what day she'd seen him, or even if she'd seen him at all. She even said that she'd seen him there on more than one occasion. She's a nice old lady, but she is a little senile. She calls the cops all the time with noise disturbance complaints, but when we show up, it's usually her own television that's makin' the noise. I have a cop followin' Jimmy Lonewolf just to keep tabs on who he talks to. Maybe he'll slip up."

"Doesn't Jimmy work for John Deere? I read in the paper that some commercial grade cyanide was missing from there recently. Isn't it possible that Jimmy Lonewolf stole the cyanide?"

"It looked like that was a possibility, but John Deere has dropped the charges against him. They claim that it was all a big misunderstanding."

"Sounds like public relations damage control to me. What about that ski instructor? Have you found out anything more about him?"

"You know that what I'm tellin' you is confidential. I shouldn't even be havin' this conversation with you. If my boss knew, he'd can me. I'm only tellin' you stuff about the case because we're workin' toward the same goal. Otherwise, I'd never tell you about a pending case. I have your word that you won't spread any of this to the press, right?" I assured Tim that I would keep his divulgences secret, although I felt a pang of guilt for bending the truth.

"The ski instructor had a iron clad alibi for last Friday. He was heliskiing that day in the backcountry. He went out for drinks and dinner that night with the clients he took skiing. We've tracked down the clients in California and they gave a similar account of the day, so he's off the hook."

"Call me when you find out more about Jimmy Lonewolf. I think he could be a key player." Tim hemmed and hawed on the line for a few moments, obviously wanting something, but not sure how to ask. As the moment of silence droned on, I feared the worst.

"You free for dinner tonight?"

My worst fears were realized. Tim had been too chummy, sharing too much inside information with me. I wanted to say, "No thanks, let's just be friends, but could you please keep feeding me the inside scoop on this investigation?" I thought through my inventory of excuses: I needed to wash my hair; it's my night to play basketball at the YMCA; I'm having dinner with Mrs. Duncan; I still have work to do. I decided to go with the work.

"Thanks, that's really nice of you to ask, but I've got a ton of work to do. This ordeal with Lela has really put me behind around here."

"Oh, okay. I understand. Been workin' like a dog myself. Just thought we could compare notes over a bite. Maybe over the weekend?"

"Maybe" I said.

* * *

I checked my e-mail. I had one from Greg:

> "Hi, pretty woman. Found out more about the Maine paralegal found in the Kennebunk River. Our investigative reporters have learned that she was married, but that she'd been separated from her husband for a few months. Apparently, her estranged husband moved out of their house a few months ago to a remote region in northern Maine. There were rumors of abuse and that the estranged husband might have had a heroine habit. When I learn more, I'll forward the info.
>
> Love,
>
> Greg"

Since I was already online, I logged into Lexis and clicked on "People Locator." I typed in "Amanda Silver" and found out that Greg was right.

She'd been caught with cocaine in Utah and had served two years in a federal prison, which was probably a slap on the wrist based on the quantity of drugs in her possession at the time of her arrest. I wondered how she supported herself financially, so I called the private investigator that we use to do asset searches and asked him to check her out. I envisioned her as a spoiled rich kid who'd been given everything from a college education to nice cars and expensive vacations—in other words, the opposite of Lela Duran. I couldn't imagine how the two of them could have hooked up, or more importantly, why? *Why would Lela have an altercation on the sidewalk with Amanda?* Over Bain? Maybe. But why the threatening letters? Lela wrote three letters to Amanda telling her that if Amanda didn't keep her promise, that there would be hell to pay. What did Amanda promise Lela? That she'd leave Bain alone?

A few minutes later, my asset search rang in over the fax machine with Amanda Silver's social security number, along with the account numbers and balances for her bank accounts. No wonder Amanda was selling drugs. Daddy's trust fund had run dry.

* * *

In the middle of my on-line search, I heard my computer chime that I had incoming mail. I toggled to my e-mail screen and read another note from Greg.

> "Like I told you earlier, the Kennebunk estranged husband moved out of their house a few months ago. While he was living in northern Maine, she started dating someone new–someone with a lot of money and a fancy car. When her estranged husband found out, he came back to town looking for her. Witnesses say that he followed her around and threatened her. She got a restraining order against him, but he must have caught her on her way to her car after work. There was evidence of a struggle near her abandoned car, and the cops think they've found her estranged husband. Dead. He disemboweled himself near the edge of the river, not far from where he must have shoved her downstream. His guts were lying all over the place. I just wanted you to know as soon as possible so that you didn't go on a wild goose chase for a copycat crime when it looks like this is a murder-suicide–unrelated to Lela's murder."

I called Greg on his cell. After reading the Kennebunk River story, I felt especially lonely. I wanted to hear his voice, to sooth my nerves and to feed my aching soul. "I miss you," I said to Greg.

"I miss you too." Greg had the voice of a rock star–sultry and deep and sinfully sexy. Just hearing his voice awakened nerve endings I'd forgotten existed. I yearned for his touch two thousand miles away.

"Listen, I'm going to be on assignment in California for the next few weeks to cover a missing child case. Is there any way you could get away for a weekend and meet me? I have a million frequent flier miles. I'd be more than happy to get a ticket for you. The case is in Sacramento, but I could meet you in San Francisco for a long weekend. Maybe even introduce you to my folks."

Meet his folks? That sounded serious. We'd only been dating a few months. How serious does a relationship have to be to cross the threshold of meeting the folks? I was flattered and surprised at the same time.

"They live in the city. Nob Hill. But don't worry. They're normal people," Greg continued.

"I don't know if I can commit. I'd love to, don't get me wrong. But I'm not sure what's happening around here with Lela's case still unresolved." I pictured us walking on the Golden Gate Bridge, hand-in-hand, breathing in the misty air–or riding a trolley down a steep hill. I hadn't taken a real vacation since I started working for Harry seven years ago.

"We could go to the theatre and out dancing. Or, if you'd prefer, you could fly into Sacramento and we could drive up to Napa Valley together and do some wine tasting. You could get a Calistoga mud bath and a massage. What do you think?" He wasn't giving up. "Or there's Lake Tahoe. You name it, and I'll arrange it. Think it over for a day or two." I pictured us soaking in a pool of mud, and then showering off together in the privacy of our suite. I imagined sipping crisp, full-bodied wine late into the evening, making love early into the morning. Room service and maid service. I wanted to be with him more every day.

"I would love to join you. Let's do our best to make it happen. A lot depends on Lela's case."

* * *

I walked into the Teton County Courthouse the next morning promptly at eight thirty for a plea bargain hearing before Judge Sheryl Furmer, the same judge presiding over John Harrison's probable cause hearing. When I approached the podium, Judge Furmer gave me a cool nod.

"People v. Rosefelder," the bailiff called out. I stepped behind the defense table. Ronald Rosefelder, comfortably sporting his bright orange jailhouse jumpsuit and a pair of handcuffs was escorted to my side.

Ronald Rosefelder was no stranger to the courtroom. This was his third arrest in less than a year for drunk driving. At this point, we had little room to bargain. Jail time was mandatory, along with drug rehab.

"Counsel state your appearances for the record," Judge Furmer commanded.

"Mary MacIntosh on behalf of the defendant, Your Honor. The defendant has been counseled regarding the charges pending and is willing to agree with the prosecution's plea bargain."

"Who says I'm willing to *accept* the prosecutor's recommendations?" Furmer said. I stiffened. Judge Furmer did not look to be in a particularly good mood this morning. Her hair was slightly flat on one side, as if she didn't have time to get a shower. Her makeup was sloppily applied and she wasn't even wearing any jewelry.

"Your Honor, this isn't a matter of national security. You've always been willing to go along with the prosecutor's recommendations on this sort of crime. Our client is willing to admit culpability and will serve the requisite time, including additional community service. He's already started the county's alcohol treatment program. He's committed to do what is right."

"Ms. MacIntosh, you're not in charge of deciding what the appropriate sentence is for a third-time offender. Last time I checked, I was the one wearing the black robe." Normally, the prosecuting attorney would back the defense lawyer up on something like this, but the prosecutor today was a young lawyer who'd recently passed the bar examination and was nowhere close to rising to his feet to bail me out.

"With all due respect, Your Honor, I'm not suggesting that I'm in charge of anything in your court. However, it's custom and practice for the county attorney's office to make certain recommendations. We've accepted those sentencing recommendations and have relied on them. We've enrolled our client in the requisite programs and he has surrendered his driver's license."

"He's a public nuisance," Judge Furmer snarled, with her upper lip curled back.

"Your Honor, Mr. Rosefelder realizes that he's made a terrible mistake. He must reduce his work hours and sales territory due to the surrender of his driver's license. He depends on his sales territory to feed his family."

"He should worry about his family when he's binging. Mr. Rosefelder, do you understand the charges against you?" Judge Furmer asked, peering over her reading glasses, making eye contact with him for the first time. He nodded hesitantly, unsure of what to do. "Mr. Rosefelder, you must make an audible response for the record," she barked. "Speak up!"

"Yes, ma'am."

"You've been before me two too many times. You have a wife and a family to support. You'd better get your act together right now, before it's too late. If I see the whites of your eyes in my courtroom again, you'll regret the day you took your first drink. Do we understand each other?"

"Yes, ma'am."

"The court accepts the plea bargain as outlined, and I hereby issue you a one-year jail term, crediting you for time already served. You must tender your driver's license and fulfill the community service as agreed. You will be guaranteed probation after you've successfully served out your punishment, and you will have to submit to random drug testing during your probation. Take this time in jail to figure out your priorities and get them in order before you waste your life away in a bottle."

"Yes ma'am."

"This hearing is adjourned," she said, making notes on the file and setting it aside. As I packed the Rosenfelder file into my attaché case, Judge Furmer said, "From now on, counsel, I expect you to be less insolent and more respectful or I'll issue a contempt order."

Chapter 19

"We've recovered the gun," Tim said on the voicemail message. "Call me when you get in."

Just as I was about to pick up the phone, Harry darted into my office. "They found the gun," I blurted out. "Tim left a voice message."

"Just got off the phone with him. The blood in Amanda's hotel room matched Lela's DNA. They're dusting the gun for prints as we speak. Looks like she did it, Mac. I knew that John was innocent. I knew it. He would never hurt Lela. Tim said that it was your idea to get the warrant for the Wort Hotel. What made you think of that?"

"When Greg and I went to The Pines restaurant for dinner, Greg mentioned that someone had broken into the safe at the Wort and stolen the master key to the rooms. The thief wasn't interested in jewels or cash - just the master key to the hotel rooms. After Camille was here and copied some of Lela's computer files to disk, I went back through her personal files on the computer. I found several threatening letters that Lela had written to Amanda. I heard through the grapevine that Amanda and Lela got physical on the sidewalk earlier in the day on Friday, so I put the two together and called the Wort to confirm that she checked out early Friday morning. I think she popped the safe to get a master key so that she could go back to the same room she'd stayed in and clean up after disposing of Lela."

"How would she know how to pop a safe?"

"She's been in prison, Harry. I'm sure she's learned all kinds of tricks."

"But if she had the master key, why not use a different room?"

"Because if her DNA was found in a different room, it would be suspect. Her DNA would naturally be found in a room she'd already stayed in."

"Right," Harry said, nodding in agreement. "But why steal a master key? Why not just keep an extra room key? They usually issue tow keys upon check-in."

"If she didn't return both keys, the hotel would have to change the locks before re-letting the room. This way, she was guaranteed to get back in her room. She could get a shower, get rid of the evidence, and no one would know the difference."

"Why in the hell would Amanda Silver kill Lela? What possible motive could she have?" Harry asked, his eyes welling with angry tears.

"I'm not sure, exactly. From the threatening letters, it looks like Amanda owed Lela money."

"What for?"

"I'm working on it," I said. Harry raised a brow at me.

"Don't dig yourself into a hole. That's what the police are for. Amanda was convicted for drug possession. I'm not saying that Lela was into drugs, because as far as I'm concerned she wasn't and never has been, but it's possible that she was in over her head. The fact that she was associating with someone like Amanda is suspect. Maybe you should back off this a little. I don't need you to end up like Lela."

"Just give me a little more time. I promise to be careful."

"Be very careful. It's not your job to solve her murder. I appreciate how much effort you've put into it to make sure that John wasn't falsely prosecuted for a crime he didn't commit, but I don't want to see you get sucked into something dangerous. Jane would never forgive me if something happened to you."

"Is John off the hook?"

"No, but I expect the charges to be dropped anytime. Jill St. Clair hasn't confirmed it yet though. I knew all along that John didn't do it, Mac. He loved her. He would never kill anyone, but especially not her. I feel bad for being so hard on him. I really blasted him the other night and I feel awful about it, but I just couldn't believe his predicament. He was with her right before she disappeared and then he didn't come to the house. He was vague and had no alibi. He lied to the police. I was terrified that he was going to be convicted of her murder. He's made such bad choices since high school. This nightmare has made me realize just how disappointed and angry I've been about him."

"It's all right that you're angry. John has let you down, but I know that he's trying to redeem himself." Harry nodded, wiping the tears with the back of his hand. "Is Tim ready to issue a warrant for Amanda's arrest?"

"Pretty soon I think. They're still waiting to see if they can match the gun to the casings found at the campground. Tim said that they've impounded Amanda's rental car and are searching it. He's trying to link the type of tires on her rental car to the tire tracks from the campground. Once he's finish testing the evidence, Tim said that he'd call us."

The phone rang. Harry picked it up. He cupped his hand over the receiver and yelled to me, "Turn on the television in the War Room. Jane's on the line. She says that the local station is covering Amanda's arrest." I hurried to the War Room, snagging my pantyhose on my chair in my haste. I flipped on the local network to witness Amanda Silver being cuffed in front of her father's ranch. Federal agents flanked Amanda on each side. Her long, dark hair flooded her face as she held her chin firmly to her chest. Her partially buttoned Chanel white blouse gripped her lean body as the agents carefully guided her head into the back seat of the squad car.

* * *

"I saw it on the news today," Greg said to me. "Rumor has it that she was having a fling with Bain and that she caught him in bed with Lela. Is it true?" By his tone of voice, I wasn't sure if he was confirming a lead story or simply asking a question. Our relationship had an inherent conflict of interest.

"I don't know what happened yet. The police are still testing evidence. Like I told you the other day, Bain has admitted to sleeping with Amanda, but denies ever having sexual relations with Lela. Hard to say at this point what happened."

"Does Amanda have local counsel in Jackson?"

"I have no idea. Why?"

"I heard that she hired a lawyer named Steadman Johnston."

"I know Steadman Johnston. His main office is in Cheyenne, but he has satellite offices all over the place. He works for lots of politicians and likes high profile cases. Everyone around here calls him 'Studman' because he's a real braggart. He rarely loses a jury trial."

"Wouldn't Harry and Steadman be on the same side of a case?" Greg asked. "They're both defense lawyers."

"Hopefully, John's indictment will be dismissed and Harry won't be involved in this anymore."

"What if John was still on the hook. What would happen then?"

"Hard to say. Harry and Steadman would each be pointing the finger at the other for blame, most likely. That's usually how it goes."

"Have they ever been up against each other before?"

"Twice. In both cases, Harry's client walked away with a not guilty verdict, while Steadman's clients were left holding the bag. If you've ever heard him interviewed, you'll notice that he doesn't talk about those cases. He only brags that he's never lost a jury trial when his client was the *only* one accused of the crime. Harry loves to rib him about it."

"Sounds like good news coverage."

"Is that what this call is about? Will CNN be covering Amanda's case?"

"A decision hasn't been made from up high yet. Amanda Silver isn't as high profile as Michael O'Connor, but being the daughter of Samuel Silver does boost her profile, even if she is a parolee."

"Could you be assigned to the case?"

"No, I'm already committed to the Sacramento child abduction case. Looks like I'm booked in California pretty much for the next month or two. Speaking of California, have you given my offer any more thought?"

I had been thinking that I needed a break. "It would be fun to spend a day or two in San Francisco and then maybe drive up to Napa Valley for a day."

"Sounds great. I'll check our camera shoot schedule and see which weekend would be best and make sure it works with your calendar before I book your tickets. I know of a romantic place near Union Square if you want to stay in the city, or there's a great Inn over near Sausalito, not to mention the quaint B&B's in Napa."

Romance seeped into my brain like a delectable sip of merlot. The image of Greg lying next to me, touching my bare shoulder while kissing the nape of my neck sent a rousing thrill up my spine that lasted for a blissful moment, until it was interrupted by the sound of the fax machine churning. I walked over and picked up the forensics report from Dr. Calvin Rudolph. The results from the fingerprint analysis sent a chill down my spine. I grabbed the forensics report and ran to the War Room where Harry was still watching the coverage on Amanda Silver's arrest. He was sitting on the edge of the conference table eating out of a steaming Chinese carton. I traded him the report for the cashew chicken. "Dr. Rudolph just faxed this," I said, stuffing chopsticks in my mouth.

"The fingerprints on the .38 don't match Amanda's?" Harry asked, surprised. "How could they have secured an arrest warrant for her when the prints don't match?"

"Let me see that," I said, re-reading the report. Forensics could only get a partial fingerprint from the gun found in the dumpster behind the Wort Hotel. They sent it to a FBI fingerprint expert for ridge comparison using IAI qualifiers. The FBI used a process called the Langsbury Ridgebuilder to build up the fingerprint to help assess to whom it belonged. The prints were compared to Amanda Silver's fingerprints on file from her arrest in Utah, but the prints did not match.

"Let me call Dr. Rudolph," Harry said as he hit the speaker button and dialed. Rudy answered. "Harry here. Got the fingerprint report. When did this come in?"

"About an hour ago. You didn't get it from me, remember? If her prints aren't on the gun, then to whom do they belong? Did you see the news? They just arrested Amanda Silver."

"We saw it. What's the word in forensics? Does other evidence point in her direction?"

"I don't know about all of the evidence, but the blood evidence in her hotel room was the ticket for the arrest warrant. We're still waiting for tire and fiber analysis on her rental car and we sent that cigarette butt to an outfit in Canada that has a new technique called 'double swabbing' where they can get DNA from saliva on a cigarette butt. If it comes back positive, it puts her at the crime scene."

"So what happens now?"

"We turn over all analyses to the prosecutor's office. It's out of our hands at this point."

"Thanks for sending us this. I know you've stuck your neck out for me on this."

"I know how much Lela meant to you, ol' boy. I'm really sorry about what happened to her. How's her old man taking it? I've known Ed Washakie Duran since he was a boy. I feel very sorry for him."

"Ed's crushed. He's seen a lot in his lifetime, but nothing has rattled him like this. He's hardly speaking to me. I know that he's very upset that I was representing John at the indictment hearing."

"That's just grief talking, Harry. Don't take it too personally. He's angry and distraught and he wants someone to blame. You'd be the same way."

"Got to run—another call is coming in. Keep me posted." Harry clicked on the blinking light. "Harrison and Associates." It was the first time in seven years that I'd heard him answer the phone professionally.

"This is Steadman Johnston's office calling for Mr. Andrew Harrison. Is Mr. Harrison available to speak with Mr. Johnston?" his secretary asked over our speakerphone.

"This is Harry. Put Steadman through." While Harry and Steadman caught up on recent events, I marched into my office to prepare for tomorrow's docket. I had another hearing before Judge Furmer on the Samuel Silver palimony case. Luckily, our private investigator had just emailed a report that Silver's mistress had never formally divorced her previous husband, so in the eyes of the law, she was still married to another man. I anticipated Judge Furmer ruling in my favor, for a change.

Chapter 20

The next morning, I arrived early at the office to the smell of coffee brewing. Since Harry never made coffee for himself, I dropped my briefcase and coat in my office and headed toward the break room, but stopped short when I heard Jane shouting. I was surprised by the venom in her voice, not because I'm a stranger to marital arguments–my mother and stepfather had many yelling matches that made "Crossfire" look tame, but Jane was not the type to lose her composure.

"You've been selling him short since high school," Jane shouted. "Forty years of marriage and I'm still defending my son."

"That's because *your* son has been selling himself short since high school. Rooming with Duane Towns. Drunk driving. And now this. What in the hell was he doing giving Amanda Silver money in broad daylight? I'm sure you have an excuse ready for him."

"Oh, is that what I do? Provide excuses for him. I ran into Ed Duran yesterday at the market and he could barely make eye contact with me. And that goes for half of the rest of this town. I'm the one who's out there, dealing with the public, while you hide in this office, and you have the nerve to criticize me? People talk in this town. You're the tough guy–nothing bothers you, but it bothers me, Harry. Call me sensitive or whatever flippant adjective you'll drum up, but I care what people think. I live in this community. I'm the volunteer at the hospital, the benefactor at the library, and the chairperson for the animal shelter. I'm out there, blowing in the wind for people to gossip about, but you just sit here in this office hidden from the public, criticizing every move I make when it comes to John. He's all I have . . ."

I watched Harry walk around his desk and grab Jane's hands into his. "Honey, I'm as sorry as you are. Maybe part of it is my fault. Maybe I put too much pressure on him to succeed. Maybe I made him out to be bigger than life when he was the high school quarterback. I'm not saying that it's all his fault. But John's an adult now and he has to face the music. We can't bail him out of every jam he gets himself into, and this jam is a big one. He's lied to the police and to us. It's time that we let him learn his lessons the hard way. I'm not saying that I won't help him, because you know that I will, but I'm not going to lie or cover up for him. He needs to learn to be accountable for his own actions."

Jane's face relaxed a bit as she leaned into Harry. He wrapped his arms around her shoulders and pulled her in close to his chest. He whispered to her and she nodded, wiping the tears from her cheeks. It seemed like a good time to dart past his office for coffee. On my return, Harry waved me in.

"Got some bad news," Harry said. He turned in my direction to talk, while Jane walked over to the tissue box on Harry's desk and grabbed a few squares of Kleenex. "Looks like John knew Amanda. Since her arrest, two witnesses have reported seeing him with her. One witness says that he saw John handing her an envelope and Amanda handing him something in exchange."

"She's served time in prison for drugs," I said. "Has John ever -"

"Of course not! My son's not some coke head," Jane said, spinning around on one heel with a tissue still wrapped around her nose. Harry gave me one of his looks—a roll back of the eyes coupled with a slight shrug of the shoulders, directing me in his silent way not to press the subject in Jane's presence."

"Have you talked to John yet? Maybe there's some rational explanation."

"No. He's not answering his phone or his door," Jane said. "I don't blame him. I'd hide too if everyone was out to get me."

"Have you checked the dealership? Maybe he's working today."

"He has today off."

"Does he still have your Yukon?"

"His truck is still impounded."

"Did you look to see whether your Yukon was at John's apartment?"

Harry looked to Jane for the answer. She shrugged her shoulders. "I didn't think to look for Harry's car when I drove by this morning. I was looking for his truck. I forgot that the police still have it."

"Let's go pay John a visit."

* * *

Harry's Yukon was parked around the back of John's apartment complex when we arrived. I bounded up the steps, two at a time, with a sinking feeling in my stomach. I'd been worried about John for days–like his fuse had been lit once too often. John was a complex soul–smart and talented, yet lazy - sweet and honest, yet cunning. His contradictions confused him more than his truths, and more often than not, he sided with the demon perched on his left shoulder. I pounded on John's door, but he didn't answer. "Break it down," I shouted to Harry. Jane held up a hand in protest, but Harry ignored her, lowering his shoulder like he did during his glory years as a Stanford linebacker and tackled the door.

The place was a disgusting mess, reeking of rotting food and human odor. There were empty Styrofoam containers dangling over the garbage can, littering the kitchen floor and cockroaches the size of grasshoppers roaming in every direction. I followed Harry and Jane to John's bedroom where we found him, in the bathroom, passed out naked in the fetal position next to the toilet. I turned back to his bedroom and searched his nightstand, which was littered with a heap of white powder and a half-empty bottle of sleeping pills. The drained bottle of Jack Daniels was titled sideways on the floor, pointing in the direction of the bathroom.

"Call 9-1-1."

* * *

Any time I hear a siren, I cringe, thinking that someone I love has been hurt or killed. I'm sure that my fears are a consequence of my father's death, but I can't be certain of the roots of my anxiety. When the paramedics arrived at John's apartment, I saw the lights flashing and heard the sirens blaring, but this time, for some odd reason, I felt comfort. As we rushed into the emergency room, Harry told me of the horror when John was a two-year- old—he'd swallowed half a bottle of the tiny, round pink baby aspirin when a babysitter was in charge. Back then, the doctor made house calls and stirred together a concoction of baking soda and water, making little John drink it until he threw up all fifty-some tablets. I looked in on John, a grown man, some thirty years later, as his stomach was once again being exonerated from drug poisoning.

John's balding head bashed the gurney with every heave of suction from the pump. The attending nurse didn't seem too concerned—as if she'd seen one too many overdoses in her life. When the severe retching episodes were over, and it was clear that John had voided his stomach of all contents, the doctor and nurse gesticulated that John was going to survive. I left Harry and Jane at their son's side. John was obviously in need of therapy. His actions screamed for attention. What was John running from, I wondered to myself as I drove back to the office? What was he trying to tell his parents?

* * *

"John was buying methamphetamines from Amanda," Harry announced as he rounded the corner of my desk, catching me in a daydream. The words reverberated in my ears, like an echo lost in a canyon.

"It figured it was either meth or coke by what I saw on his nightstand."

"He said that he went over to Lela's last Friday to deliver a message from Amanda. Amanda told John that if Lela kept it up, she was going to suffer the consequences."

"Was *Lela* doing drugs too?" I asked. Lela had never shown signs of a person on drugs. Her party life was plain to see, and it was clear that she enjoyed cocktails, but up until a few months ago, she was never late for work, or showed any other sign of being hooked on a drug.

"I don't know."

"What was the exact message?"

"Something along the lines that if Lela ever sent a threatening letter to Amanda again, that it would be the last letter Lela ever typed."

I thought about the letters I'd found on Lela's computer, and wondered what Lela had on Amanda? "How'd she come in contact with Amanda in the first place?"

"I don't know but Jill St. Clair will have the time of her life telling the jury that John was buying drugs from Amanda and that he did Amanda a favor by passing along a threat. If he was able and willing to pass on the drug dealer's threat, then he was probably able and willing to help carry out the threat."

"That's a stretch. John would never do that."

"He lied to the cops. He lied to you. He's doing drugs -"

Harry slammed his fist on my desk. "Give the kid a fucking break! Whose side are you on anyway? The kid's stretched out on a hospital bed right now wishing he could just sleep this whole nightmare off. Instead, he's telling the truth and you're ready to lock him up -"

"I'm just being straight with you. John needs help, and I hope you see that he gets it. But just because he's finally coming clean doesn't mean that he hasn't been involved in something. How can you be sure that he's telling the truth now?"

"I'm sorry," Harry said, putting his head in his hands. "I don't know why I'm defending him. The kid's done nothing but dumb ass things for so many years. I'm so disappointed in him that I can't see straight. But, he's my flesh and blood and I love him so much that I want to protect him. But, I can't. You're right. He's got to face up to this. He's obviously got himself mixed up with some bad company."

"Can you talk to Steadman? Maybe he can fill in the gaps."

"Right. If I even crack that door, Steadman will turn it around and paint John as the drug dealer. Or the crack head. I'm not breathing word of this to Steadman."

"You seemed so chummy with him last night -"

"I'm chummy with him when I need to be, but that doesn't mean that we're not adversaries. He's here to do a job, and so am I. He'll use whatever means necessary to get his client acquitted. I need to do the same."

"Fine," I said, "but you're going to have to play your cards wisely. You think that Michael O'Connor's case was a media frenzy? This will be worse. CNN and the national networks probably won't cover this, but our local stations will be marooned on our doorstep. The Shoshone tribe will rally behind all efforts to put a white person behind bars for murdering one of their own. We're the establishment to them. They co-exist with us, but that doesn't mean that they accept us. Ed Washakie Duran will be made a local hero. We're going to have to plan accordingly and come up with a defense strategy that paints Amanda as a rich wasted daughter of a Hollywood actor. Her affliction with drugs must be center stage. But with that will come the skeletons in John's closet. He's not going to walk away from this squeaky clean."

Harry shook his head violently. "I don't want Jackson Hole to know that my son's been buying meth. Jane will fold if the whole town knows.

Maybe we should move for a change in venue."

"No way. This is the most favorable venue John will ever have. You and Jane are highly respected citizens. John is still remembered for his victory in the town's only state football championship. No way are you going to get better treatment anywhere else. Let's take a deep breath and formulate strategy. I still think that we should call Steadman and work as a team."

"No. Steadman is not on our team. We'll share with him what works in our favor. We won't be teammates. Our goals are different. If we share with him what we know so far, he'll point the finger at John during trial. Don't give him the ammunition."

"He's going to find out."

"So?"

"So, Steadman's going to try to pin this on John no matter how much we cooperate. Let him do his own legwork. Between defending John and keeping up with our case load, we have enough on our plate," Harry said, taking off his Herringbone jacket and draping it across the back of the brown leather chair. "I want to play it 'Oliver North-style,' meaning that I think we should say that we're unaware of any issues with drugs and that the trial will prove John's innocence. If we try to split hairs at this point, we'll only be cutting our own throat."

"Playing dumb usually backfires."

"I know."

"Jane is going to have to deal with the embarrassment."

"I know."

"He could be convicted."

"I know."

"Jane needs to know the reality of this. Embarrassment isn't the worst thing that can happen here." I hesitated, waiting for Harry's response, but he was silent. "Does John have other vices?"

"What do you mean?"

"I don't know, Harry. Does he do coke? Does he smoke crack? Does he shoot up heroin? I really don't want to be graphic, but we need to know everything. When Amanda is indicted, which will be soon, she might talk. We need to know what illegal activity he's been engaging. In other words, Harry, you need to get to know your son better."

"Oh, thanks. Coming from you?"

"What's that supposed to mean?"

"Nothing. I'm sorry. I'm really sorry. I shouldn't have said that. It's been a shitty week."

"It's been a shitty month, Harry, but don't take it out on me. I'm working around the clock for you. Don't bring my past into this."

"*Your* past?"

"Yes. You know what I'm talking about."

"No. I don't."

"My dad -"

"Believe it or not, Mac, but this isn't about you—or your dad. This isn't a good time to play the orphan card."

"The orphan card? Since when do I play the orphan card? I'm not an orphan, may I remind you. I was raised by my mother and stepfather -"

"You were born and raised in Colorado. Your dad died when you were little. Your mom quickly remarried and raised the four of you—including the step kids—basically as a single mom. You're stepdad was a jerk. You had to put yourself through college. Am I missing something?"

I shrunk down in my chair, feeling the weight of my self-pity collapsing in my lap. "I'm sorry. I misinterpreted what you said."

"Forget it. Like I said, it's been a bad week."

"What did you mean by the 'orphan card'?"

"Nevermind." Harry grabbed his jacket from the chair and headed toward the door to my office.

"No, really. I want to know what you meant by that."

"I didn't mean it like that. What I meant to say is that you don't play the victim card. I hired you because you passed my interview. I only asked one question. Do you remember what it was?"

"You asked me what I was going to do with my life when I decided that I made a mistake in becoming a lawyer."

"Do you remember your answer?"

"I told you that I was going to work in an orphanage in Africa."

"Exactly. I knew then that you'd survive. No matter what curve ball was thrown your way, you'd position yourself to strike at least a base hit."

"What were the other interviewees' answers?"

"Every one of them said that they hadn't made a mistake in becoming a lawyer. You were the only one that could see your way out. That's a sign of a good lawyer."

"That's the nicest thing you've ever said to me."

"No, it's not," Harry said, reaching over to give me a warm pat on the back. "I need to get home. John's been released into our custody for the time being, and I'm afraid that Jane is going to crack up alone with him in the house. She'll demand answers from him when I'm not around, and then defend him like hell when I ask him the same questions. Can you hold down the fort for the rest of the day?"

"Sure. Lock the door behind you when you leave, please." Harry waved to me on his way out, briefcase in hand. Hours later, and deep into a pile of paperwork, Greg called.

"Turn on the news," Greg said. I ran to the television and flipped it on, then picked up the extension in the conference room.

"Amanda Silver Detained," was the headliner. The broadcaster told of her previous arrest record and her father's celebrity status. John was not mentioned in the coverage.

"I bet that Bain is shaking in his wing-tipped shoes," Greg said. "What was he doing with her anyway?"

I wanted to tell Greg about John and his involvement with Amanda, but I couldn't breathe a word of it. Greg would be compelled as a journalist to pursue the story, regardless. I wanted so much to have a regular boyfriend–a man that I could share everything with who would understand how I felt. Greg was smart and would understand, but he had a job that required him to snoop the story. His allegiance as a lover and friend might always be compromised.

After hanging up with Greg, I watched the remainder of the broadcast and then called Tim Marshall to see if he had any more leads on Lela's case. I'd already left him a few messages during the day, but he hadn't returned my calls.

"Listen, Mac, I can't talk to you about the case right now. Things are heatin' up," Tim said.

"What do you mean?

"I can't say. Listen, I've got to go." The line went dead.

Chapter 21

When the phone rang a minute later, I assumed it was Tim Marshall calling me back, but instead, it was Harry on the line. He sounded half-crazed. "John's been arrested. The sons-a-bitches popped him on our front lawn in front of God and everyone. Charged him with conspiracy to commit murder. The arraignment is set for morning. Be there at eight thirty, sharp.

You need to draft a motion for separate trials tonight—we need to file it before the arraignment hearing tomorrow. I don't want John tried with Amanda. Also, be prepared to argue bail. Unlike Amanda, John is not a flight risk and he can be released into my custody. Do not, and I repeat, *do not* argue that he's a good citizen or anything like that. I don't want to discuss his criminal record at the arraignment. Judge Furmer has already heard all about John's criminal past. If this case is assigned to her, we might want to think about papering her." Harry was talking about a preemptory challenge. Each side gets one complimentary "boot the judge" card—one of the perks of jurisprudence. If a lawyer feels that a judge has a prejudice against his or her client, he or she has one chance to get rid of that judge—no questions asked.

* * *

"People of the State of Wyoming versus Amanda Silver and John Harrison. Case number WC0329975. Counsel, state your name for the record."

"Jill St. Clair for the People, Your Honor." A gray and white checked suit hugged Jill's thin frame like a tight glove. Her hair was buzzed even shorter than usual around her ears and was crisply spiked on top. She looked more like a drill sergeant than a prosecuting attorney.

"Steadman Johnston on behalf of Amanda Silver, Your Honor." Steadman's navy pinstriped suit hung squarely on him like a navy's captain's uniform. His crisp white dress shirt bounded his thick neck while his brick red tie hung from its knot like a noose. His thinning strawberry blond hair was parted in the middle and combed back, forming the shape of the wings of a ptarmigan in flight.

Amanda stood next to Steadman wearing her long, dark hair pulled back sharply in a ponytail. Her cream pantsuit clung to her shapely figure, revealing cleavage from under the v-shaped plunging neckline. The four-inch stiletto open-toe sandals showed off her French manicured toes.

"Mary MacIntosh on behalf of John Harrison." I felt John swaying side to side, his tweed jacket bumping up against the shoulder of my black suit. Black seemed to fit my mood this morning–somber and serious like a heart attack. I knew in my heart that this hearing, like the last one, was mostly procedural and that Judge Furmer had likely already made up her mind regarding bail, but I wanted to prove to Harry and Jane that I could effectively represent their son. I glanced at John long enough for him to get the message to stand still. He looked like shit. His face was pasty white–suggesting the unhealthy lifestyle that he maintained. The fast-food, booze, drugs, and late nights were haunting him like a bad dream. The pungent odor of his cheap aftershave overwhelmed my senses, causing me to question whether he'd showered this morning. John was like that. He'd show up to an important affair dressed in nice clothes, but without a shower and a shave. Such indiscretions caused a rift the size of the Grand Canyon between him and Harry.

"Your Honor, we've agreed to bail for John Harrison," Jill St. Clair said. "If the bail arrangement pleases the court, we agree to release him into the care and custody of his father, Andrew Harrison, until the time of trial. However, the State has not and will not agree to the same terms for Amanda Silver. We respectfully request that bail be denied and that she remain in custody until trial." Furmer nodded.

"Mr. Johnston, you may address the court regarding bail," Furmer said.

Steadman, who was seated to the left of John, rose to his feet and unbuttoned the top button of his size forty-six jacket. "Your Honor, I respectfully disagree with the State's accusation that my client poses a flight risk. She has family here in Jackson, much like John Harrison. Amanda Silver pledges not to leave the state until after the trial is completed–that is, if the State has enough evidence to pursue trial on the merits, which we don't think that it will. Nevertheless, we will agree to a higher bail, if necessary, in order to assure the court that Ms. Silver will abide by your rulings." Steadman nodded at Judge Furmer, half expecting her to agree with his suggestion.

"I don't agree with your recommendations, counsel. I don't believe that a million dollar bail order is going to keep Ms. Silver's feet firmly planted on Wyoming soil. Granted, she has family here, but her father owns a private plane. Who's to say that she won't skip town. Her former conviction for possession of drugs in the State of Utah has been placed on the record via the State's request for judicial notice. Bail is denied."

"Your Honor, -" Steadman started.

"Bail is denied, counsel. I'm not taking further oral argument on the matter."

"But Your Honor -"

"Have a seat, counsel."

"Seems to me that you're hometowning me," Steadman grumbled, loud enough for the judge to hear.

Furmer squared off in his direction and removed her reading glasses. "Counsel, I've issued your client a fair and impartial ruling. Now I'm going to issue you a fair and impartial warning: Do not, and I repeat, do not disrespect this Court and the rulings issued herein. I take this job quite seriously and do not make rulings based on the locale from which a lawyer resides. Such an accusation is without merit and only serves as grounds for contempt. If you plan on continuing to represent the defendant before this forum, you will conduct yourself with integrity. Do I make myself perfectly clear?"

"Gin clear," Steadman said arrogantly.

"This arraignment hearing is adjourned," Judge Furmer stated. "Bailiff, take defendant Amanda Silver into custody." The bailiff bounded to his feet and placed handcuffs on Amanda's slender wrists, taking his time to ensure that the cuffs were not too tight. He grabbed her gently by the elbow and led her through the criminal's threshold - a secret entrance to and from the courtroom that only the accused had access. Some lawyers used this entrance to avoid the media, but they did so at their own risk. I watched Amanda leave the courtroom in her stiletto sandals and spring-tight suit. I wasn't the only one in the courtroom to notice her tattoo that was visible through her white pants. As she left, she turned her head back and gave me a fleeting glance. Or was it a grin?

* * *

"The tire treads were not a match," Tim Marshall whispered to me at the local police hangout—a coffee shop downtown near the precinct. Tim wore blue jeans and a yellow and brown plaid shirt. "I'm sorry that I couldn't talk last night. I was issued a gag order from my boss."

"Isn't it your day off?" I asked, noticing his apparel. He nodded and shrugged his shoulders. It was balmy for Jackson in late May - high sixties without a puffy cotton ball cloud in the sky. Summer was beckoning and any other soul in their right mind would have been hiking or biking or resuscitating their lawn from winter scorn, but not Tim. I wanted to tell him to get a life, but I thought the better of it, remembering that he was giving up his precious time on his day off to help me. "What do you mean that the tires don't match?"

"The tracks at the campground were different from the treads on the tires of Amanda Silver's rental car," Tim said, taking a gulp of his steaming hot coffee. "The treads are from a Goodyear tire. The tires on her Ford Taurus rental are Firestones. No match."

"You have her on the blood, Tim. Maybe that's enough to convict. Remember the O.J. case. Too much evidence can be a hindrance. Are you worried about the treads?"

"No. I'm not worried. But the rental is clean. No fiber evidence."

"Speaking of fiber evidence, did you ever test Dr. Miller's car?"

"Damn," Tim said, looking at me with a cocked head, rubbing the z-shaped scar on his forehead. He uncrossed his jean-laden legs and moved to the front of his chair. "You know what? I'm glad you said that. We combed his car and bagged the fiber samples, but we put it on hold because we found Amanda Silver's rental. I forgot to tell the lab to start workin' on the doctor's car. Excuse me," Tim said, standing. "I need to make a call. Captain will ring my neck if he finds out that I forgot this one," Tim said under his breath as he walked over to the coffee shop counter and asked to borrow the phone. While waiting for him, I used my cell phone to check my messages at the office. He returned to the table as I was listening to my last voicemail message.

"You need one of these," I said, pointing to my cell phone.

"I hate those things. Give ya' brain cancer," Tim said. *Coming from a man who smokes two packs a day.* "Wanna know what my prediction is on this whole mess?"

"What?" I asked, awaiting a dissertation on brain cancer and cell phone use.

"John's gonna turn Amanda in. He's gonna rat her out for it. He'll walk, Amanda will serve time."

"I thought we weren't going to discuss the case."

"Hard not to. If it's not the case, you won't discuss anythin' else with me."

"What's that supposed to mean?"

"You know. Been tryin' to ask you to dinner for weeks. You always have an excuse. I figure that if we have a case to talk about, at least we're talkin'."

"Then let's talk. Amanda is not going to rat John out because there's nothing to rat about. She'd lie through her teeth before she'd admit to anything. Anyway, she doesn't seem like the type to narrow her options."

"If her options are limited, she might. She's facin' thirty years to life for parole violations."

"Whoa." I'd forgotten that she must be on parole. Her smug attitude belied any preconception that she might need to be humble before a judge in fear of further jail time.

"That's right. Don't count her out. The only way she's seein' the light of day is an acquittal or a plea bargain. She's no dummy."

Maybe Tim was right in his assessment–maybe Amanda was street-wise, but she didn't give the impression that she was the least bit concerned about her most recent arrest. To the contrary, she seemed flattered by the notion that people in town knew who she was. The fact that she was being shackled after an arraignment hearing seemed to be beside the point.

"Steadman will squeeze her out of this somehow."

"Is that what you think?" Tim said, obviously shocked by my assertion. "Furmer's not afraid of Steadman Johnston or anyone else. She'll throw the book at Amanda Silver, if she can. Got that Supreme Court seat waitin' for her. My father says that she's the sternest judge he's ever seen, and he's been a cop around here for some forty years. That woman is tough as nails. It's no wonder that she's been through three or four husbands."

"I only know of two."

"Your behind in times. She's had herself a few more. One was this youngin' straight out of college. Outdoors-type. The other was much older–a walkin' life insurance policy about to pay off. Neither could stand her for more than a few months."

"Her personal life doesn't have much bearing on her ability to be a good judge, Tim. Some people are just bad at being married. You were married once, weren't you?" I asked, knowing the answer to my question, and not allowing Tim enough time to answer. "Marriage is tough. Maybe she makes poor choices in that department, but I think she makes solid rulings on the bench, overall."

"She don't seem to like you too much."

"She's given me a hard time lately. I don't know what I've done to aggravate her."

"Don't take it personally. It ain't about you. Rumor has it that she was hot for Harry some years back and that he kept true to his vows. She didn't like the rebuke. She probably takes it out on you."

I'd never heard that rumor before, and Jackson locals aren't shy about spreading gossip. Harry was a good catch and I could see the possibility of Furmer hitting on Harry at some bar association gathering, and I could also see Harry backing away shyly, like a wolf confronted by an aggressive grizzly bear. The more I thought of it, the rumor made sense. Jane expressed disdain about her, so much so perhaps, that Harry was willing to bump Furmer with a preemptory challenge. It was all becoming clear, in that split second of conversation. Sometimes, the faintest bit of truth can paint a completely different landscape on the canvas of facts before you.

"Listen, I need to get back to work. Let me know if you hear anything about the car," I said as I grabbed my purse and headed for the coffee shop door.

* * *

After leaving the coffee shop, I walked down the street a few blocks when I recognized the swing of Sheila's hips stretching every seam of her blue jeans. Her bubble-gum pink tank top was so tight that I could see the etchings of her lace bra from a block away. Her frizzy blond hair was pulled back in a clip, revealing large hoop earrings swaying in the breeze.

"Sheila, wait up," I yelled, running to catch up with her. She turned my way for an instance, and then turned back and started walking at a brisk pace in the opposite direction. I yelled to her again, but this time she didn't turn my way. By the time I reached her, I was completely out of breath, but managed to grab her by the arm and twist her in my direction. The minute she locked eyes with me, she pulled away.

"I can't talk right now," she said, jerking her arm away and briskly stepping up her pace. I ran to keep up with her. "They're watching me," she whispered. I noticed the rings of dark shadows encircling her eyes and the overall opaque pallor of her skin. She was thinner than usual and looked spooked.

"Who's watching you?" I asked, curious to see if I'd heard her correctly. She was not the paranoid type, if my memory served me right, but I'd never spent much time with her outside the confines of a local tavern, and usually after a few drinks.

"Amanda's guys. Don't talk to me in public. If they see me talking to you, they'll get me."

Sheila rushed off toward her car. As she locked herself in, I pulled out my Blackberry and retrieved her cell number and called her on her cell. She answered. I could see her in the front seat of her car, crouching down as low as possible with her cell phone clamped to her ear.

"What's going on?" I asked, hoping that she'd know it was me calling.

"You don't want to know. This is a big fucking mess."

"I need to know. Does it involve Lela?"

"Yeah. It involves me and Lela and a whole lot of others. You need to drop it. The more you dig up the dirt on us all, the more we're gonna get nabbed. It ain't no joke. It's a fucking mess. That mother fucker ain't messing around. He knows how to fuck with you–make you wish you were never born. Fuckin' bastard thinks he can -"

"Who else is involved?"

"None of your business, if you know what's -"

"It is my business. Our friend is dead and my boss's son is being accused of murder. Prove to me that it's not my business."

"I ain't gonna prove to you nothin. You don't get it. You live your little pristine life with you good-payin' job and your nice apartment. Some of us ain't got medical insurance, let alone a decent car or a place to live. Don't be ordering me around, princess."

"I'm not ordering you around. I'm just trying to help figure this mess out and understand what went wrong. I want to help you -"

"You can't help me. Everything got fucked up around here when Lela decided that she didn't want to go along with the program. She screwed it up and now she's dead, and the rest of us are sittin' ducks left holdin' the bag."

"Sheila, you're going to have to help me out here. Talk to me. Tell me what's been going on and how we can help you out of it."

"No way. If I talk to you, then you talk to the cops, then I'm floatin' the Snake without a raft. That's how it works."

"Is that how it worked with Lela? Did she tell someone something that she shouldn't have? Is that why she was killed?"

"Don't play stupid with me. I've known you long enough to know that you've figured this whole thing out. You're just waiting for one of us to screw up."

"Who's us?"

"You know who 'us' is. You're just trying to get me to tell you 'cuz you're probably tape recordin' this and you're turnin' me in. I may be a dumb checker at Albertsons, but I ain't no idiot after all. I got this whole thing under control, if you'd just keep your stupid nose out of it. Don't call me no more and get the fuck away from my car."

"I'm not recording this. I'm just trying to solve a crime. I would think that you'd want to help. Lela was you're best friend, wasn't she?"

"Sure. She *was* my best friend, until she screwed up."

"How did Lela screw up?"

"What do you think?" Sheila asked, her voice slightly calmer. "Her neck was shot off, wasn't it? Don't you think that was a message to the rest of us to shut the fuck up?"

Chapter 22

"They found two strands of Lela's hair in the trunk of Dr. Miller's car," Tim said, gleaming with self-importance. He slid his way into the back booth of the coffee shop where we'd met earlier. I watched in amazement as he added three large creamers into his thick sludge of coffee, stirring it repeatedly, until it attained a light brown color. "No hair was found in the interior of the car."

"People don't always shed hair every place they've been, do they?"

"No, but it's not likely that someone would leave hair in a trunk of a car, unless they were back there, know what I mean? Your hair just doesn't show up in the trunk of a car, leadin' Camille to believe that the hair could not have been accidentally transferred from the passenger compartment to the trunk."

"What if he had some of her hair on his jacket and then threw the jacket in the trunk? Aren't there a number of explanations?"

"You sound like a defense lawyer."

"I'm just playing devil's advocate."

"I don't have to solve the crime. That's for the county attorney. Alls I do is collect the evidence. And when it comes to certain folks, it's easy to be suspicious. Dr. Miller is one of them guys that I've been suspicious of since he moved to town. He doesn't seem right to me. He doesn't fit in around here. He ain't swift enough to serve the high-rollers that live around here, and he's not down-to-earth enough to serve the rest of us."

"He gives me the creeps too, but that doesn't mean that Lela was in the trunk of his car. Rumor has it that she was meeting him every Friday during her lunch hour. I'm not saying that she wasn't getting a facial or some other legitimate treatment, but it's also possible that the two of them were an item.

"How do you know him?" Tim looked at me with the suspicion of a jealous high school boyfriend.

"I had a spa treatment with him last week. I'm telling you, he's creepy." I wanted to deflect any inclination that I was suspicious of Dr. Miller. Some vagrant notion inside of me told me to hold back–that if I told Tim everything that I felt or knew, that it would somehow backfire against John.

"He was shifty during our first interview," Tim said, taking another gulp of his thick coffee, then swallowing the rest of his blueberry muffin in one bite. With crumbs lacing his chin, he wiped his face with his shirtsleeve and said, "What else do you know about Dr. Miller?" It was as if Tim had a sixth sense about me. He knew that I wasn't telling him everything that I knew, but he was too polite or smitten with me to press too hard.

"Just what I told you. I went to his office to check him out."

"Why? Why would you go to his office? Have you been there before for spa treatments?"

"No. I just decided that I needed a facial."

"Bullshit."

"Okay. Sheila told me that Lela went to see him every Friday afternoon and it seemed strange to me. She wasn't the type to spend that kind of money on herself for spa treatments, so I decided to book an appointment and check the place out."

"Shit. There's my boss," Tim said, as he hid his face behind a large laminated menu. I looked behind me, spotting the Sheriff sitting down at a booth across the café. He had a lit cigarette dangling from his mustache-laden mouth, and ashes were flicking in every direction as he told the waitress what he wanted to eat. Tim peered around the menu at me and said, "I'm not supposed to be talkin' to you about this case no more. Been told that I could get a suspension for it. I'm slippin' out the back door. We'll talk later."

I watched as Tim ambled out through the back door. I snuck up to the counter to pay for my tea, hoping not to be noticed by the Sheriff.

After leaving the coffee shop through the back door, I climbed the steps to our office and shoved my key in the lock. To my surprise, the door was not bolted. I pushed through the door and called out for Harry, realizing that he must have come back to the office earlier than expected, but I got no answer, so I called out again. Still no answer. A chill ran up my spine—like the one you might feel when watching a scary movie that you'd already seen before. You know something bad is about to happen, and you hear the music that reminds you that it is going to be just terrible and gory, but you can't remember the exact details of how awful the scene might play out.

I picked up a stapler from my desk and walked through the office quietly, checking behind every door. Since we'd had two other break-ins recently, I couldn't afford to be careless. I tiptoed into Harry's office, shoving the door so hard that it banged into the wall as hard as possible, ricocheting back toward me. I was hoping to smash anyone lurking behind the door, but all I did was manage to make a huge mark in Harry's upgraded select wood paneling. I then snuck into the War Room, looking behind the door and under the conference table. Then I heard a noise in the coffee break room. I grabbed a black, metal three-hold punch from the conference room desk and armed with office supplies, headed in the direction of the noise.

I quietly crept into the break room and flipped on the lights with the urgency of awakening from a nightmare. I held the three-hole punch up, ready to defend myself, when I heard another noise -- nearby. I turned to my right, squatted and then looked under the table, imagining that there were two beady eyes staring back at me. Then I hear the noise again, louder this time, and all too similar to be menacing. I realized that the noise was the ice machine inside the refrigerator freezer, making a fresh round of ice. I sighed in relief, embarrassed at myself for my paranoia.

Maybe Harry forgot to lock up, I thought to myself. He certainly wasn't acting like himself these days. Maybe he was distracted and left without bolting the door. But just to be safe, I checked around the office—under every desk and behind every door. I looked under Lela's desk and noticed that something was missing. The computer screen was still sitting on top of her desk and her laser printer was next to it, along with the facsimile machine, but the central processing unit what was normally under her work station was gone.

I stared in disbelief, realizing that someone had been in the office, and might still be around, lurking, waiting for the prime opportunity to finish what he'd started months earlier. And then a light went on in my head–whoever broke in the office right after Lela was killed was looking for something. They rummaged through Lela's desk and tried to log into her computer. They didn't know her password, so they were unable to get the information they were looking for. This time, they had a key to the office and stole her computer. I hurried to my office and called Tim at home. He said that he'll be right over.

I opened Lela's drawer where she kept her personal files and started snooping. One file said "taxes." I opened it and found last year's tax return. To my chagrin and dismay, Lela made more money than me, but this was not the point of my search. As I read on through the return, I realized, to my great relief, that her income wasn't solely from her legal secretary salary. She received a governmental stipend from her Shoshone status. She also had a decent investment portfolio, much better than my own.

As I put the tax file back, I noticed a file on the bottom of the drawer, covered up by all the hanging files. I pushed the hanging piles aside and grabbed the lone file called "Plumaze." After perusing the invoices and then comparing them to the file I'd previously found called "Dr. Miller," I whispered to myself, "Oh Lela, what did you get yourself into?"

Chapter 23

"Who else has a key to this office?" Tim said, arriving ten minutes after I called him. He was panting from running up the steps and beads of sweat swarmed his brow. He darted in and out of each office, making sure that no intruder was lurking before giving the first degree of questioning.

"Harry, Lela, me. The Bank's cleaning crew. Maybe the security officer for the Bank. I'm not sure who all has keys."

"The Bank's cleaning crew also cleans your offices?"

"Once a week. On Sunday night a husband and wife come in and vacuum and dust the place."

"Who has the master key?"

"Probably Harry. He's in court this afternoon. I'll have to ask him when he gets back."

"Where's Lela's key?" Tim took out his notebook from his pocket and started scribbling on the pad.

"I'm not sure. It's normally on her key chain. The last time I saw her key chain was in her apartment the night we discovered her missing. I think that Ed Duran took her truck to the ranch, so he probably has it."

"Why don't you call him right now and ask him," Tim said. I called.

"Is Lela's office key still on the ring?" I asked Ed.

"What's it look like? There are about ten keys on her ring." Ed said. I pulled out my keys from my purse to make sure that I was describing the key correctly.

"It's a thick gold key with an insignia from Smith Locksmith on it. It should have a red rubber protector on it."

"Nope. There's no key like that. Only truck keys and her apartment key and then some small keys that look like they go in a filing cabinet or suitcase lock. No other big keys."

"And you haven't removed any keys from her ring, right?"

"Right."

"Can you bring the key ring into town at your earliest convenience?" Ed reluctantly agreed, after giving me a dissertation on how Lela would never have loaned her office keys to anyone and that she couldn't possibly have lost the key. After Ed was convinced that I wasn't blaming Lela for losing the key, he went on to tell me what he thought about John Harrison and that he and his tribe would punish whoever killed Lela, since so far, the justice system wasn't getting the job done. I listened patiently.

"Maybe someone removed Lela's office key when they paid her a visit at her apartment that night," Tim said. "She must've had her key that mornin' to go to work, right?"

"I guess," I said. "But I don't know. Harry's usually the first in the office in the morning, and that Friday night when Lela disappeared, I was the last person to leave the office, so she didn't have to lock up. Who knows when the last time she used her office key? Obviously, there's something here that someone wants." Tim nodded in agreement. "What if they took my computer too?" I blurted out. I hadn't checked yet. I dashed into my office, but my computer was still there.

"What's wrong?"

"I just thought that maybe my computer was stolen too. Our computers are networked, so the same information is stored on both units. Luckily, the zip drive is on my computer. I do the nightly backups before I leave and I usually take the zip drive tape home with me on Fridays for safekeeping. I'm going to take some time this afternoon and go though the files and see if I can figure out what this thief was after. You'd think that if he or she was after something on the computer, that he or she would take the computer with the back-up system." I was more thinking out loud at this point than talking to Tim. "I'll call you if I find anything."

"I'll submit a police report for the missin' computer and the missin' key to your office. I recommend that you call a locksmith immediately to have the locks changed."

* * *

After Tim Marshall left, I examined more closely the file that I found hidden in the bottom of Lela's desk. It looked like Lela had been accepting shipments from the Swiss company via the Shoshone private airstrip. She received shipping invoices evidencing what had been shipped to her and then created her own invoices on the computer, but Lela's invoices showed fewer quantities of Plumaze being shipped. I looked to me like Lela had been presenting Dr. Miller with her invoices and keeping the surplus products for resale to another dermatologist in Denver, Colorado. She was cheating him. Maybe he figured it out.

I booted up my computer and perused the files stored on the hard drive. She'd obviously been creating false invoices for Dr. Miller on our computer system. Perhaps she had a file on him stored on the hard drive. I did a search for "Miller," but came up with a "no files exist" message. I also looked under "Plumaze," but there was nothing. So I decided to scroll through her directories, in hopes of finding something out of place.

Every file in the directory was labeled with the last name of each client we'd represented. As I scrolled though the client names, I came to a file called "Popo Agie," a name I'd heard before, but Popo Agie was not a client of our firm. Lela had told me that Popo Agie was a Crow Indian word pronounced "po-PO-zha," and that it meant "Beginning of the Waters." There's a place on the Wind River Reservation where the Shoshone Indians were relocated over a century ago, where the Popo Agie River plunges into a cave called the "Sinks." The Shoshone consider this place sacred.

I couldn't imagine why Lela would have a file on Popo Agie, so I opened the directory. The subdirectories contained files named "John," "Amanda," "Sheila" and "Miller." I opened each of the subdirectories, one at a time, and with my mouth agape, printed documents that would irrevocably change many lives.

Based on my shocking discovery in what I read in the Popo Agie files, I made an emergency appointment for a facial with Dr. Miller. When the receptionist at his office informed me that Dr. Miller was only doing Botox and Plumaze injections that day, I agreed to Botox injections.

* * *

The spa treatment room was vaguely illuminated with soft lighting. Mozart triumphed through the stereo system while water splashed over the fountain on the wall next to the door. I reclined in the chair with a hot compress over my face in preparation for the injections that would lead to instant muscle atrophy.

"You're going to just love, and I mean love, Botox!" the receptionist said, bouncing around the treatment room, preparing a tray for the doctor. "I do it every three months. Can't move a muscle in my forehead. Isn't it great? I've never looked younger. And just look at my eyes. My crow's feet were deeper than the crags of the Tetons. Now, you can't even see them." I peeked out from under the washcloth on my face. She smiled. She was right. I couldn't see her crow's feet or any other crease in her face. The entire upper portion of her face was frozen in time. Ice Age. Not a muscle moved.

"I'm worried that if my muscles don't work, that sooner or later they will give up and then droop to my chin," I said. I was just making small talk, to be honest. I didn't plan on being injected more than once in my lifetime. The receptionist took my flippant comment quite seriously.

"Botox is entirely safe and has been used in Europe for years. You don't see French women with droopy faces, do you?" she snapped. "It's clinically proven to be a safe and effective product in the war against aging." She finished cleansing my skin and abruptly left the room.

About five minutes later, Dr. Miller walked in. His shoulder-length, brown hair was pulled back into a ponytail and his mask was dangling around his throat, revealing a distinctive dimple in his chin. His eyes were lapis blue on the ridges, but faded to brown specks near the pupil. He shook my hand and congratulated me for taking a step in the direction of youth.

182

"I will be placing an icepack on your skin to chill the site briefly before I make the injection. You will feel a slight pinch and after I'm done injecting, I will be quickly massaging the area to ensure accurate dosage and to alleviate bruising. It is possible that you may bruise around your eyes. About ten percent of my patients do. It might be slightly red around the injection point for the first few hours. It is your job in the next two hours to move your forehead up and down as often as possible. The more you move the injected site, the more potent the Botox will be at paralyzing the muscle and eliminating the wrinkle." He walked around to the sink and washed his hands. He then put on his latex gloves and grabbed a syringe from the tray next to the sink. The sight of his large hands in latex gloves holding a syringe triggered a panic button my mind. I'd seen those latex-wrapped hands before. But they hadn't been holding a syringe. They'd been holding a gun!

He applied an ice pack to the center of my forehead just slightly above my eyebrows and pressed down. The coldness set in like dusk in winter as my capillaries constricted like a coiling serpent. Before the headache set in, I opened my right eye slightly, fixating on the hand, the glove and the syringe. As I watched Dr. Miller's hand move, I realized that the syringe was not roving toward my forehead as he promised, but heading straight toward my right shoulder. Right before he made contact, I lunged with my left leg, kicking him squarely in the jaw. I then rolled off the left bank of the reclined chair and darted toward the door. Just as I was about to grab the handle, Dr. Miller grabbed my ankle and jerked me to the ground. He jammed my calf with the syringe and I screamed out in pain. I jerked my leg away before he could inject the serum in me, ripping the syringe out of my leg and throwing it across the room. I squashed my high heel into the palm of his hand, applying as much weight as I could. He shrieked in pain, swinging his right leg around, connecting at my mid-thigh, dropping me to my knees.

Certain that Dr. Miller was the thug who'd attacked me at gunpoint in my office in December, forcing me to strip and stand handcuffed and naked, I knew that he was not going to let me get away this time. He'd probably broken into our office back then to find Lela's files on Plumaze or Popo Agie. He probably stole Lela's computer this time. He must of known who I was the first time I came into his office. He was clearly on to me–he knew what I was up to.

But I knew what he was up to also, and anger pumped up my adrenaline like some supernatural force. I swung my left leg over the chair, scrambled to my feet and grabbed my purse that was on the chair. I swung my purse at him, knocking him down and without giving it a second thought, and relying on my karate skills from kick-boxing, I kicked Dr. Miller in the throat with the high heel of my right shoe. I laid him flat, gagging for air, as I ran for the door. Just as I grabbed for the handle, he grabbed my left heel again and jerked me to the back to the ground. I landed on my left knee with a thud, but managed to get the door open enough to crawl out of his office, screaming, "He tried to kill me. Dr. Miller tried to kill me."

Chapter 24

I kept running, past the receptionist and out the door. When I reached my car, I dove in and locked the doors as quickly as I could. I seized my cell phone and called Tim Marshall.

"Where are you?" Tim shouted into the phone, after I told him what had just happened.

"In his parking lot," I managed, completely out of breath.

"Get the hell out of there. I'll send squad cars immediately, but get the hell out of there." I started my car and screeched out of the parking lot, holding the cell phone to my ear with my shoulder. As I looked in the direction of traffic as I entered the main highway, the cell phone slipped and dropped to the floor, near the accelerator. I reached down to grab it, causing me to overcorrect and I ran off the road, skidding into the gravel. I swerved back on the pavement, sending my Honda Accord into a three hundred and sixty degree spin. I slammed on my brakes and slid across the road again, coming to a stop in the middle of the highway. Cars were veering at me in both directions, so I jammed the stick shift back in gear and squealed back around on the pavement. I put my cell phone back to my ear.

"You shouldn't have gone there alone, Mac," Tim said, unaware of the fact that the phone has been on the floor for the past minute. "We've been watchin' that guy for the past week. He's under surveillance from the FBI and his medical license is being reviewed for unlawful practices. I can't tell you any more about it because it's top secret, but he's a dangerous man. Desperate people do desperate things and -"

"I'm on the road now," I said, finally able to breathe.

"Are you okay?"

"I'm freaked out and scared out of my mind, but otherwise I'm fine. I think he was trying to kill me with that syringe."

"We'll search his office for it, but my guess is that he's probably gotten rid of whatever was in there, but at least now we have exigent circumstances to justify an extensive search of his premises. We might be able to get a warrant for his house, too."

"I think he's the man that assaulted me in the office last December."

"Why do you think that?"

I was about to explain when my cell service broke up and I could only hear every few words Tim said. "I'll talk -- -- more about -- later. I'll----- -a formal statement from you -- -- -- on -- way------Miller's office now," Tim said as he hung up.

* * *

"He tried to kill me, Harry," I said, as I bounded into his office, out of breath and hysterical. "He tried to kill me!"

Harry looked up at me with the concerned eyes of a parent, befuddled with my hysteria. "Slow down. What are you talking about? Who tried to kill you?"

"I found these invoices in Lela's desk," I said, handing the papers over to Harry, who was seated at his desk. He put on his reading glasses and looked at the invoices. "I think that she was picking up the Plumaze from the reservation for Dr. Miller. But instead of delivering a full shipment to him, I think she was stealing a little of the product from each shipment. She created new bills of lading or invoices on the computer and then delivered the stuff to him on Fridays.

"I also found a file on the computer called 'Popo Agie.' It ties Dr. Miller, Amanda, John and Sheila to the shipments. After reading the computer files, I went to Dr. Miller's office to check it out, agreeing to a Botox injection. As I lay there, I realized that I'd seen his gloved hands before, here, in our office that morning when he held me at gunpoint and made me strip. He was supposed to be injecting me with this tiny needle in my forehead but I noticed out of the corner of my eye that a huge syringe was heading toward my shoulder," I said, gasping for a breath.

"Slow down, Mac. What the hell are you trying to say? You think that Dr. Miller was your assailant last December?"

"Yes, yes. Yes, I think he was the guy. I think he figured out that Lela was screwing him on his shipments and broke into our office to find her paperwork on the Plumaze. I think that I surprised him, and that he faked a sexual crime in order to throw the authorities off. No one would suspect a doctor of such a thing. He decided in that split second to make it look like a rape or something. I don't think that he intended to rape me, because he certainly had enough time to do it if he really had wanted to. He made me stand there naked for a few minutes before you entered the door. I think he was here to either get documents or to confront Lela. He did have a gun, after all and he-"

"Did you report this to the police?" Harry asked, in an ubiquitous, fatherly tone. I nodded.

"Oh, I left out the good part. When I came back to the office after lunch, the door was unlocked. Did you leave the office unlocked?"

"No. I bolted the door before I left."

"The door was open and Lela's computer is missing. I reported that to the police also. Someone broke in here today and stole her computer. That's why I searched my hard drive. Our computers arc networked. That's how I found the Popo Agie file."

"What?"

"Someone broke into our office today!"

"When? Why didn't you tell me?"

"I just did. God. So much has happened today that my head's spinning." I sat down and sucked in air. "I came in after lunch and found the office unlocked and Lela's computer was missing, so I called Tim Marshall and reported the break-in. That's when I decided to search my computer to see why someone would want to steal Lela's. That's how I found the Popo Agie file with Dr. Miller's name on a subdirectory, as well as John's."

"Okay. Okay. Calm down. Take a breath." I took a deep breath as Harry continued. "So, how does John fit in?" he asked, peeling the reading glasses from the bridge of his nose.

"Lela had subfiles on each of them. I'm not sure what they mean yet. Come with me to my office. Maybe you can help me figure it out."

"Do the police know about this Popo Agie file yet?"

"No. Just about the computer. Why?"

"I don't want them to have any more evidence linking John to Amanda. I hope we can keep that under our hats a few days."

"Harry! That's obstruction of justice." Harry shook his head, grimacing.

"I don't need a lecture from you."

"I'm not lecturing you."

Harry sat down in my office chair and rubbed his eyes, which were now wet with tears. "It's been a long couple of weeks, Mac." Harry rambled on, unable to get a hold of himself.

"Back in the old days, we got a good case, worked it up, fought hard but fair in court and the jury reached a verdict. There were discovery battles and words exchanged, but at the end of the day, we were all gentlemen and walked away with a handshake and a nod. These days, people fight to the bitter end over the exchange of documents and call each other names before slamming down the receiver. And now our secretaries get killed, we get beat up and our lives are on the line for trying to do our jobs."

"Harry," I said, putting a hand on his shoulder, "none of this is really related to the profession. Lela got involved with some bad characters and it's coming home to roost, that's all. Yes, the profession gets ugly sometimes and yes, it should be more civil. But the reason we have Dr. Miller in our lives is because of a stupid decision *Lela* made. I know how much she meant to you, but she was messing up her life and it caught up with her. Unfortunately, she probably got your son involved in her mess. Now our job is to try to save John while we figure out who killed her."

"What do you mean, 'who killed her?' Amanda Silver is sitting in the clink now for murder. You've said all along that you thought she was involved. Are you changing your tune?" The anger in Harry's voice alarmed me.

"I think she's involved, but I don't think she did it alone. She clearly had opportunity, but I'm not convinced of motive. I need to talk with her. If only she could tell us what was going on. None of it fits. This Plumaze stuff might be the new miracle cosmetic wrinkle fixer, but it certainly can't be so big to merit an illicit drug ring–and that's exactly what this looks like–a drug ring. But if Plumaze is easy to import from Europe, despite the fact that it's not FDA-approved, it's not *illegal,* for Christ's sake. There's got to be more to this. Even if Lela was shorting Dr. Miller or Amanda, it wouldn't justify killing her, would it? I need to know what this Popo Agie thing is really all about. Amanda could enlighten me."

"Oh right. Like Steadman will let you talk with her. He'll guard her like she's the Taj Mahal."

The phone rang. Harry picked it up on the speakerphone. It was Bain on the line.

"Steadman called you?" Harry asked. "What did he want?"

"It's no surprise that Jill St. Clair is the head prosecutor in this his case," Bain started. "The woman hates me. We've been working together for almost ten years and she's hated me for the past nine and a half. I made the mistake of commenting on her hairstyle once and she's never forgiven me. At any rate, she's trying to get Amanda to rat me out–to say that I was the mastermind behind the murder or that we were in cahoots. She's offered Amanda a plea bargain if she'll turn me in. Steadman called me to give me the head's up, but he says that his client is not dealing."

"There's no validity to St. Clair's offer, is there?" Harry asked. Harry liked Bain, and I think he felt sorry for him

"Of course not! I've told you, I had nothing to do with this. Nothing. I feel like I'm living in the Twilight Zone here. I slept with the daughter of a movie star and my life has suddenly come down like a mudslide. Sleeping with Amanda wasn't a crime. I had *nothing* to do with Lela, I swear!" Bain screamed, nearly irrational.

"Is there anything I can do to help?" Harry offered. "I've known Steadman for a long time. Maybe I can talk some sense into him."

Bain took a loud breath into the receiver and spoke in a more controlled tone. "I'd really appreciate it. I'm scared out of my mind that perhaps Amanda did do it and that she's going to accuse me of being involved so that she gets a reduced sentence. I know the system. I know how these deals get done and how innocent people can be framed. I'm telling you, I'm scared shitless and for the first time in my life, I don't know what to do. The system that I work in is maneuvering me." I could hear the desperation in Bain's voice. He was right. The system was inherently flawed by overzealous prosecutors (like Bain, sometimes), and by lazy cops looking for someone to blame, and by desperate defense lawyers grabbing at any plausible straw to save his or her client. Judges could be bought. Deals could be made with ex- cons, willing to lie to get out of jail sooner. Bain knew that he was in trouble, and the only way to win was to beat the system.

* * *

"He's down here at the station, Mac, and he denies everythin' you said. He says that you came into his office for Botox injections and that he was about to inject you when you freaked out and assaulted him. He's pressin' charges," Tim said.

"He's *what?*" I yelled into the phone, shocked by Tim's assertion. "He's pressing charges against *me?* That's absurd. I want to press charges against *him* and I want the police force to investigate his whereabouts last December eighteenth. He's the one that broke into our office and assaulted me, I swear it is."

"Calm down. I'm just the messenger here. I can't stop him from pressin' charges. We can't find any syringe like the one you said he had. He had a small syringe in the examination room that you were in and he turned it over to the police. We searched his entire office and came up empty. You're welcome to come down to the station at any time today to give your statement and to press any charges you see fit, but he's entitled to the same privileges."

"You don't believe me."

"It's not a question of who I believe. I'm not the judge. I'm just doin' my job, that's all."

"I'll be down later to give my statement." I put my head in my hands. Ten days of hell with Lela and months of trial work stress were crashing in around me. The floodgate of tears was more than I expected, uncontrollable and unrelenting, like a thunderstorm in June. I felt exhausted and defeated. I reached for a tissue and wiped the torrent of mascara from my cheeks, trying to gain composure. My breath was shallow yet rapid, like that of a child.

As I wiped my eyes, I looked out the window -- at the beauty of spring. Nature, in the midst of it all, had painted the trees and the gardens in violet and apricot, magenta and melon. I saw a glimpse of color, flying again near my window, beckoning me to lift my spirits. It looked like the butterfly I'd seen the week prior, beckoning me to gather myself. I never gave much thought to reincarnation until this moment, but the way that creature looked at me reminded me of Lela, head to toe. From a mere three-second interaction with nature, my anguish was unraveled. I had cases to prepare and a murder to solve, and nothing was going to stop me, especially a wormy Dr. Miller.

* * *

"Is that your entire statement," Tim said to me as I looked over the typed version that I'd prepared. It wasn't my *entire* statement. My entire statement would have included information about the files from Lela's Popo Agie directory on her computer. If I'd turned the Popo Agie files over to Tim, he would have believed every word I said. But I couldn't turn them over . . . yet. I'd promised Harry.

"Yes. After I sign it, can I have a look at Dr. Miller's statement?" I asked. I knew that I was stretching professional courtesy, but I figured that the worst thing that Tim could say was "No."

"You know that I can't do that. I would if I could, but I can't."

After leaving the police station for the umpteenth time in the past week, I decided that it was time for some exercise. I felt like a worm in an apple and I needed some air. I grabbed my gym bag out of my car and changed into my running clothes. When my feet hit the pavement, I felt stiff and weary at first, but after the first mile, my mind filtered out the stimuli of life and all I could hear were my shallow breaths growing deeper, and as my mind grew sharper, it was in this moment that I figured out who killed Lela Duran.

Chapter 25

"Harry, I'm right. It's the only thing that makes sense. Read this." I handed Harry the rest of the documents that I'd printed. "You've got to trust me on this one."

Harry read the documents, shaking his head. I watched him intently, wondering what he was thinking. Harry's motto had always been: "No surprise is a good surprise." I had the feeling that he was surprised. "Oh, my God," was all he could manage.

"You need to call Steadman. If I'm right, and I'm pretty sure that I am, we can prove this." Calling Steadman was tantamount to waiving the white flag for Harry, and I doubted he would even consider the option.

"Mac, I'm not calling Steadman. He's such an arrogant bastard. Let him figure it out on his own. To be perfectly honest with you, I don't give a damn how this turns out any more. Nothing is going to bring Lela back. All I care about now is saving my son from injustice."

"How could you say that? You're the king of justice. That's what sold me on you! That's why I came to work for you in the first place. God knows it wasn't for the money or the plush office. It was because you believed in the system and what it stands for. Don't bail out on me now." He looked away, as if he'd given up. He'd spent most of his adult life seeing to it that his clients were treated with utmost fairness, yet when his own legal web was tangling before his eyes, he wanted to surrender. He closed his eyes slowly.

"I'm tired, Mac. I'm tired of this game and the players. I'm tired of seeing the system screw up. I'm tired of trying to figure out how to play a judge or a jury or a prosecutor. I'm tired of knowing that doing the right thing might not lead to the right result. I'm tired of fighting -"

"What are you talking about? Just ten days ago you were at the top of your game, giving closing arguments in the Michael O'Connor trial. What's happening to you? You don't really believe what you're preaching. You just need a break. A vacation. When was the last time that you had a vacation, Harry? You haven't taken one in years."

"This isn't about you, Mac. It's about her," Harry said, his voice trailing off to a whimper. He looked up at me with red, swollen, earnest eyes and said, "I knew she was involved in something, but I didn't do anything to stop her. I overhead too many conversations to just ignore it, but I didn't want to tell her what to do. She made it clear long ago that I wasn't her father and that I was to stay out of her personal business. So, I did. It's my fault. I should have questioned her. I should have intervened. I shouldn't have lent her money when I was pretty damn sure that she was using the money to bail herself out of some mess. John knew about it too. He didn't say as much, but he hinted often that she needed an intervention."

"It's not your fault, Harry. Lela was a mature woman making grown-up decisions. I don't know how she got involved in this, but she made the decision. She was certainly making good enough money here that she didn't need to get involved in illegal trade to make ends meet." I thought about Lela's expenses. Her apartment couldn't have cost more than five hundred dollars a month. I don't know what her monthly payment was on her truck, but it couldn't have been more than a thousand dollars. Was she in over her head financially? She did put a lift kit on her truck, jacking the truck several feet higher, and she put huge tires on. She liked new clothes and she like to go out partying. "Maybe she had a drug habit?" I blurted out loud. The mere mention of drugs brought Harry to his feet.

"Lela did *not* have a drug habit!"

"Harry, I'm just thinking out loud. I can't figure out why she would have agreed to illegally import drugs for Dr. Miller. And I can't imagine if she did do it, why she would then risk screwing him on the deal. Both decisions seem to be out of character for her and I'm trying to put the pieces together." I walked over to the window in Harry's office and looked out into the darkness.

"I should have told you earlier, but you must understand that I've been sworn to secrecy on this for years," Harry started. "It's such a long story, and I don't know where to begin, but I'll start by saying that Lela dropped out of high school at age sixteen because she was pregnant. She didn't want to have the baby, but Ed Duran insisted that she not have an abortion. So, she was reclused to the ranch until after the baby was born–which was when all of the trouble started.

"Lela wanted to return and finish high school, but when she tried, she was treated harshly by the kids. There had always been a big rivalry between the Indians and the whites, but Lela's baby sparked something deeper.

"During her pregnancy, we had no idea that John was involved. And after Lynette was born, Jimmy Lonewolf claimed that *he* was the father. Well, that sparked off a tribal issue between the Shoshone and the Arapaho, because Lonewolf is Arapaho. But soon after that argument heated up, John stepped up and claimed that Lynette was his. You wouldn't believe what happened at that point. The inter-tribal fighting became an inter-racial war, and as the rivalries heated up, John and Jimmy Lonewolf got into many fights, and Lela just couldn't handle the pressure of constant badgering. She dropped out of school and secluded Lynette to the protection of her parents' ranch.

"Like I said, I should have explained all of this a long time ago, but I figured that you and Lela were friends, and she would tell you what she wanted you to know. Frankly, I'm surprised in this small town that you haven't heard it by now, but after eighteen years of heartache, the news isn't that exciting anymore. When John first learned that Lela was pregnant, he was the captain of the football team and had no interest whatsoever in being a responsible father. Jane, John and I met with Ed and Lela and discussed it, and it was agreed that Lela would have the baby and that the baby would be raised on the ranch as a Shoshone. John would not make any claims on the baby, and Lela's family would raise it.

"But when Lela started showing, Jimmy Lonewolf claimed paternity, and that's how the war started. Lela claimed that John more or less forced himself on her at a party and that she tried to fight him off, but he'd overpowered her. Of course, John's version was quite different. He claimed that they were partying together and that she threw herself on him behind a haystack.

"When the baby was born, we wanted a paternity test, but Lela refused. She decided that the baby was hers, and hers alone, and that she didn't need a father for her child. Her mother agreed to raise the baby on the ranch so that Lela could finish high school, but, after a few months of motherhood demands, coupled with relentless hazing from classmates, Lela dropped out of school and motherhood. Of course, when she asked for a job, I gave her one immediately, to keep her close to us, in hopes that she'd soften, and eventually agree to a paternity test. That never happened."

Harry got up and poured himself a cup of coffee. "So, did she ever agree to paternity?" I asked.

"No. After leaving the ranch and moving to town, she got a taste of freedom—freedom from the demands of motherhood, and freedom from the constraints of living under her father's thumb. She loved earning her own money, and, frankly, she spent it foolishly, mostly on clothes and cars and partying. She allowed her mother to raise little Lynette, who by now, as you know, is of legal age."

"Is Lynette still living on the ranch?"

"Still on the ranch, living with Ed and his wife, under their fierce protection."

"How much of this does Lynette know?"

"I don't know. We've been invited to Ed's ranch many times over the years, and John has always had a good relationship with Lynette, but I don't know whether Lela ever told her the truth."

"Why wouldn't Lela allow a paternity test? That doesn't make sense."

"Because of the racial issues, or at least that's what she's told us. Believe me, we've tried everything to convince her. Hell, I employed her for nearly twenty years. And now you can understand why I did it. And why I've always been so protective of her. And why John has never let his flame for her die out. He really did love her. And he wanted to marry her. That's why he never pursued his college scholarships. He wanted to be a family with Lela. He gave it all up for her, but she never agreed. Maybe she didn't love him. Maybe she was afraid that Lynette would be shunned. I don't know the answers. I only know the years of heartache."

"When you say 'racial' issues, do you mean that Lela was worried that Lynette would be teased because she's half Caucasian?"

"No. That her child might be half Arapaho."

"Shoshone, you mean?"

"No. Arapaho. Jimmy Lonewolf is Arapaho. Lela's a Shoshone. The tribes despise each other. She refused the paternity test because she never wanted to exacerbate tribal tension. There was always the possibility that Jimmy Lonewolf was the father. He was her boyfriend at the time."

I couldn't believe my ears, but it explained so much of the history between Lela and John and Jimmy Lonewolf. But is also raised more questions than I could imagine. "Does any of this have to do with Lela's murder?"

Harry set his coffee mug down and closed his eyes tightly. "I don't think so, but I don't know. I don't see how it could."

"Does Tim Marshall know?"

"Yes. He knows now."

Chapter 26

"I Didn't Kill My Child's Mother," was the headliner on the local evening news. Jimmy Lonewolf's suggestion of paternity to Lela's child made a giant ripple through the community, sparking an age-old rivalry between the Shoshone and the Arapaho.

After watching the evening news, and having more questions than answers, I drove out to the airport to talk to Sheila's brother, Sam. Sam happened to be the manager of the Avis rental car agency, and Sheila promised that Sam would be working the late shift. Since Sheila was Lela's best friend, I figured that Sam might cut me a little slack and at least tell me whether Dr. Miller rented a car the day Lela was killed.

If it wasn't for the private jets surrounding the terminal, one might think that the airport was a large hunting lodge, decorated with the spoils of nature. Picturesque artwork and bronzes of the Wild West were prominently displayed to greet the adventuring travelers. I walked into the terminal and looked around for the rental car agencies. Since there was no one standing at the Avis counter, I rang the night bell, summoning an overweight, male version of Sheila from the back office. His hair was mousy-brown, unlike Sheila's bleached blond, and was long and ugly. He wore an Avis cap backwards and a red shirt with a company logo. "Sam?" I said, as he approached the counter.

"That's what my tag says."

"Hi. I'm Mary MacIntosh, Sheila's friend. She said that you'd be working tonight."

"What can I do you for?"

"Around the time that Lela was murdered, I think that a man named Dr. Garth Miller rented a car. I need to know what kind of car he rented, or more specifically, what kind of tires were on the car that he rented. Do you think you can help me?" I asked, leaning a little forward over the counter and flashing a warm smile.

"Uh, sure, I guess I could look it up, but I'm not supposed to do it," he said with a slight sneer. The chewing tobacco sheltered by his lower lip was now exposed; revealing his deeply stained lower teeth. He looked at the computer screen and rolled the mouse around, clicking. "What was that guy's name again?"

"Dr. Garth Miller." Sam typed it in again and asked for a correct spelling, but the computer did not have a match. "Try Saul Steinberg," I said, using the name on the Popo Agie files. Still no luck. "Do you have access to any of the other rental car agency's information?"

"Sorry. No can do. Hope you find what you're looking for," Sam said, on his way back around the customer service desk.

I looked around the corner at the Hertz desk, but no one was manning it, so I snuck around to the computer and typed in Dr. Garth Miller, but the computer flashed a "No Match Found" message. I started to type in Saul Steinberg, but I heard a voice, so I ducked under the computer desk and hid. The voice was getting closer. It was Sam talking to someone.

"Sheila told me not to help her, so if she noses around your desk, don't help her out, okay?" Sam said to someone. I heard a voice agree. "There's a case of beer in it for you from Sheila if you don't cooperate with this broad."

"I won't help her. Anyway, it looks like she left," the other voice said to Sam. I waited for a few minutes, but didn't hear any other voices, so I crawled out from under the computer terminal. I hit the button after Saul Steinberg's name and after a few seconds, the computer screen flashed his rental car agreement. I hit the print button and crouched down next to the printer, hoping that it wouldn't make too much noise. As soon as the printer stopped, I ripped the piece of paper from the paper tray and read it. He rented a Chevy Tahoe with Goodyear tires. The vehicle was rented on Friday, May seventeenth at two o'clock in the afternoon. It was returned at six o'clock Saturday morning. Goodyear tire tracks were found at the campground where Lela's body was dumped into the Snake River, but there were lots of different types and sizes of tires. I needed to find out exactly what kind of tire we were talking about. Just as I was about to dart out of the Hertz booth, I heard the voice again. "I heard my printer," someone said.

I had to run for it. I stuffed the printout in my purse and ran out the back entrance to the airport. A security alarm went off the minute I opened the door. Sirens were blaring as I ran to the parking lot where the Hertz rental cars were parked. I looked for a white Chevy Tahoe with the same license plate as the one noted on the printout. I found it in space number forty-seven. I took out my Blackberry and squatted down to take a closer look. I had my mini Maglight in my purse and I shined it on the tires. "Goodyear Wrangler RT/S radial tubeless tires. P245\75R16\109S." I scripted the serial number of the tire into my Blackberry and then I crawled around to the back of the SUV to get the license plate. The Tahoe had Wyoming plates with the number "22" for Teton County, then a Wyoming bucking bronco (called "Old Steamboat") and then the numbers "4556." As I made a note of the license plate, I heard the sound of a motor running. I jerked my head to the left in time to hear tires screeching and to see a car with no headlights careening toward me at a high rate of speed.

I dove in between the two Tahoes parked in spaces forty-seven and forty-eight, and when I heard the car screech to a stop and the door open, I crawled in front of space forty-eight and then made a mad dash to the next row of cars. I listened for a minute to see if I could hear footsteps. I reached into my purse for my cell phone, but it wasn't there. I must have left it on the passenger seat of my car. I crawled through the next row of cars and then dashed again, trying to get closer to the terminal. I could still hear the car engine running in the distance, but I couldn't see anyone, so I slowly peeked up over the Chevy Cavalier that I was hiding in front of when I saw him standing two cars to the right of me. Time froze, like an alpine lake in winter. I took off like an elk on opening day of hunting season, dashing from row to row, not even trying to hide myself, only trying to get back to my car.

As I sprinted across the next row of cars, I heard a loud crack and felt something whiz past my head. I dove to the ground, skidding across the asphalt, causing the contents of my purse to spill out. I desperately collected everything and scrambled to my feet when another shot grazed my purse, jettisoning it out of my hand. I bolted into my car, sliding through the passenger side door as another round of gunfire engulfed me. I crawled over to the driver's side and slid the key into the ignition, praying that my old car would start. It didn't. I pushed down harder on the clutch, joggled the gearshift and tried again. This time, the engine backfired as it turned over at exactly the same time as the back window exploded. I slammed my foot on the gas jettisoning my car over the curb and as fast as I could, sped away. I peeled onto the highway, skidding sideways before careening into a reflector pole. I heard the passenger side panel crunch as I jammed on the gas. I glanced in the rearview mirror and saw the headlights of a SUV gaining on me.

I quickly snapped on my headlights and carved a sharp right out of the airport parking lot and onto Highway 191. The gravel spun beneath my tires as I sided into the center line, accelerating south. The SUV was bearing down on me, so I gunned the Honda into fifth great and held the pedal to the floor. My eyes remained fixed on the road but my mind focused on who was behind the wheel of the SUV. *Who wanted me dead? Did they know about the videotape? Was it Dr. Miller? It must be him, but how did he find out?*

As I approached Gros Ventre Junction, still six miles north of Jackson, the SUV caught up with me and made its move. I downshifted to second and swung hard to the right, careening into the Jackson Hole Golf and Tennis Club parking lot. The SUV shot past, unable to make the hard right, and came to a screeching halt a quarter mile down Highway 191. I saw the white taillights as the SUV started back up, so I instinctively turned off my headlights and waiting in a parking stall. As the SUV creeped through the lot, I gunned the accelerator and shot back on the 191, without headlights. I sped towards town and as the 191 turned into North Cache Street, I dodged in and out of side streets until I crossed Pearl Avenue, where City Hall was located.

* * *

I don't know whether it was Tim's mocking tone or his accusatory manner that set me off, but something inside me snapped. "How dare you suggest that I made this up? How dare you suggest that I'm lying? This guy is a fricking maniac, Tim. He tried to kill me." I got up from the bench and started pacing the carpet, trying desperately to collect my thoughts.

"Let's go for a ride in the squad car."

* * *

"I measured the skid marks by space forty-seven," Officer Green interrupted as he walked through the terminal door. "They're about nineteen feet long."

"See, I told you. I'm not making this up." Tim walked over to Officer Green and together; they compared notes before resuming conversation with me.

"Okay, I'm sorry. It's just that it seemed a little too convenient." Tim made a note in his spiral and looked me in the eye, squinting a little, as if he was about the squeeze the truth out of me. "So, what were you doing here in the first place?"

"I came out here to see if I could find out what kind of car Dr. Miller was driving when Lela was killed."

"How did you know that he rented a car? Hesitantly, he asked, "Did he rent a car?"

"Yes. Under his real name." Tim looked at me sideways, confused. "I figured it out from a file I found on Lela's hard drive." There's a file on there with a name on it that I didn't recognize, so I took a chance and asked the rental agency if a car was rented on the seventeenth of May under Saul Steinberg." I handed Tim the rental car documents. He looked at them. "I wanted to check it out for myself first before I came to you, because I didn't want you to think that I was sending you on another wild goose chase. The tires are at least the same make," I said, pointing to the rental agreement. "I think that they should be tested against the tire mold you took from the scene of the crime."

"Where did you get this rental car agreement?"

"I . . . I . . . let's just say that I found it."

"Why didn't you come to the police with the information from Lela's computer files?"

"I wanted to check some things out myself first."

"You wanted to be the hero, didn't you?"

"I guess so," I lied. I didn't want to be a hero. I wanted to honor Harry's request not to turn over the information, but I also wanted to check out my suspicions first-hand.

"Follow me," Tim said. We walked out to his squad car and he reached inside the window and pulled out his radio, calling dispatch, requesting paperwork for another impound. "We'll impound the car and do tire and fiber analysis," Tim said, "but you'll need to come down to the station again to make another statement. Two assaults in one day. You tryin' to set some kind of record?"

"I think someone's trying to send me a message."

"Maybe it's time you tell me everythin' you know. Someone obviously wants you out of the picture, and it's high time you got the message, Mac. You're messin' with some pretty shady characters and instead of letting the police do their work, you think you're Wonder Woman. You're goin' to end up on a slab in the morgue if you keep it up."

* * *

"You look like hell," Harry said to me when I walked into the office the next morning. I started to tell him what happened at the airport, but Harry held up the local paper and pointed to the "Police Report" column, a rap sheet detailing every crime or incident reported in the past twenty-four hours in Jackson. Theft, fights, domestic disturbances, and drunk driving arrests were the most common entries. I rolled my eyes at Harry and collapsed into the chair.

"I didn't sleep at all last night."

"You seem to be on some mission to get yourself killed. Why didn't you tell me that you were going to the airport? I would have gone with you."

"You have a lot on your mind, Harry, and I had this hunch that I needed to check out." I told Harry about Saul Steinberg a/k/a Dr. Garth Miller and what I believed happened on May seventeenth. He listened intently, and even agreed that perhaps it was time to meet with Steadman.

* * *

We walked into the lobby of the Ranch Inn where Steadman was staying and proceeded into the miniscule conference room, which was not much bigger than the interior of Harry's Yukon.

In the few days that Steadman had taken roots, he'd turned the place into a roving cyclone of files, pens and paperclips. I could smell stale coffee smoldering on the bottom of the miniature Coffee Mate, which was surrendering to an army of half-empty Styrofoam cups. When Steadman offered us something to drink, I quickly opted for bottled water.

"To what do I owe the privilege," Steadman started, trying hard to offend.

"We have information that may prove favorable to your client," I said, sounding too official for my own taste.

"But before we go much further," Harry interjected, "we think that it would be most helpful if we had this discussion in the presence of Amanda. The information will likely help her defense, and she might be able to fill in the gaps that don't quite make sense to us." Steadman looked at Harry as if he had two heads.

"Why in the hell did you come here to tell me this? You've could've saved yourself the time by telling me this on the phone, to which I would have told you that you have a snowball's chance in hell of meeting with Amanda." Steadman stood and opened the door, escorting us out.

"Don't be so contemptuous, Steadman. We're here to help both of our respective clients. Why would we take the time out of our busy schedules to meet with you if we didn't have something good to offer? If you change your mind and want to save yourself a lot of leg work, call me." Harry attempted to shake Steadman's hand, but Steadman withdrew, like a petulant child.

As we crossed the street on the way back to our office, I turned to Harry and said, "Why's he so rude? Why wouldn't he want our help?"

"Steadman is a piece of work, let me tell you. On the one case that we did both represent defendants, when we could have been on the same team, he was an absolute idiot. He refused to share any discovery with me. I tried to split the costs of depositions with him and he flat-out refused, noticing his own depositions. It was ridiculous. We've offered the olive branch. Now the ball is in his court."

Just as I was about to step up the curb in front of our office, an ambulance screamed by, red lights flashing and sirens blaring, catching me by such surprise that I tripped over the curb and fell hard on my right arm. I heard a crack as I landed.

* * *

The emergency room at St. Joseph's was relatively quiet, thank goodness, and it only took about an hour to confirm the break and cast my right arm to the elbow. More than anything, I felt stupid for the accident. In all my years of mountain bike wrecks, skiing accidents, karate blocks, and falls from rock climbing, I'd only suffered sprains and bruises. I'd never had a broken bone before.

The cast was heavy and uncomfortable and it was to stay on for six weeks. It was nearly impossible for the emergency room nurse to slip the sleeve of my silk blouse over the cast. My navy suit jacket was not going to fit. Putting on pantyhose for tomorrow's court appearance would be interesting. So much for the romantic weekend in San Francisco with Greg, I thought to myself.

"Ms. MacIntosh, here is your insurance card back," the nurse said. Her nametag read Betty Kanowski. I recognized her last name.

"Doesn't your husband work for John Deere?" I asked.

"Why, yes. Do you know him?" Betty asked in her gingerly voice.

"I don't know him personally, but I've heard of him. Doesn't he work with Jimmy Lonewolf?"

"Oh, yes he does. That kid has been nothing but trouble. The latest fiasco is that he's been stealing from the place. He's been given time off without pay while they investigate it. Stole some cyanide and some other stuff."

"Cyanide?"

"You know. Fertilizer stuff. It ain't the first time that kid's stole. My husband is his supervisor. Wanted to fire him lots of times, but I guess the owner feels sorry for the kid. God knows why. If it was my store, I'd fire him and press charges." Betty leaned a little closer. "I guess I should watch what I say around here. His mother works in the accounting department. She don't like me much and she's been giving me the evil eye lately. Don't care. But the walls have ears in this hospital."

"When did Jimmy steal the cyanide?"

"Last week, I think. I'm not sure. Why?"

"Just curious. Thanks for your help getting me dressed. I don't know how I'm going to dress myself in the morning."

"It'll take twice as long, but you'll manage. The hardest part is washing your own hair. You can't get this cast wet, darling. You'll have to wrap your arm in plastic before you bathe," Betty said. She helped me into the wheelchair and escorted me to Harry's car. The minute she walked away, I told Harry about my conversation with Betty.

Harry dropped me back at the office and then he headed directly to the prosecutor's office to talk to Jill St. Clair about the cyanide and Dr. Miller's rental car. His demeanor was dyspeptic, and I was fairly certain that Jill St. Clair was in for a lecture.

I carefully settled in my chair and attempted to log into my e-mail, realizing for the first time that I do just about everything with my right hand, which was now in a cast and sling. After rifling through the usual stack of letters and pleadings, I came across an unusual-looking letter in a plain manila envelope with no return address. Normally, I would have thrown this type of letter away, assuming that was junk mail, but the postmark was from Vancouver and the letter was addressed to Amanda Silver, c/o Harrison & Associates. I sliced open the envelope and pulled the plain white sheet of paper out, reading it twice before I understood. The words were composed of letters that had been cut out of a magazine and pasted together on the paper. It read:

"WhAt ComeS AROunD GoES ArouND."

* * *

"What happened to you?" Tim Marshall asked when I showed up at the precinct with the letter.

"Someone broke into my apartment last night and I had to defend myself," I said, with a half smirk. He squinted at me and then cocked his head to the right, trying to determine whether I was telling the truth. "I'm kidding. I tripped on the curb this morning and broke my arm."

"You're havin' a helluva week," Tim said as he walked around his desk with a black Sharpie pointed at me. He sat on the edge of his greenish- gray metal desk, pulled the lid off the pen and told me to roll up my sleeve. I had to laugh at the sophomoric gesture, but in a way, it was cute. Tim drew a skull and cross-bones on my cast with the word "DANGER–HANDLE WITH CARE" written under it in all capital letters.

"I wasn't aware of your artistic abilities."

"There are a lot of things about me that you aren't aware of," he said, putting the lid back on the pen and then gently pulling my sleeve back over the cast. He held on to my arm for a few seconds longer, pretending to study my injury. "You know, Mac -"

"What do you make of the letter?" I interrupted, hoping to change the subject.

"The letter," Tim said, moving back to his side of the desk. "Anyone could've sent this, and I have no idea what it means. It's probably just a prank. Why? Do you have someone in mind? You seem to be highly insightful these days."

"No, but I thought that you could run a fingerprint and DNA test on the envelope."

"I'm not sure that it merits a lab test–like I said, it's probably a prank. DNA testing is expensive, and we have expended considerable resources on this case already." He paused, analyzing my reaction, and continued. "But, if it will make you feel better, I'll see about sending to the lab." His intercom buzzed. "Listen, I've gotta run. I have a meetin' with the Chief. Do you have dinner plans later?"

"Bar Association meeting tonight," I said as I followed him out of his office.

"Rain check?" he asked. I nodded. "I'll let you know about the letter. I'm goin' to give a copy of it to Amanda Silver's lawyer. Amanda might know who sent it."

* * *

A voicemail message from my mom awaited me when I returned to the office. Since I hadn't talked to her in weeks, I decided to do away with the convenience of sending an e-mail and picked up the phone.

"I'm fine mom. It was a clean break and it should be healed in a few weeks." I asked her what's she'd been up to, reclining in my chair, knowing that an open-ended question beckoned a very long-winded answer. She told me about the house that she was redecorating for a client on a seemingly unlimited budget, her golf game, her tennis match, and the trip she'd been planning to take to Australia. As she rattled on, I reflected on my relationship with her.

I suppose that the fondest memories that I have of her is when I was a little girl, maybe six or seven years old. My mom and her two sisters would go to Gram's house and they would do their annual canning. They would make raspberry jam and strawberry jelly and wonderful apple pies with little cinnamon candies inside. I would sit and help them wash the fruit and peel the apples and mash everything together while listening to them talk about their husbands and their projects and the other things they liked to do. I felt so grown up during those warm fall days. To this day, something about the transition from summer to fall makes me feel wholesome and connected.

"Mary?" my mother said.

"Yes, mom."

"I'm really sorry about Lela. I know what a good friend she was. Keep me posted on your arm. I love you."

As I set the receiver down, I heard Harry stomping down the hallway. He poked his head into my office.

"I met with Jill St. Clair," Harry said. "She wants to meet with Steadman and us together to discuss the case. She said that Jimmy Lonewolf was indicted today for theft of cyanide. He's got a court-appointed lawyer.

Tim Marshall sent her copies of the Popo Agie files from Lela's computer. She also has the autopsy report and DNA analyses. Also, Amanda wants to meet with you. Steadman called a few minutes ago. He's not happy about it, obviously, and he's counseled her against it, but apparently she's made up her mind."

"You mean with us, right?"

"No. Only with you."

Chapter 27

Why would Amanda Silver want to meet with me alone? She was paying Steadman a King's Ransom to defend her, and Steadman wasn't the type of lawyer to let his client call the shots.

After being patted down in the holding area, I was escorted by a guard down a cinderblock corridor to a door marked "Attorney Room." The air smelled thick and stale–decades of cigarette smoke still lingering from crimes of the past. The guard unlocked the bolted door, showing me into a space not more than five feet wide and ten feet long, with cement walls painted sea foam green. I could hear the clanking of institution sounds around me as I entered the conference space, where Amanda was sitting in a plastic yellow chair wearing a burnt orange jumpsuit with plastic shower shoes. Her dark brown hair was slightly greasy at the roots and her normally radiant skin looked ruddy, as if it was starving for its usual dose of moisturizers. Her lips were chapped and splotched, lacking their accustomed mauve sheen.

"I heard about the letter," Amanda said as I sat down across the table from her. Without any makeup, Amanda looked younger to me than she had on the day that I ran into her at the police station. She put her hands on the table and began picking at one of her acrylic fingernails that was beginning to peel away from the cuticle.

"Who do you think it's from?" I asked.

"The truth?"

"It might save time, Amanda, if you tell the truth." I rested my hands on the table with hers–signifying that we were on a level playing field. I wasn't there to play games, or to hide anything from her. If she wanted to tell me something relevant to the case, that could help her or John, I was willing to listen. I felt like I needed to befriend her, but didn't want to appear too chummy.

"I'm not sure who it's from, but it could be from this woman that I served time with in Utah. She was a prison butch–the ringleader up there. I did everything in my power to stay out of her way, if you know what I mean. I bought her cigarettes and got her some other stuff too. Illegal stuff. Of course, being the fool that she was, she got caught with it. She had to do more time. She threatened me, so they moved me to a different ward of the prison for the rest of my time there, but plenty of her bitches on minimum security passed on the threats."

"So you think she's threatening you again now?"

"No. She's just letting me know that she's knows where I am and what's going on."

"Why would she send *me* the letter? I'm not your lawyer. Why wouldn't she send it to Steadman?"

"Don't know–don't care. I don't sit around trying to figure out why other people do the things they do. People are screwed up." She flipped her hair behind her shoulder and sneered. "Maybe it was a warning."

"To whom?" I asked. She didn't answer, shrugging her shoulders in patent disconcern. Without giving the assurance that her warning caused me trepidation, I asked, "What else did you want to talk to me about?"

Amanda looked at me long and hard. "Nothing."

"So, why am I here then? You wanted to talk with me. I assume you wanted to talk about something other than the letter."

"No. I just wanted to size you up."

"What do you mean?"

"Just wanted to see what you're like. I told my lawyer that I wouldn't discuss the case with you."

"Then you're wasting my time." I stood up, prepared to leave. While she continued to pick at her acrylic fingernails, I knocked on the window for the guard to let me out. Before the door closed behind me, I poked my head back in and said, "By the way, what shade of lipstick do you wear?"

* * *

"She was just messing with me," I said to Harry when I returned to the office. "She had no intention of talking about the case."

"She must've told Steadman what happened, because he called to apologize, which is a bold move for him," Harry said. "He said that she wants to talk again, with all of us present, about the case this time. She claims to have information -"

"Count me out. I don't want to waste any more of my time. I need to prepare for the videotaped deposition tomorrow in the Samuel Silver case. By the way, do you know where Lela kept our spare video cassettes?"

"In the storeroom, where she kept everything else. I think you should reconsider meeting with Steadman and Amanda Silver. She obviously knows something."

"Good. Then you meet with her. I'll take a deposition for a paying client." I walked down the wood-paneled hallway into the storeroom, which was no bigger than a broom closet. I flipped on the lights and opened the silver metal cabinet, looking on each shelf of office supplies, trying to find videotapes. I finally spotted them on the bottom shelf, most of the tapes still in the cellophane wrappers. Next to the tapes lay a solitary small key—one that might fit in the lock of a filing cabinet or desk drawer. The key had a ticket attached to it with the numbers "456" written on the front and "downstairs" written on the back.

I grabbed a blank videotape and the key and yelled down the hallway as I walked toward Harry's office. "What's this key to?" I handed him the key and he examined it.

"I don't know, but it looks like a safety deposit box key. I have a box in the vault of the Bank, and my key looks just like this. Why? Where'd you find this?"

"In the storeroom, next to the videotapes. It says 'downstairs' on the back of the tag. Maybe we should check it out."

Harry agreed and followed me down the flight of stairs to the foyer of the Bank of Jackson Hole, which was bedecked in emerald green marble flooring and mahogany furnishings. Harry'd had his accounts with the bank for years, and the tellers knew him by name. He walked up to a young woman at the teller window and showed her the key. She examined it and agreed that it was likely a key to a box in the vault. She picked up her telephone and called the manager over to accompany us to the vault. A short, pudgy man in a navy suit soon greeted us, shaking Harry's hand while leading us to the back.

The vault looked like a large, silver donut on the back wall, encased with high-tech security panels. The manager punched in a code on the panel and then held up a card to the red eye beam, which quickly blinked to green. He then put a key in the vault door and it clicked open. He led us to a vast wall lined with silver rectangles, each numbered in sequential order. Pointing to a box two feet from the ground, we saw the numbers "456." The manager put his key in first and turned it, and then Harry put the second key in. The lock clicked open and he pulled the box from its slot, set it on the marble table behind us, and quickly pried it open. Inside was a black videotape labeled "Popo Agie - Saturday" and an envelope with Harry's name on it.

Harry opened the note and shared it with me as we silently read together:

"Harry,

If you've found this, then I'm sure that something bad has happened. I made this tape to document what really was going on—to protect myself and the people I love from the lies. I never meant for things to get so out of control. I tried to stop it, but it was no use. They said they'd kill Lynette or you or Mac or members of my family if I turned them in. I'm sorry, Harry. I didn't mean for this to happen. It started out as a way to make a little extra money so that Lynette could go to college. But I got in too deep with the wrong people. Please forgive me.

Love,

Lela"

We grabbed the tape and the note and ran upstairs to the conference room VCR, and pushed the play button. The date at the bottom of the tape flashed "Sat May 11" on it before the film started to roll. We watched the tape together in disbelief.

Chapter 28

Steadman sat down at the square table in the Attorney Room of the jail next to Harry. Moments later, the guard escorted Amanda in wearing the same orange jumpsuit, but a new addition to her appearance–large, black and swollen bruises on her left cheek.

"You have a hard time making friends in jail, don't you?" I said to her as I watched her slowly inch into her chair. Harry nudged me under the table with his foot, silently urging me to be less impertinent.

Steadman cleared his throat, causing the many layers of his jowls to rattle, before removing his thick glasses and holding them up to the florescent light, inspecting them for dust and fingerprints. He then rubbed them clean with the thick end of his scarlet striped tie before replacing them on the bridge of his bulky nose. "Thank you for meeting with us. Again, I apologize for the incident before–my client wasn't trying to play games. She was simply trying to determine how she fit into this team. She didn't mean to offend anyone. Regardless of what has transpired, we're here today to strike a deal." He looked to Amanda, who was shaking her head affirmatively.

"Go ahead," Harry said.

"Amanda will agree to testify that John had nothing to do with Lela's death so long as you turn over the tapes."

Harry shot a look at me while holding up his finger, cautioning me not to say a word.

"What tapes?" Harry said

"Don't play dumb with us. Either you give up the tapes, or Amanda is going to testify that killing Lela was John's idea and that he's the one that did it."

"That's blackmail!" Harry shouted, pounding his fist on the table. "That's tantamount to perjury, Steadman. You can't be serious?"

"I am. Amanda has an alibi, remember. Bain has testified that she was with him the night of the murder. John has no alibi." Harry stiffened.

"He may not have an alibi, but he has no motive. You, lady, have plenty of motive. You also had opportunity. You weren't with Bain all night," Harry said, as if he were in a schoolyard fight.

Amanda inched forward in her chair, opening her mouth to speak. Steadman held out his left hand. Amanda sat back, taking his admonition.

"Tell us about Popo Agie," I said.

"What about it?" Amanda blurted out in a snarly tone, before Steadman could stop her. He reached over and grabbed her arm, whispering sternly in her ear. I figured that he was reminding her that the attorney-client privilege only applied to her discussions with him, not us. We were not her lawyers. We could testify in court against her regarding anything she admitted to us during our discussion. "I'm not here to discuss Popo Agie."

"Here's what I'm thinking," Harry said. I knew from his tone of voice that he was not concerned with amenable social skills. "I'm thinking that you killed Lela out of rage for cheating you on a business deal. You're in the drug business with Dr. Miller. You found out that Lela was undercutting you. You threatened her and she sent you a threatening letter back, telling you that she had computer files incriminating you for selling the drugs. She also told you that she had videotape of you meeting the airplane at the Shoshone airstrip. So you killed her, and then you screwed the prosecuting attorney so that you'd not only have an alibi, but an ally in the judicial system.

"I think that when you arrived at Lela's on that Friday night, she offered you a glass of wine. You accepted. You spiked her glass with the cyanide that you got from Jimmy Lonewolf. After Lela passed out from the drug, you planted Bain's semen in Lela's bed, making it look like he was sleeping with her. A love triangle gone bad? You figured that if you framed Bain for a murder, there was no way you could be prosecuted. You then dragged Lela to your car, drove her to the campground, shot her in the throat and dumped her body in the Snake River," Harry said, his face a lighter shade of crimson; his eyes a deep shade of jade. "How am I doing so far?"

Amanda appeared to be following Harry's version of the truth precisely. She even nodded a time or two. But the craters on Steadman's ruddy face flushed with rage. Rising to his feet, he shouted, "This negotiation is over. You sandbagged me, Harry. I thought we were meeting today so that we could strike a deal–not badger and humiliate Amanda. If I'd known you were up to just some of your old tricks, then I'd never have subjected my client to this -"

"Dirty tricks?" I interjected. "We heard that you offered *Bain* a deal like the one you just offered John. You're trying to play both sides, seeing who'll give you the best deal. Don't lecture us about sandbagging."

"That's none of your business," Steadman said, waiving Amanda off. *Was this a signal to her to deny any deal made with Bain?* Instinctively, Amanda pulled back from Steadman, grabbing the rubber band out of her hair, allowing her long mane of dark hair to fall freely over her shoulders. Amanda's hair shone like a placid lake illuminated in a full moon–her beauty calculated and precise. She looked at me squarely, as if she wanted to say something, but Steadman glared her down.

"Tell us what you have on John. Maybe we can work something out," Harry said, sounding more biddable.

Steadman, still standing, looked to Amanda, who, in turn, looked back at him with a cunning glare.

"What kind of deal?" Steadman said, lowering himself back into the chair. "Tell us what you have on John and maybe we can work it out."

"No deal. I'm not in the *mood* to deal," Amanda shouted, her tone irritable and cold.

"Well, I hope you're in the mood to be convicted of murder and I certainly hope that spending the rest of your life in prison sounds good to you. You seem to be making friends fast," Harry said, as he walked to the door.

* * *

"That was fantastic," I said to Harry on our way out of the jail. "You have Steadman exactly where you want him now–squirming. He's going to sit there with her for the next hour interrogating her to death."

"My hope is that she'll tell Steadman why our story is wrong, and in doing so, tell him the truth," Harry said. "I'm sure that she's playing games with him too. Now that he knows that we know about Bain, maybe he'll reconsider his alliances."

"You mean with Bain?"

"I mean that Steadman will figure out that Bain is not Amanda's ticket out of this. The alibi with Bain is not ironclad, by any means. Maybe he'll want to make a deal regarding John."

* * *

Right after we found the Popo Agie tape in the bank vault, Harry had called Ed Washakie Duran and had him come to the office to view the video. After our jailhouse visit with Amanda, we had an appointment with Ed to visit Popo Agie. He agreed to meet us on Highway 191 and accompany us to the Shoshone National Forest.

The drive was longer than we expected, permitting Ed to fill us in on the details we couldn't get from the video and to acquaint us with the Popo Agie Wilderness and the cave. "The Pope Agie Wilderness once b-b- belonged to the Shoshone. The jagged peaks and deep valleys were once our homeland. The Popo Agie River sinks into a c-c-cave. It emerges again about a half-mile downstream in a m-m-massive spring. We call the spring the 'Rise.' We call the sinking area the 'Sink.' This time of year, with the snowmelt being so s-s-severe, Shoshone expect that the river flow above ground. It may not sink now. Our ancestors tell stories that a river disappearing can be a sign of b-b-bad luck. Since the Pope Agie rises again, this means reincarnation, which is sacred to our people."

"Have you been to the cave?" I asked.

"Yes. Many times. When I was a young b-b-boy, we went there often, but I haven't been there in many years. I took Lela and her br-br-brothers there when they were children."

"Is the cave big enough to walk in?"

"Yes. I will show you."

When we arrived, Ed enlightened us with more details about the Wind River Range and how the Shoshone once freely roamed the area. He told us how they were forced to share land with the Arapaho, further describing the ongoing feud between the tribes. He smelled the air and touched the earth after we got out of Harry's car. "Hold on," Harry said, "I need to get a few supplies before we go." Harry retrieved a flashlight from the emergency supply kit kept in the rear of his Yukon and handed us each a bottle of water and a Power Bar.

We started our trek into the Sinks Canyon State Park, an area thick with pine trees and willows. The peaks surrounding us were jagged and high.

"See over there," Ed pointed to his right, "That's Warbonnet. N-N-Next to it is Pingora, then Sharks Nose, Camels Hump, Lizard Head, and Watch Tower." I followed Ed's finger as he pointed to each distinct mountain peak. Camels Hump did, in fact, look like the hump of a camel, but the rest of the peaks didn't resemble their respective names.

At the ranger station, Ed showed the park ranger his identification and advised the ranger that we intended on exploring the cave.

"The cave is very popular these days. No one comes here for months, and then, all of a sudden, I can't keep the traffic out," the ranger said, clad in a forest green shirt and tan slacks.

"Any of the cave visitors repeat customers?" Harry asked.

"Yeah. A young gal has been coming here weekly. Sometimes she brings a friend."

"Can you describe her?" I asked.

"Long, dark hair. Pretty."

I showed him a picture of Lela. "Does this look like her?"

"That's her. Friendly gal. Said that she could help me with some paperwork that I need to file in the courthouse. My granddad passed on and he deeded some property and -"

"Has she come here with a boy that looks like this?" Harry asked, showing the ranger a picture of John from his wallet.

"No. She comes here with another girl," the ranger said. Harry raised his eyebrow to me.

"What did this other girl look like?" I asked.

"Pretty young lady with a nice shape. Don't know her hair color or nothing like that 'cuz she always had a hat on, but she had a pretty face."

"Follow me," Ed said, mid-way through the ranger's description. I waved to the ranger as we set out on the trail. The ranger nodded, watching us as we followed Ed on a narrow trail skirting the banks of the middle fork of the Popo Agie River. The trail was wet and muddy, making each footstep perilous in jogging shoes. Harry and I hadn't anticipated trekking, and hadn't packed proper hiking gear. "The cave is only a m-m-mile or so up river." It was a long mile. We walked for another hour before we reach a tiny opening in the ground. "This is the Sinks."

"*This* is the cave?" I said, staring down at the tiny hole in the ground. "There's no way that we can fit it there. The opening's only a foot wide."

"I know of the s-s-secret opening," Ed said, pointing us west as we follow behind him.

"I can't see the river any more," I said, nervous that we were walking over a cave, feeling the squishy feeling of earth under my feet. It felt like the ground was going to yield at any moment.

"That's because the river s-s-sank into the ground."

"The entire river seeps underground?" Harry asked with a bowed head, as if he couldn't possibly believe such a wonder of nature.

"Almost. Some of it stays above g-g-ground, but it's too marshy to walk through. Moose love it. Over here." Ed led us to a hole in the ground at the nape of a hill, which was sprinkled with tender new spring grass. "There's the ladder," Ed said, pointing to a thick braided rope tied to a large pine tree. "We'll climb down one at a time. Me first." Harry and I watched as Ed slid down the robe and disappeared into the darkness. "Mac, your next," Ed's voice echoed from the bowels of the cavern.

"Give me your flashlight," I said to Harry, uncomfortable with the notion of sliding into the black abyss of earth. I slid carefully down, and as my foot touched the ground, I felt Ed's gentle hands guide me to even footing. I fumbled to catch my balance, embracing the damp smell of nature and hearing the echoes of water dripping nearby. I flicked on the flashlight and waved it up to the ceiling, watching Harry traverse the rope in complete horror, looking like a child who'd climbed up farther than he'd expected on playground equipment. Relief settled on his face when his feet found solid ground.

The cave was narrow and cool and water dripped from the earth above us. "The limestone is very porous," Ed said. "It's called 'Madison Limestone.'"

The white limestone had long icicle-like objects hanging from recesses of the cave. "How far back does this go?" I asked.

"This is the biggest chamber. There are many side chambers up ahead. Then it g-g-gets too narrow to pass through." We followed Ed into the first side chamber, where the sound of the dripping water intensified. I shone my light above us, peeking into every dark crevice. Ed scowled at me.

"I'm looking for bats."

"Bats don't live in this cave."

"Good. I don't like bats. They remind me of mice . . . with wings." We continued to follow Ed to the second chamber, where the sound of the water echoing was considerably louder. The air felt thicker, yet it remained a cool, constant temperature.

"Those are called soda straws," Ed said, pointing to tiny columns of limestone hanging from the ceiling. "Look in the c-c-corner," he said, directing my flashlight to my left. "Those are called the draperies. Next to them are the ice-cream c-c-cones. Over here we have what they call a strand of pearls." Each formation of limestone was distinct and beautiful. "The formations take hundred and even thousand of years to form. Wait here.

I need to backtrack for a minute. I'll be right b-b-back." Ed disappeared into the blackness of the previous chamber. We waited for Ed to return for a few minutes before Harry started looking around.

"What's that?" Harry asked, grabbing the flashlight from my hand and shining it into the corner of the cave. I followed Harry to the corner, where we found piles of burlap sacks stacked on top of each other. He shined his flashlight on the stack and, with his pocketknife, slit one open. "White powder."

"Drugs?" I asked. As Harry dipped his finger in to test the powder, we heard a loud noise coming from another chamber of the cave.

"What was that?" I said in a whisper.

"I don't know. Let's get out of here." Harry shined the flashlight to his face and then held his finger to his lips, signaling for me to be quiet. He clicked the flashlight off and grabbed my casted arm and gently led me back the way we'd come in the cave. We stepped slowly over the rocks, careful not to make any noise. The darkness was so dark, that I couldn't see a thing. I felt like I'd been condemned to hell.

"The rope's gone," Harry whispered.

Just then, Ed reappeared. "Here you are. I was l-l-looking for you."

Harry flicked the light back on. "Who'd take the rope? You said that it's been here for forty years. Where have you been? We heard a loud noise."

"I heard it too. I was ch-ch-checking it out."

"Probably the owner of the white powder back there," I suggested.

"How are we going to get out of here?" Harry said in a panic, showing signs of his claustrophobia.

"I have my cell phone," I said, pulling it from my back pocket and dialing 9-1-1. The phone beeped at me, flashing a "no service" message.

"Damn," Harry said, hitting the flashlight on the palm of his hand. "The batteries are dying." Within a few seconds, everything turned pitch black again.

Chapter 29

"I'll be back," Ed said as I heard feet shuffling again.

"Ed?" Harry shouted, waiting for an answer. "Ed?" I followed Harry's voice, reaching out into the darkness with my arms stretched straight like Frankenstein. When I jabbed Harry's side, he yelled.

"You scared me."

"I just wanted to stand next to you. Where'd Ed go?"

"I have no idea. I have a bad feeling about this, Mac. Maybe this was a set-up."

"Not Ed? He wouldn't set us up." *Or would he? Maybe he was in on this too. Maybe he knew about Lela's dealings all along.* "What if the drugs belonged to Lela? What if she was dealing? If Ed knew about it, he wouldn't want anyone else to know about it. But he wouldn't just let us rot down here, would he?"

"Jane said that he's given her dirty looks around town in the last few days and you saw him at John's hearing. Maybe he sabotaged us."

"The park ranger knows that we're here, right?" I wanted to believe that there was a search and rescue crew on its way to save us.

"That can easily be explained away. Ed could say that we're hiking and that he's picking us up down the trail, or something like that."

"But your Yukon is parked in the lot."

"With the keys on the fender well. Ed knows where the keys are. He saw me stash them there."

"Why do you put your keys in the fender well, anyway?"

"I always do. That way, I don't lose them when I'm skiing or hiking or whatever I'm doing."

"But someone could steal your car."

"In Wyoming? It's never happened in the twenty years that I lived here. Granted, I would never have done it when I lived in San Francisco, but here, I don't think twice about it. Hell, we rarely lock the house, unless we're going away for the weekend or something."

"I hear something," I said, pulling Harry's arm in close to me. "Do you hear it?"

"You two okay down there?" Ed said, standing over the hole up above us. "I'm going to throw down the rope ladder. I found it in the bushes. Step aside." Before I could move, I heard a whooshing sound and then a plop. I reached for the rope.

"Go ahead," Harry urged as he thrust the rope ladder into my hands. I started climbing up the rope, inch by inch, hoisting myself slowly up. My right arm was still in a cast, making it nearly impossible to grip the rope well enough. Ed told me to hold on as best as I could while he hoisted me up.

Compared to the darkness of the cave, the bright sun was blinding. "How'd you get out?" I asked after Harry had made his way to the top.

"I followed the water upstream to the tiny h-h-hole we saw when we first got to the Sinks. I wedged my way out. Someone must've followed us," Ed said, pointing to the muddy ground. "There's footprints here." Large waffle-like boot prints were wedged deep in the mud. "I found the rope over here," Ed said, directing us to a cluster of willow bushes. Just then, the bushes moved and we could hear a groaning noise.

"Something's in there!" I shouted, watching the branches sway again. "Let's get out of here!" I took off running in the direction from which we came, peering back to see Ed huffing behind me. Harry passed me on the right, sprinting like he was on his way to the end zone.

"Moose!" Ed yelled. I peered back over my left shoulder and saw a cow moose running at us at full speed with her head lowered, looking mad as hell. In the distance stood a baby moose, peeking out of the willows at his mother. "D-d-don't look back. Run. Split up. G-g-go in different directions," Ed huffed, his hefty belly impeding him. Ed dashed to the right, breaking away from us, but since I didn't know my way around, I continued on the trail, trying to catch up with Harry.

The sound of the moose's hooves striking the mud grew louder, like the cadence of a beating drum. I darted behind a tree, hoping that she'd run by me, but instead, she stopped dead in her tracks and froze, snorting like a pig on its way to the butcher. I wanted to yell to Harry but he had disappeared up the trail. I considered edging around the tree to see where the moose was, but I was afraid that she'd spot me. I'd heard that moose didn't have great eyesight, and that they rely heavily on their scent of smell to detect danger, so I decided to dodge from tree to tree. After a few moments, I edged around the tree and saw the hind end of the moose, making its way back to her baby. She must have sensed me because she turned around, glared at me eye-to-eye, and then she stomped her front right foot three times into the soft earth.

* * *

I found a confused Harry wandering around the parking lot of the Sinks Canyon. "Where's your car?" I asked. Harry threw his arms up in disbelief.

"This is where we left it, isn't it? This *is* the right parking lot." Of course it was the right parking lot. Someone had stolen his car. "Wait here for Ed," Harry said. "I'm going to go have a talk with the Ranger. Maybe he knows where it is." I tagged along while Harry interrogated the Ranger. Despite his denials, the Ranger clearly was hiding something. He admitted that he might have heard another vehicle in the parking lot, but denied that anyone else had entered the park since our arrival. When Harry asked to borrow his phone to call the police, the Ranger quickly agreed to make some calls on his two-way and within a few minutes, we had answers.

"Someone wrapped your Yukon around a tree a few miles up the road. I'll take you to it, but I gotta use the john first."

While we waited for the Ranger, I asked Harry, "What's his story? Do you think he knows who took your car?"

"The Ranger? Possibly. He acted weird the minute we got here. All I know is that someone didn't want us out of that cave alive."

"What was in the burlap sacks in the cave?" The temperature of the cave was probably perfect to store drugs–consistently cool with low humidity.

"I'm not sure what kind of drugs, but I think we should go to the airstrip and poke around. Whatever's down in that cave was probably flown in and maybe someone who works there can tell us something."

"I don't know about going to the airstrip right now, Harry. If the stuff is being flown in, maybe the airstrip employees are in on it too. Someone obviously followed us to the Sinks, and whoever it was didn't want us to come back up alive. Maybe we should report this to the sheriff and let him handle it."

"I would report it if it wasn't for the fact that the cave is on federally managed land and the Bureau of Indian Affairs has easement rights for sacred purposes. With two federal agencies vying for the right to investigate whatever is down there, and the County Sheriff asserting dominion if it is tied to Lela's murder, can you imagine the mess?"

* * *

We headed north on Highway 131 after the Ranger winched Harry's Yukon out from the ditch. Miraculously, the car suffered little damage and started on the first try, and despite making a substantial noise, it seemed to be running all right. Ed told us on the way to the airstrip how he'd run through the trees to escape the moose. He claimed that he had no idea who'd thrown the rope into the bushes and he agreed with Harry that telling the authorities about the white powder in the cave would be a mistake.

"The airstrip is p-p-private. Only the people who live on the Wind River Indian Reservation have permission to use it," Ed said. "Lela wouldn't have used the airstrip."

"But she would have had permission to be there, right?" I asked.

"I can't see why she w-w-would. She had no business there."

"According to the 'Popo Agie - Saturday' videotape, she'd been there on more than one occasion," I said. "She kept documents in her desk that indicated that she was helping import a cosmetic drug called Plumaze for Dr. Miller -"

"I know who Dr. Miller is."

"Ed, it's possible that Lela was importing something other than Plumaze. She could have been importing cocaine or methamphetamines, based on what we saw in the cave," Harry said.

Ed rocked his head back and forth, cradling his head in his hands. "It's all my fault," he said, moaning like a sick child who'd been left out in the cold. "She wanted Lynette to come and live with her and I refused. I didn't want Lynette to be polluted by m-m-modern society, but Lela wanted her to go to college. We fought many times about it. Lela said that she was g- g-going to save enough money so that they could move away and make a new life."

"It's not your fault, Ed."

"It is my f-f-fault, Harry. Many years ago, Lela wanted to marry John and take Lynette away from us and move away for a new start. I refused to let her have Lynette. I told her that we would find them and take Lynette back, no matter what. I threatened her. I've made so many mistakes. I pushed her so far away and this is where it landed her–in her grave. I'm as guilty as the murderer. I helped k-k-kill my own daughter -"

"Ed, that's nonsense. All parents make mistakes. Hell, look how hard I pushed John in sports. It backfired too. Maybe if we'd both left them alone, they would have run off and been happy. But maybe not. We both tried to do what we thought was best for our children. That's what parents do." Harry reached into the backseat and patted Ed on the knee.

With tears flowing down Ed's cheeks, we pulled up to the airstrip hangar -- a white metal rectangular building with steel siding. We parked the Yukon by the chain-link fence surrounding the hangar and entered discreetly through the rear door labeled "Employees Only." A woman who looked to be in her early forties wearing faded blue jeans and a neatly pressed tan cotton blouse approached us immediately. Looking alarmed by our intrusion, she swiftly set her reading glasses on the end of her nose and set down a clipboard full of paperwork. "Can I help you?" she asked in an inhospitable tone.

"I'm Ed Washakie Duran. Chief of the Shoshone. This is my friend Andrew Harrison and his associate, Mary MacIntosh." The woman looked us up and down, measuring our sincerity with each fleeting glance.

"I'm Connie O'Riley," she said, reaching out to shake Harry's hand.

"Nice to meet you." Harry reached into his wallet and pulled out a business card, clearing his throat before continuing. "I'm sorry to be so blunt, but Ed's daughter was killed about two weeks ago and we have reason to believe that she was conducting some sort of business out of this airstrip. Do you recognize her?" Harry said, holding up a picture of Lela. Connie took the picture from Harry's hand and grimaced.

"I might have seen her. Why?"

"What was she doing out here?"

"I don't understand your question," Connie said, looking down at Lela's picture for a place to rest her eyes.

"I think I should call my manager," she said, as she scampered toward an office in the back of the hangar. She slammed the door behind her and pulled the plastic Venetian blinds closed. We could see two figures behind the blinds gesticulating. A loud clanking noise in the corner interrupted the confrontation. A young-looking man with slicked back hair was working on the engine of a parked airplane. He leaned over to grab the wrench that he'd dropped.

"Let's go see if he knows anything." Harry approached the mechanic in his usual congenial manner and said, "Hi, son. My name's Andrew Harrison, but call me Harry. You work here?"

"Uh, yeah. Why?" he asked, poking his grease-laden face out from the engine of a small Cessna.

"I'm an attorney in town and we're out here investigating a matter. I'd like to introduce you to my old friend, Ed Washakie Duran. Ed's the Chief of the Shoshones. His daughter, Lela was murdered a few weeks ago. Let me show you a picture of Lela. She was a beautiful lady. Does she look familiar to you?" Harry asked, jostling Lela's photo in font of the mechanic's face.

"Yeah. I've seen her around her."

"What's your name, son?" Harry asked.

"Billy. I mean, Bill. I go by Bill. Bill Watkins." His short, lean frame was well delineated by a slate-blue jumpsuit covered with grease. His thin, sandy hair was slicked back off his forehead, covered by a red bandana fastened above his ears.

"Have you worked here long, Bill?"

"Few years, I reckon."

"When did you see her last?"

"A week or two ago. She used to come here on Saturdays."

"Did she come here alone?"

"No. She came with another girl and sometimes with a guy. There were two guys sometimes."

"Did one of the guys look like this?" Harry asked, pulling a picture of John from his wallet.

"Yep. That's one of them. He didn't come out here too much. The other guy was here most of the time.

"Was the other kid an Indian with long hair pulled back in a ponytail?"

"Eh, yeah, I think so. He had a ponytail and was short and skinny and wore his baseball cap backwards. Punk-like."

"What did the other girl look like?" I asked.

"Hard to say. She wore a ski cap."

"Small breasted or big?"

"Big. Big ass too." Bill snickered to himself, as if he'd blurted out a secret he'd sworn to keep.

"Did another dark-haired woman ever come out here with them?"

"One of them had dark hair–the one that you showed me a picture of. That's the only dark-haired one that I ever saw I think. But I can't be too sure now 'cuz they've been coming and going so much that I've learnt to ignore 'em. So maybe there were two chicks with long dark hair, but I can't be for sure."

"What were they doing?"

"Hauling shit off a plane. Every Saturday a Cessna like this one here would land around lunchtime and they'd unload the plane. It didn't even gas up or nothing before it took off again."

"What were they unloading?"

"Don't know. Couple crates. I didn't take much notice. I learnt the hard way not to meddle my nose into other folks' business."

"What did they load it into?"

"Trucks."

"What kind of trucks?"

"Excuse me," Connie said, one hand thrust against her hip, the other grasping a hold of a clipboard. "The manager has asked that you leave the premises immediately. Or I'm calling the cops."

"Now wait here a minute," Ed started to say, ready to assert his seniority, but Harry pulled him back, assuring him that a squabble with the manager would not facilitate matters. We'd found out what we needed to know from the mechanic and it was far more important to leave quietly than to stir a fight.

Chapter 30

"I didn't know they were pulling drugs off that plane," John swore to Harry. Lela called me a couple of times and asked that I help her out, so I followed her out to the airstrip and helped her load both of our trucks with crates."

"What did Lela say was being offloaded?"

"Medical stuff for Dr. Miller. She didn't tell me all the details, because once she told me that it was a favor for Dr. Miller, I told her that I didn't want to help anymore. She said that I shouldn't be jealous since there wasn't anything going on between them, but I didn't believe her. She was doing too many favors for him for me to believe that something wasn't going on and -"

"Where did you take the crates?"

"I followed her to a storage shed west of town on Powderhorn Lane."

"Take us there," Harry demanded. "Ed, do you have Lela's car keys?"

"I d-d-do."

"Good. We may need them."

* * *

When we arrived at the rental storage facility, John took us to unit B- 212 around the back side of the peach stucco adjoining garages. Harry asked Ed for Lela's keys and then fished through the key ring until he found a key that looked compatible to the padlock on the storage shed. The second key Harry tried worked. He yanked the lock off and heaved the roll-up garage door. Inside, dozens of wooden crates were stacked against the back wall.

"Are these the crates that you delivered?"

"I've only helped her once or twice. Each time, it was only one or two crates. There's got to be twenty crates in here."

Harry summons us inside, flicked on the light and then closed the garage door behind us. "Let's open one."

Chapter 31

"Coffee?" Harry said, ripping the lid off the crate. These crates are full of coffee!

I reached deeper into the coffee and felt around, knowing that Lela was not in the java business. I searched deeper, until I felt something hard. I unearthed a knapsack, bound tightly with hemp string. As I struggled to pull the string apart, Harry handed me a pocketknife. I drove the knife deep into the knapsack, scattering the contents all over the floor. "Holy shit!"

"Jewels," Harry yelled, diving after the emeralds, rubies, sapphires and spinels that decorated the concrete around our feet.

It all made sense to me now. Lela was an expert on gems. It amazed me how she could spot a rock on a woman's finger and name the gemstone. She could even tell from where it was mined. She would say, "See that red spinel on that woman over there? It's from Sri Lanka." Or, "See that brilliant cut ruby? It's probably from Myanmar." I didn't know where half of the places were on the map and when I asked her how she knew so much about jewelry, she told me simply that gems were her passion.

Harry glared at John. "Did you know about these?"

John looked down at the jewels and then looked back at Harry without saying a word.

"Of course you did," Harry continued. "You and Lela were planning to -"

John straightened his shoulders and interrupted. "I'll tell you what Lela and I were planning to do, Dad. Years ago, we were going to elope and take Lynette, but when Ed made it clear that he wasn't going to let that happen, we decided to save up enough money to at least be able to send her to college, so that maybe she'd have a chance at the life neither of us had -"

"You had a chance at college, John, but you screwed it up by -"

"Just let me finish, Dad. I know I screwed up. That's not the point. We wanted our daughter to have opportunities that we didn't take advantage of. So we made a pact to save money for her future. Lela didn't love me—she was never going to marry me. But at least we had a daughter together. It was the link that kept me in her life. So, when this opportunity came up with Dr. Miller, I agreed to help her. He said he would pay her cash if she allowed his private plane to land on the Shoshone airstrip. Then Dr. Miller talked her into offloading the crates from the plane for extra money. That's why she bought the truck. So, Lela offloaded the crates of Plumaze and took them to the storage shed. Inside this shed, she pulled out the bags of Plumaze and made deliveries to his office every Friday."

"If he paid her cash for the Plumaze, explain the jewels at our feet," Harry interrupted.

"It's a long story, and I don't know half of it, but Lela told me that at first, she got paid cash with every shipment. But as time went on, there were discrepancies in shipments and lots of arguments between her and Dr. Miller. At one point, he said that he was short on cash, but offered her jewels to settle up. But then, some shipments came in and he stiffed her again, and that's when she started a tracking log of shipments and deliveries."

"Did anyone else come with you to this storage shed?"

"No."

"Just Lela?"

"Yes." John looked confused, but Harry pressed on.

"Sheila never came here with you? Or Amanda? Or Jimmy Lonewolf or anyone else?"

"No, Dad. I came here with her alone. Just the two of us."

"You never saw what was in the crates?"

"I saw the Plumaze. They were little viles of liquid wrapped in a burlap sack."

"What about drugs? Did you see crates or packages of drugs?"

There was a long hesitation before John answered. "Lela didn't have anything to do with the drugs. That was Amanda's deal."

"So you knew about the meth."

"Lela told me about it. She was furious. There was never supposed to be illegal drugs–just the Plumaze. When Lela figured out that Dr. Miller and Amanda were importing cocaine and meth, Lela panicked, and she even threatened to turn them in. At first, they offered her a cut, but she refused. Maybe that's where the jewelry came in, because all of a sudden, she seemed to lighten up about the whole thing. Then, things got ugly again. Lela and Amanda got into a fight -"

"What was your role in this? Were you receiving a 'cut' too?"

"I wasn't getting anything. I was just doing Lela a favor. I was doing it for my daughter -"

"Why in the hell would you get involved in something like this? You *had* to know that importing the Plumaze was illegal."

"No, I didn't know that the Plumaze was illegal. She told me that it was wrinkle cream for the face. Why would I think that was illegal? I did it to help Lela out, that's all. I loved her," John said, buckling to the ground in tears. "Chief, I didn't hurt Lela. I would never have done anything to hurt her. Please know that."

"Look at this," I said, pulling a hand-written note out of the knapsack. It's from Lela.

> "If you've found this, I'm probably on the lamb–or dead. I'm sorry to those of you that I've hurt. It wasn't my intention to hurt anyone. I have documented this nightmare on another videotape labeled 'Popo Agie–Friday.' Bruce has the tape. Lela"

I handed the note to Harry and after glancing at it, he handed it to Ed. Ed swiped the tears from his cheeks and said, "I know where Bruce is."

Chapter 32

Bruce Picnic Ground was located a mile above the Popo Agie Campground. "I b-b-brought Lela here years ago for a p-p-picnic. We played a game called 'find the treasure.' I'd hide a treasure, and then she'd find it. Then she'd hide a treasure and I'd find it. I remember where she hid her treasure." We followed Ed through the thick pine trees just beyond the two picnic tables to a place where a hollowed log was surrounded by crimson Indian Paintbrush flowers. Ed leaned down to one knee and fished in the hollow log with his right hand. I heard a scraping noise as he pulled out an object wrapped in plastic.

"Bingo," Harry said, ripping the videotape from the container marked "Popo Agie–Friday."

* * *

"You have to see it to believe it," Harry said to Tim Marshall over the phone. Come over here right away."

Tim Marshall's nearly six-foot frame happened into the War Room like a bolt of lightening. His face was unshaven and his ruffled hair was masked by a baseball cap. The air surrounding him wafted cigarette smoke, and, perhaps, stale beer from last night's poker game.

"Is this Lela narrating?" Tim asked, as he glared over his sunglasses at the television screen.

"Yes. I'll rewind it to the very beginning. She does a self-portrait and identifies herself first, and then gives a history of what's been going on," Harry said, while pushing the rewind button. Lela reappeared on the screen, telling us where she was and why she was there.

"Where's this airstrip?" Tim asked.

"On the Wind River Indian Reservation, not far from Riverton. It's a private airstrip. Look, that's the plane landing," Harry said, pointing to the screen. A Cessna bounced to the ground, kicking up dust as the wheels slammed down. "Watch. Amanda Silver's about to enter the picture." In the next frame, Amanda Silver walked out of the airplane hangar to greet the plane, her long, dark hair blowing in the wind. She was wearing black leather pants and a white mid-riff halter-top. Lela zoomed in to focus on Amanda's skull tattoo with butterfly eyes, and then panned back out to the pilot.

"Who's the pilot?" Tim asked, squinting at the screen. After taking a closer look, he whispered, "Dr. Miller." I nodded. We watched Jimmy Lonewolf swagger onto the scene, his shiny silver tooth gleaming in the sunlight.

"What's *he* doin' there?"

"He's their new delivery boy, now that Lela is dead. Lonewolf backed his truck on the airstrip and loaded the crates. His short, skinny frame was hardly a match for a heavy crate. He grimaced with every step. When he finally dragged the last of the crates into his pickup, he approached Amanda again.

"I can't hear what they're saying," Tim said.

"It's hard to hear. We might have to have the tape enhanced.

"We have a good video specialist workin' for us at the police station. She's the lady that videotapes all of the confessions during interrogation. I could have her take a look at it." Tim's thought was interrupted. Sheila appeared on the screen with a clipboard in her hand and greeted Amanda and Dr. Miller. She then looked at the crates, making notes on the sheet of paper. As we continued to watch the scene unfold before us on the video screen, Tim said, "The lab compared the tire prints overlays from the plaster sample we got at the campground to the Goodyear tires on the Tahoe at the airport. They're a match. Also, a few strands of Lela's hair were found in the SUV.".

"Was any other fiber found in the SUV?" I asked.

"Yes. Hair from another source, but we don't have a match yet."

"Compare it to the DNA from the cigarette we found at the campground," I blurted out. Tim looked at me, confused.

"What cigarette?"

"Remember the cigarette I found in the bushes at the campground? Camille was going to send it to a lab in Canada that does double swabbing in order to get saliva DNA." Tim nodded. "Compare the DNA from the hair to the DNA in the saliva."

"Do you know somethin' that I don't know?" Tim asked.

"Let's meet tomorrow morning at eight o'clock at Jill St. Clair's office. You get the DNA compared, and I'll call Jill."

Chapter 33

The morning air that seeped through my bedroom window was fresh and crisp, awaking me from a deep dream. In the dream, I was driving along the highway when I saw smoke up ahead. As I got closer to the smoke, I could see a car on fire on the side of the road. I pulled over and jumped out to make sure that no one was in the burning car. As I approached, I could see a woman (who looked like Lela) inside, so I yelled at her to get out of the car, but she just turned toward me, grinning, as if she didn't care that her flesh was about to melt. I tried desperately to open the driver's side, but when she saw me reaching for the door handle, she quickly locked the door before I could depress the handle. She waved to me as her long dark hair was engulfed in flames. I started screaming at her to let me help her. I pounded frantically on the window, when I was suddenly jolted out of my dream by the sound of the alarm clock.

Feeling sick to my stomach, and in need of fresh air, I tied my shoelaces and hit the pavement for a quick jog before our meeting with Jill St. Clair.

I met Harry at the coffee shop before our meeting and discussed strategy. We hopped in Harry's Yukon at ten to eight and headed for City Hall.

City Hall's parking lot was full because they allowed the jurors to park there for free, so we had to park in the alley behind the office building. I had two copies of the videotape with me—one was in my attaché case, labeled "Popo Agie–Friday," ready to hand over to Jill St. Clair, and the other was hidden in the inside pocket of my long brown leather coat. Harry insisted on making yet another copy of the tape, and asked Jane to deposit it into their safety deposit box at the Bank of Jackson.

Harry and I got out of his Yukon and proceeded through the narrow alley toward the back entrance to the public building. The sun was not yet high enough to crest the top of the brick building, making the alleyway dark, cold and moist. As we passed the large, green garbage dumpster, I heard a rustling noise. I expected to see a raccoon rummaging through last night's tossaways, when a man in a navy ski mask grabbed me by the left arm and shoved a gun to my head.

"Give me the tape," he said in a deep growl. Harry turned around, alarmed and bewildered, as the gunman pointed the gun at Harry. "Either give me the fucking tape or I'm going to kill the bitch." Harry stopped dead in his tracks, staring down at the muzzle of the .357 magnum. "Put your fucking hands in the air!" he shouted. "Both of you. Now! Put your hands in the air!" The gunman jerked my arm behind my back so hard that I could feel my clavicle separating from my shoulder. I screamed in pain as he shoved me closer to Harry, pressing the nozzle of the gun deep into my skull. "She's gonna die unless you give me that mother fucking tape. Get it?" Harry nodded, unable to speak.

"You're not going to get away with this, Saul Steinberg," I said, in a faint whisper of a voice. The pain in my shoulder was horrendous, practically stealing my breath. The gunman jerked his head in my direction, aiming the gun back at the back of my head with his right hand, while patting Harry down with his left. When he was satisfied that Harry didn't have the tape, he pointed the gun back at Harry and turned toward me.

"I liked it better when you stripped for me. Guess we don't have time for that this morning."

"How dare you," Harry started, and as the two men started shouting at each other, I slowly reached into my attaché case and pushed 9-1-1 on my cell phone.

"You're a sick bastard," Harry said to Dr. Miller. "How could you -"

"Shut the fuck up."

Dr. Miller turned back toward me, his fidgety eyes darting at me through his ski mask. I figured that he would look for the tape in my attaché case, so I voluntarily lowered the case to the ground and reached inside my coat for the second copy of the tape.

"Hands in the air!"

"The tape is in my coat pocket. I'm just trying to get it for you," I said as loud as I could, hoping that my voice might be detected on my cell phone. "You can get it yourself if you want. Please, don't shoot me. I'll give you the videotape, or anything else you want. I don't want to die in an alley behind the prosecutor's office -"

"Shut up!" Miller yelled. "Don't move a muscle," he shouted at Harry, as he approached me. "Hands up!"

With the cast on my right arm and the pain in my shoulder, it was impossible to stick my arm very high in the air, but as I slowly started to lift my arms, he reached inside my coat and grabbed the tape. As he pulled back, I swung my right arm down at him as hard as I could, connecting with the back of his head. Already off balance, he buckled at the knee and fell to the ground. Harry pounced on top of him, tackling him like a professional NFL player. They rolled into an oil-laden puddle in the center of the alley when I heard the gun go off.

The sound of the shot was deafening, noise reverberating from the tall brick walls encasing the alleyway. Harry rolled off Dr. Miller, clutching the side of his chest. Blood gushed from his jacket through his fingers, down onto the pavement.

"Get in the van," he yelled, pointing to an unmarked white van in the lot next to the alley, "or the next one will be in the head." He pointed the gun over Harry's head while grabbing me by the hair. He yanked me into the van and closed the door. He ran to the driver's side and sped away, leaving Harry in a pool of blood in the alley to die.

Chapter 34

As soon as we were out of town, Dr. Miller pulled the van over and grabbed a rope from the back. He yanked my arms together behind me, causing me to scream out in excruciating pain. He then duct-taped my mouth shut with thick, silver tape, and drove for over an hour until we got to the Sinks Canyon Campground. He yanked me from the van and marched me passed the Visitor's Center. When the Ranger came out, Dr. Miller peeled a few greenbacks from his pocket and handed him the bills. The Ranger turned the other direction and walked back into the Visitor's Center. With the gun wedged into my temple, he marched me to the bottom entrance to the Sinks cave and ordered me inside. With my arms tied behind my back, I had to crawl on my knees through the opening, and as I inched my way past the first set of sharp rocks, Dr. Miller shoved me to the ground. My face splattered against the pebbles covering the wet earth.

"Keep moving," he yelled. I tried to get up but I felt faint and dizzy, blood trickling down my forehead and dripping into my mouth. He jabbed at me again, swearing that if I didn't move, he'd shoot. I crawled over the second set of sharp rocks and into the second chamber. As I rounded the bend that separated the first two chambers of the cave, I saw John and Jimmy Lonewolf lying in the corner, blindfolded, shackled and gagged, with Sheila standing guard. The burlap sacks of drugs that had been there yesterday were gone.

"What took you so long?" Sheila whined. "You said you'd be back in an hour. I've seen sitting here with these idiots for three hours. I'm freezing and I need to take a piss -"

"Shut up. You're worse than my first wife and I think I told you where she ended up." Dr. Miller shoved me toward Sheila. "Tie her up. Sorry to report that I had to shoot her boss." I heard John let out a whine, knowing that his father was probably dead.

Dr. Miller shoved me again toward Sheila and I fell. Sheila grabbed me by my broken arm, sending a volt of pain down my spine that rivaled electric shock. I screamed out and tried to make eye contact with her, but she quickly averted her eyes and forced me to the ground next to John and Jimmy. She blindfolded me and then tied hog-tied my feet to my hands.

Sheila and Dr. Miller started arguing again, and she finally convinced him to leave the cave. John, Jimmy and I sat there in the dark silence for hours until they returned.

* * *

"I say we torch 'em," Dr. Miller said.

"You torch them. That's disgusting. I'm not going to set anyone on fire. It was bad enough shooting someone. It's your turn to do the dirty work."

"You seemed to enjoy shooting Lela. I didn't hear you complaining when I shoved her in the river."

"I didn't *enjoy* shooting Lela. It was horrible. I did it for . . . for us."

"How romantic. When are you going to figure out that there is no 'us.' You'll be the fuel for the human bonfire if you don't do as I say. Now, take the wood from the crate and build a fire like a good little girl scout and douse it with the gas."

"But -"

"Do it now!" Sheila swore a few more times before I felt a plank of wood land on my left leg. I scooted as close to John as possible, and rubbed the back of my head on his elbow, shifting my blindfold down so that I could see. His hands were bound behind his back too, and if only I could nudge myself closer, maybe I could untie him. I inched closer and tried to maneuver around, but Sheila threw another plank and it hit me square in the jaw. Dr. Miller handed her a red metal can with a rubber tube jetting out. Sheila doused the wood without blinking an eye. Dr. Miller lit the match.

The flames immediately shot to the ceiling, engulfing us in a raging inferno. "Let's go," he yelled, as their silhouettes darted out of the second chamber.

The smoke quickly filled my lungs, making it nearly impossible to breathe. I anchored my elbow into John's hip, trying desperately to reach for the ropes around his wrists, but he rolled away from me before I could connect. His torso was entirely engulfed in flames as he rolled back and forth trying to put himself out. The flames exploded higher, to the point where I could no longer see. I rolled the other direction. I could smell burning flesh and I could hear the whimper of screams muffled by duct tape, and that is the last thing I remember of the bonfire.

* * *

"Breathe!" a familiar voice shouted at me from above. "Breathe!" I filled my lungs with a painfully scorching gasp of air and coughed violently. I opened my eyes and saw Lela standing over me, wiping my face with a wet cloth. I knew that it was over–I was in heaven with her and she was taking care of me. I remembered what had happened–the cave–the fire. I tried to talk.

"John," I tried to say, but Lela shushed me.

"John is here. So is Jimmy."

Heaven smelled familiar, like the grassy plains of Wyoming. I drifted back to sleep.

Chapter 35

"We don't have time to wait for an ambulance. They n-n-need to get to the hospital now." I peeled my eyelids open again and saw Ed Washakie Duran standing over me. Lynette was at his side.

"He's right, Tim. Let's load them in Ed's truck and we can radio ahead to the ambulance. We'll meet them on the way and they can get them to the hospital," Greg shouted to Ed. "Come on! Time's a wasting. John's not going to make it if we don't hurry." Greg was kneeling next to me, holding my head. "Hey princess," Greg said, "you're going to be okay. We're taking you to the hospital now."

Tim and Ed loaded John and Jimmy in the cab of Ed's truck. Lynette jumped in and they sped off. Greg carried me to Tim's patrol car and we followed, sirens blaring.

"I thought I was in heaven," I said to Greg. "I saw Lela. She was wiping my face with a wet towel and telling me to breath."

"That was Lynette. She was wiping your face when we found you. She and Ed rescued you from the cave."

"How did they know we were there?"

"Ed had a vision, he said. He went into his sweat lodge and saw you and John in the cave."

"How did you get out here?"

"Your 9-1-1 call," Tim answered from the driver's seat. "The dispatcher heard your conversation in the alley with Dr. Miller and also heard the gunshot -"

"Harry! Oh God, is Harry okay?"

"He's in the hospital," Greg said. "When we left, they were wheeling him into the operating room to remove the bullet. He'd lost a lot of blood."

* * *

"All rise," the bailiff said, bringing the court to order. "People v. Jimmy Lonewolf."

Jill St. Clair, wearing a black pantsuit and a pumpkin-orange blouse, jumped to her feet, dominating the prosecution table. She set down her three- inch binder and declared her appearance for the record. Jimmy Lonewolf, on crutches and bandaged, was escorted by the sheriff to the defense table.

"Mr. Lonewolf, do you understand that you've been charged with a felony count of larceny for stealing cyanide from your employer?"

Jimmy looked up at Judge Furmer and quietly uttered a sincere, "Uh huh."

"Uh huh is not an audible response, Mr. Lonewolf. Address this court with either a 'yes' or a 'no'." The public defender whispered in Jimmy's ear.

"Yes."

"And do you understand that you've also been charged with a felony count of transporting an illegal controlled substance?"

"Yes."

"I understand that a plea agreement has been arranged between you and the prosecutor. Is this correct, Ms. St. Clair?"

"Yes, Your Honor," Jill St. Clair said. "The People have agreed to reduce the felony count of transporting a controlled substance in exchange for Mr. Lonewolf's testimony in a case that's currently being worked up for prosecution. We expect charges to be filed within the week."

"Mr. Lonewolf, do you understand the plea agreement that you are about to enter into?"

Jimmy looked at the public defender, who nodded to him to affirm.

"Yes."

"This means that you will have to testify in a court of law similar to this one about your conduct or the conduct of others. It also means that you will still be sentenced for felony larceny and misdemeanor possession of a controlled substance. You will have to serve time in jail for the felony. Do you understand?"

"Yes." Jimmy looked down again.

"This court hereby sentences you to six months in jail for larceny. Mr. Lonewolf, cyanide is a dangerous chemical. Stealing anything from one's employer is immoral and against the law. But stealing a dangerous chemical that poses a threat to human life is a serious matter. That is why I'm sentencing you to jail time. You will be transported from jail if and when you are required to testify in this other case. Sheriff, please take Mr. Lonewolf into custody. Next case."

"People v. John Harrison." Jill St. Clair remained at the prosecution table, her hair spiked and ready for combat. I escorted John to the defense table, who was wearing one of Harry's tan Armani suits with a gold and black-striped silk tie. His face and hands were covered with bandages from the second and third-degree burns he'd suffered in the cave.

"Good morning, counsel," Judge Furmer said—the first indication that she was in a decent mood. "Mr. Harrison, it looks like today is your lucky day. The prosecution has dropped the pending murder charge against you. You are being charged today with a misdemeanor count of illegal transporting of a controlled substance. Do you understand the charge pending against you?"

John cleared and struggled to speak, answering "yes" in a muffled voice. The burn unit physician told us that the burns suffered around his cheeks would tighten his skin, making speech difficult for some time. Skin grafting would be necessary.

"And I understand that another plea arrangement has been made wherein Mr. Harrison has agreed to testify in another matter in exchange for a reduced charge?"

"Yes, Your Honor," Jill St. Clair said. "We have agreed to drop John Harrison's misdemeanor count in exchange for his testimony in an upcoming case."

"This must be an awfully exciting case coming up. I hope it lands in my courtroom," Furmer said. "Mr. Harrison, do you agree to the terms of the plea agreement?"

John looked to me and then said, "Yes."

"Then the charge is hereby dismissed against you, pending your testimony as set forth by Ms. St. Clair. Next case." Jane and I escorted John through the gallery and out to the courthouse steps. The local news cameras clicked in unison as we helped John into Jane's car.

* * *

"She lobbied for the drug case during John's hearing?" Harry said from his hospital bed. His torso was heavily bandaged and a monitor was beeping over his heart. "She has no shame," Harry said, adjusting the I.V. tube taped to his wrist. The nurse stepped in to check his vital signs as he continued to speak. "Enough about Judge Furmer. Tell me what really happened after I was gunned down in the alley."

"For starters, let's just say that Jill St. Clair doesn't have spiked hair for nothing."

"What's that mean?"

"It means that when she wants things done, her marching orders are granted. After she saw the Popo Agie - Friday Videotape, search warrants were flying all over this town."

"How'd she get the tape, anyway?"

"I guess I should back up. I'll start where you left off. After you were shot in the alley, the police responded to a report of a gunshot. They found my attaché case with both videotapes in it, and my cell phone, which was still connected to the 9-1-1 call. So, Tim Marshall took the Friday and Saturday videotapes to Jill and he narrated them for her. He explained Sheila's involvement and told her how he'd requested a search warrant for her locker at Albertson's.

"While Albertson's was being stormed with warrant-clad police officers, Greg and Tim sped to Sinks Canyon to rescue me."

248

"How'd he know where to find you?"

"I'd told Greg about the Friday Videotape that morning, and described where the cave was. He knew all about Dr. Miller from an informant's tip, and he'd warned me earlier in the day to be careful. So when his buddy at CNN called him about the gunshot, Greg knew that something had to have happened to me, since I was with you on our way to the meeting in Jill's office. So, Greg and Tim put it together and raced to the cave, but Ed and Lynette apparently got there first, thank God." I told Harry about Ed's vision in the sweat lodge.

"Lynette saved the two men that have been fighting over her for years. How ironic," Harry said, lifting his oxygen mask. "What's more ironic is that Ed and Lynette have finally agreed to paternity testing. John is beside himself at the possibility of being part of Lynette's life. She even visited him in the hospital.

"So, do you want to know how they got Sheila?" I asked, feeling the warmth of Harry's presence. He nodded. "Just as we'd suspected, Sheila hid the gun at work, and they found the gun and some money stashed in the air conditioning vent of the Albertson's storeroom."

"So tell me. How did you know to tell Tim Marshall to search Sheila's place?"

"Lipstick," I said. "Remember when I found that cigarette butt at the campground?" Harry shook his head. "It had red lipstick on it."

"So?"

"I admit, I was a little star-struck with Amanda Silver when I first learned that she'd gone on a date with Bain. She's so beautiful and her dad's a Hollywood star. Anyway, when I accidentally knocked her down at the police station a week ago, I noticed that she was wearing my favorite shade of mauve lipstick–Lancôme Ginger Root Velvet."

"So?"

"So, the cigarette butt had bright *red* lipstick. The only person I know that wears bright red lipstick is Sheila, even when she's wearing a pink shirt. For whatever reason, that stuck in my mind. The lipstick on the cigarette butt was her signature to me. It put her at the scene of the crime."

"But lots of women who smoke wear red lipstick," Harry said.

"But the butt had to have been left at the campground recently. Even Helen said that with the amount of spring run-off, the rivers around here were running so swiftly. Any garbage like a loose cigarette butt at the bank of a fast-flowing river would have been swept downstream. Plus, with the amount of rain, the butt would have gotten soaking wet and would have disintegrated. Someone left that butt there near the time of Lela's death."

"Okay. Let's say that it was, for now. Let's assume that Sheila was there when Lela's body was dumped into the river. What do you think happened?"

"I know what happened. Sheila and Dr. Miller argued about it in the cave before they set us on fire. Here's the long version. Lela went to see Dr. Miller for dermatology sometime last winter, maybe around Christmas. He was the new doctor in town and his claim was that he could make women look younger without getting a facelift. Plumaze was not FDA approved, but was far better than any other cosmetic filler on the market, permanently erasing wrinkles. Anyway, Lela was one of his few Indian clients and she bragged to him that she was Chief Ed Washakie Duran's daughter. He questioned her further about being a Shoshone and inquired about the airstrip. She agreed to meet him at the airstrip and help him transport what she thought was Plumaze in exchange for cash.

"Lela said in her Friday Videotape that Dr. Miller would pay her a cash commission for every crate that she transported to the storage shed. Every Saturday, she would meet him at the airstrip and unload the crates from his Cessna. She then took the crates to the storage shed. The crates were filled with coffee to deter any smell of drugs. Lela would then take the burlap sacks of what she *thought* was Plumaze to the cave and leave them there. Amanda or Sheila would go to the cave later and retrieve the drugs.

"At first, Dr. Miller paid Lela in cash. Lela kept track of the shipments and payments on our office computer. In fact, when I first found Lela's files, I thought that she was cheating Dr. Miller on Plumaze shipments, but what I now understand is that after months of hauling crates, Lela discovered that Dr. Miller was importing cocaine and methamphetamines from Mexico and Central America. The Plumaze was just a ruse to use the airstrip."

"Well, that explains the vast quantities of coffee in our break room," Harry interjected. I agreed, and continued explaining.

"When Lela told Sheila about her discovery, Sheila begged her not to confront Dr. Miller and swore that she'd take care of things. Apparently, Sheila 'took care of things' by hopping in bed with Dr. Miller and devising a plan to axe Lela out of the picture."

"So, how did Amanda fit into this?" Harry asked.

"I was just getting to that. Amanda and Dr. Miller had been running drugs across the border for years. The FBI was on to them. Amanda still kept her drug connections while serving time in Utah. That's why she got that letter from Vancouver. It was a secret code from one of her inmate connections to send up more drugs. Anyway, once Amanda showed up in town after getting out of the Utah prison, things heated up. Amanda took over, basically squeezing Lela out of her role, but they still needed Lela in order to have access to the airstrip. Soon, Dr. Miller started stiffing Lela on payments, but since Dr. Miller was sleeping with Sheila, Lela was afraid to confront him. When Lela finally told Sheila, Sheila told Lela to mind her own business, and, at this point, Lela knew that she was in over her head and started documenting everything.

"Lela pretended to be sick during one of the shipments, and snuck off into the bushes at the airstrip to videotape the scene (the Saturday Videotape). She then confronted Amanda with the first letter. Amanda fired a letter back, telling her that if Lela turned them in, it would be the last thing she ever did. So Lela made the Friday Videotape the next week, and then wrote Amanda back, telling Amanda that she was backing out of the deal and that they no longer would be permitted to land the plane at the airstrip. This last letter was dated May sixteenth."

"How did Jimmy Lonewolf fit into this?" Harry asked.

"Jimmy Lonewolf will testify that Amanda hit on him one night at the bar and asked him if he could get his hands on some cyanide. Desperate to please her, Jimmy stole the cyanide the next day and gave it to her."

"That's his entire involvement?"

"No. He hauled some drugs for her too. But other than providing the cyanide to Amanda, he didn't have anything else to do with Lela's murder."

"What about Bain?" Harry asked.

"I'm getting to that. After the O'Connor trial, you know that John showed up at Lela's with the bottle of German wine. Lela accepted the wine, but told John that she was on her way out, so he left. Right after John left, Amanda showed up at Lela's to confront her about the videotape. Lela must have offered Amanda a glass of wine and Amanda accepted. When Lela wasn't looking, Amanda spiked Lela's wine with the cyanide. Lela must have passed out.

"With Sheila's help, they carried Lela out of her apartment and put her in the trunk of Dr. Miller's rental car. Dr. Miller and Sheila drove Lela to the campground, shot her in the throat and dumped her body in the Snake River."

"What about Bain?" Harry asked again.

"Amanda slept with Bain Thursday night before the murder. She took the sheets from the Wort Hotel and put them on Lela's bed Friday night. That's how Bain's semen ended up in Lela's bed."

"Bain was telling the truth."

"He was. Amanda set him up. She had sex with Bain on Thursday night to get the semen on the sheets and then she asked him out for dinner on Friday night to provide her with an alibi."

"And Sheila?" Harry asked from under the oxygen mask.

"Sheila's involvement in this is hard for me to believe. Her so-called best friend. After shooting Lela in the throat, she had the composure to volunteer to work the graveyard shift that night to provide herself with an alibi. She took the gun to Albertson's with her and hid it in the air conditioning vent above her locker."

"For them to plan these alibis meant that this wasn't some impetuous decision. They plotted the whole thing out, step-by-step. That brings us to Dr. Miller," Harry said.

"He was the mastermind—nothing but a clever drug dealer. I hope that Jill St. Clair can prove that he was the one that broke into our office last December. I want that creep behind bars, for good. God, this has been a nightmare. This horrible web was woven so that one drug dealer could land his plane. I hope to hell that he and Amanda both spend the rest of their lives behind bars."

"Speaking of bars," Harry said, "I could use a drink."

"You'll have to wait until the doctor says it's okay. You'll be out of here in a few days."

Chapter 36

"Check out the headline in the *Chronicle*," Greg said as he closed the door to our "Rose Chalet" room at the Casa Madrona. The view through the stained glass windows set off against the Golden Gate Bridge was a magical display of shapes and colors. Sausalito was Greg's suggestion, across the peninsula from San Francisco. It's Spanish name meant "little grove of willows," but the willows had been replaced with quaint shops and restaurants, with silhouettes of sailboats framing the skyscrapers of San Francisco.

"Amanda Silver, Daughter of Movie Star Sam Silver, in Jail for Drugs Again," was the lead story.

"Look at the picture they got of her," Greg said as he hopped back on the bed, sporting only a white terrycloth bathrobe, courtesy of the hotel. His blond hair stood on end forming a peak at his crown. After last night, I imagined that my long red curls looked like Medusa's snakes, hissing at the horizon. For once, I didn't care that I wasn't looking my best in the morning, or that he didn't either. I loved his smell, taste and feel, and just being with him.

Unable to hold the newspaper with my casted arm, Greg straddled behind me and held it for me, as we read together. I sipped room service coffee, learning how Jill St. Clair struck a deal with Amanda Silver, who agreed to testify against Dr. Miller and Sheila.

"My client is guilty by association only. She's made poor choices with whom she associated," Steadman argued in Amanda's defense.

The article went on to surmise that Sheila was the one who rented the SUV under Saul Steinberg's name. Her brother, Sam, who worked for

Avis, had his friend at Hertz change the name on the rental car agreement to cover up for Sheila. Sheila used her own pistol, a .38 special, to shoot Lela and then dump her in the river. The article explained about the drug trafficking, and the use of the Popo Agie cave to store the drugs. Another picture on page twelve showed a picture of Dr. Miller in a police car.

"He's smirking," Greg said. "I knew he was a bastard the minute I laid eyes on him. He looks just like the child molester that I'm investigating in Sacramento. Gives me the creeps." I agreed.

"So this must be Sheila." He pointed to a mug shot of her -- her bleached hair showing a dark line of re-growth at the part. Her eyes looked black from the smeared mascara under them.

"That's a terrible picture of her. She's actually not bad looking."

"She looks like trailer trash."

"Her parents split when she was little. I guess that her mom left town with another guy and her dad remarried right away to this lady that already had three or four kids from a few different fathers. It wasn't a great situation. They lived in this shack of a house outside of town. Sheila didn't have many good things to say about either of her parents, or stepparents."

"You sound sympathetic to her."

"I'm not. I still can't believe that she was behind this. She's not the classiest of gals, but she didn't seem like the violent type. Lela and Sheila had known each other since the first grade. I just can't imagine putting a gun to my best friend's throat and pulling the trigger."

"She was probably doing meth. When people do drugs like that, their minds change. They become vicious animals. Meth is as addictive as cocaine. My bet is that she was hooked on drugs and Lela's threat to turn them in put Sheila over the edge. She probably decided that it was better to kill her friend than to live without her drugs."

"That's sick."

"That's what drugs do," Greg said, perusing the rest of the article. "Look, Tim Marshall is quoted in article. He thanked his crime scene investigation unit and staff for the hard work in solving the case. And he mentioned you by name. It says, 'We couldn't have solved this case so quickly without the help of Lela Duran's law firm, Harrison & Associates. Attorney Mary MacIntosh found several key pieces of evidence that helped us, including a cigarette butt. We sent it to a special forensics lab where they able to perform a relatively new technique called double swabbing. The double swabbing provided us with DNA from the saliva remnants from the butt. The DNA was a match to Sheila Fall, putting her at the scene of the crime. Ms. MacIntosh also located the critical videotape that Lela Duran made, revealing the drug operation taking place on the Wind River Indian Reservation. The police and county attorney's office are grateful to Mac and Harry for all of their help. We know how much they will miss Lela. Putting the responsible parties behind bars is the first step in the healing process.'"

"That was nice of Tim to give me credit. Finding the cigarette butt was sheer luck."

"Putting the pieces together takes brains. You're smart and beautiful. I know I told you this before, but I'm really sorry about Lela. I know how much she meant to you and Harry." Greg leaned in and pulled me close. I could feel the stubble on his chin grazing the nape of my neck. His arms were strong and muscular.

"I'm sorry she got herself mixed up in such a mess. I'm sure it started out small. Maybe it was exciting to her. But I'm sure she never intended to be involved with drug dealers. She was pretty straight-laced. I think she just wanted to be able to send Lynette to college. She hadn't been much of a mother to her. She was going to try to make up for it."

"Not the change the subject, but how did Harry get from San Francisco to Wyoming, anyway? I read in a profile that Harry went to law school in San Francisco. Didn't he grow up in California?"

"He did. He took Jane on a trip to Yellowstone early in their marriage, I think. He fell in love with the place. He took the Wyoming bar examination not long after that and passed. But it took some convincing to get Jane to move. I guess she agreed when she got pregnant with John. Harry had worked hard for a large law firm in San Francisco and he was ready to hang a shingle, so he moved to Jackson and set up shop. He's been there a long time. But enough of this," I said, putting down the paper. "I didn't fly all this way to talk shop. I've been living it night and day for months."

"What *did* you fly all this way to do?" Greg asked, smiling. I leaned against him and began caressing him all over his body, arousing him until he got his answer.

"You steal my breath away," he whispered into the nape of my neck, sending shivers down my spine. He pulled me back on top of him, kissing my shoulder, then my arm, as he gently untied my robe. He turned me on my side, so that his body fit mine, gently caressing my shoulder. "Absolutely exquisite," he said.

I turned in his direction and kissed him passionately, engaging the silky smooth velvet of his lips, while allowing my hands to explore. I slid my hands down, pulling him closer to me, feeling his passion grow as he rocked gently against me. He cupped my chin in his hands, staring deeply into my eyes, looking fierce in his desire to make love. Instead, he pulled back, taking me gently in his arms and said, "I think I'm falling in love with you."

I wanted to tell him that I loved him too, but I didn't know how. Tears rolled from the corners of my eyes, dripping into my already matted hair, as I struggled for words to express how I was feeling. I'd never known love before, not in a passionate sense. My body was reeling with emotions and desires so unfamiliar that I wanted to scream out in ecstasy, but I was so afraid to be vulnerable and open for rejection. I wanted to tell him how desperately I needed his love, but my inner struggle with the armor protecting my heart was formidable. Somehow, somewhere deep from within, a faint whisper of conscience uttered, "I love you, too." As the words escaped my lips, I reached behind his neck and pulled his lips to mine.

* * *

"So, what happens when you go back," Greg asked, after we'd had a chance to catch our breaths and were able to look at each other without making love again. I thought about it for a moment before responding. What happens, indeed? I go back to my life as a lawyer, working countless hours defending people with adequate budgets. Harry did promise me free rein with a couple of new cases. He wants me to get acquainted with civil law–defense and plaintiff work. So far, I've only practiced criminal law and, quite frankly, the concept of anything civil sounded good right now.

"I resume the practice. Harry has more cases than he knows what to do with. I guess I've finally earned his trust after seven or eight years, so he's going to hand over the reins. And you?"

"I stay in Sacramento until this trial is over, and then, who knows? I never know where I'm going or what I'm doing next."

"Do you like it that way?"

"I like the fact that every day is different and that I have a lot of creative input. But there are downsides to all jobs, and mine happens to be rootlessness. I spend eighty percent of the year in hotel rooms, roaming the country for headlines. My New York apartment sits empty most of the time. I'm getting to a point where I'd like to settle down, have a family, and be there to help raise the kids. But in order to make it in this business, you have to be very flexible and very aggressive and basically unattached. It was great in my twenties and early thirties, but I'm closing in on forty."

I looked at Greg–adorable and smart, carefree and fun. We decided to get dressed and have a margarita at the bar. Greg ordered his blended with salt. I ordered mine on the rocks, no salt. As we were about to order a second round, my cell phone rang. I answered.

"Oh my God! Is he okay?" I asked. I turned to Greg. "Harry's had a heart attack."

"Let's get you to the airport," Greg said.

* * *

"Life is what happens when you're busy making other plans," I said as we raced to catch the next available plane.

"John Lennon?"

"Harry quoting John Lennon."

"They're both right. Life really is happening. And I feel like it's time to make it happen for us. And, by the way, Harry will be okay." I nodded.

We exchanged a hurried but passionate kiss and I boarded the plane. As soon as we were airborne I began to wonder what really would happen to Greg and me. And I wonder if he was thinking the same thing.

I sure hope so.

Epilogue

June 17th

Dear Father:

You must be gravely disappointed with the decisions I have made for myself and for our People, the Shoshone. Popo Agie is a sacred place and I have subjected it to the darker side of evil. It is too late to tell you that I ache over my poor judgment.

I cannot bear the accusation of betrayal. I have betrayed my own soul; yet, I am trustworthy and faithful as the spirit of a Palomino. Only you will understand the meaning of this passage. I hope that you find my beauty, despite the fact that I will never be pretty again. I trust that you will learn to live with failure, both mine and yours.

I will never again leave you standing alone in the ring of fire. I will remain at your side, loyal and present. You have nourished me through childhood and now it is my honor and duty to sustain you in spirit during your remaining years.

I pledge to keep you company in the vacant hours of life–when no other human company can fill your void. My mistakes of greed and desire are not that of your own. Do not feel guilt or shame. Rejoice in my successes. I am thankful that I am no longer cold and alone. I must go now. I hear my mother's song.

Love from your daughter,

Lela

Books by Maureen Anne Meehan

Dying to Ski, a Mary MacIntosh novel
Snake River Secret, a Mary MacIntosh novel
Powder River Poison, a Mary MacIntosh novel
Pandemic Predator, a Mary MacIntosh novel
Poisoned by Proxy, a Mary MacIntosh novel
The Five, a Mary MacIntosh novel
Rodeo, a Mary MacIntosh novel
60 Dates in Six Months (with a Broken Neck)
Push You Away
Let Me Be

ABOUT THE AUTHOR

Maureen Meehan Aplin received her bachelor's and master's degrees in education before becoming a lawyer. She lives with her family in Southern California, where she is a mental health judge and crafts legal thrillers, as well as nonfiction dating satire.